Praise for the novels of

SHARON SALA

"Sala's characters are vivid and engaging."
—*Publishers Weekly* on *Cut Throat*

"Sharon Sala is not only a top romance novelist, she is an inspiration for people everywhere who wish to live their dreams."
—John St. Augustine,
Host, Power!Talk Radio WDBC-AM, Michigan

"Veteran romance writer Sala lives up to her reputation with this well-crafted thriller."
—*Publishers Weekly* on *Remember Me*

"[A] well-written, fast-paced ride."
—*Publishers Weekly* on *Nine Lives*

"Perfect entertainment for those looking for a suspense novel with emotional intensity."
—*Publishers Weekly* on *Out of the Dark*

Also by Sharon Sala

THE WARRIOR
BAD PENNY
THE HEALER
CUT THROAT
NINE LIVES
THE CHOSEN
MISSING
WHIPPOORWILL
DARK WATER
OUT OF THE DARK
SNOWFALL
BUTTERFLY
REMEMBER ME
REUNION
SWEET BABY

Originally Published as Dinah McCall

THE RETURN

Look for Sharon Sala's next novel

TORN APART

Available July 2010

SHARON SALA

blown away

Recycling programs for this product may not exist in your area.

ISBN-13: 978-0-7783-2785-1

BLOWN AWAY

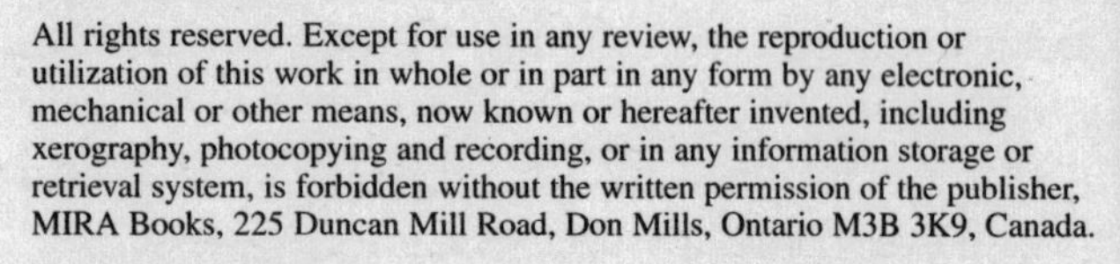

For questions and comments about the quality of this book please contact us at Customer_eCare@Harlequin.ca.

www.MIRABooks.com

Printed in U.S.A.

The only thing certain in life is that it's over too fast.
It's a fact I've learned the hard way.
As the oldest of my mother's three children,
I am the only one still alive.

As a native Oklahoman, I grew up knowing that,
for a certain period of time every year,
we will be faced with tornados. I learned young
when to run for cover, and learned the hard way
that sometimes the only way to live through one
is to be underground.

Life is full of many things,
but certainty is not one of them.

One moment someone is alive,
and before another breath can be drawn,
they are gone.

I watched my father die from health complications,
lost my younger sister less than two months later to
clinical depression, and had the love of my life
die in my arms from liver cancer.

And every time I thought I'd learned the lesson
I was meant to learn from the heartbreak,
yet another would be dumped in my life.

What I do know is that I'm still here.

There are many reasons to rejoice in being alive,
but for me, and because my loved ones are not,
it is my job to live each day that I'm given
with as much grace as I can muster.

This is why I'm dedicating this book to us…
the people left behind.

One

Sweat poured from Lance Morgan's hairline, despite the rising wind, as he continued to dig deep into the loamy earth in the woods outside of Bordelaise, Louisiana. Austin Ball's rental car, the car he'd used to get here, was just a few feet away. Lance wouldn't look at the body, rolled up in the rug behind him, which he intended to bury, or think about the fact that his great-great-great-grandmother had saved that very rug from the Yankees during the War of Northern Aggression. What he'd done, he couldn't take back, which was a metaphor for his life. It was what he'd done to begin with that had gotten him into this mess.

He stabbed the shovel back into the Louisiana loam, scooped out yet another shovelful of dirt and threw it on top of the growing pile as he thought back over the mistake he'd made that had brought him to this end.

Borrowing money from a Chicago loan shark like

Dominic Martinelli and using the family estate, Morgan's Reach, as collateral had been risky. It had been in the Morgan family for over two hundred years, and being responsible for losing it was simply not a possibility. He couldn't be known as the Morgan who'd squandered the family estate.

At first he'd had no trouble meeting his payments, and then weather and bad crop prices had combined, and he'd started falling behind on payments. He'd made excuses, sent e-mails promising money that never arrived. Before he knew it, he was six months in arrears.

Yesterday, when he'd received a phone call from Austin Ball, of Meacham and Ball, Esquire, who represented Martinelli, informing Lance that he was bringing some papers for him to sign, Lance had just assumed it was an extension on his outstanding loan.

He had prepared a lunch for two of Caesar salad, lobster rolls and some of his favorite brownies from a bakery in town. He'd even brought up a bottle of wine from the old wine cellar, and pulled out his mother's best china and crystal on which to serve the meal.

Ball had arrived on time, driving a black rental car, and sweating profusely beneath his gray worsted suit. Lance had taken some satisfaction in the lawyer's discomfort. Any fool worth his salt would have known not to wear wool in Louisiana during the month of September.

It wasn't until after the meal that Ball had announced Martinelli's intentions to foreclose and produced papers to that effect, instead of the ones Lance had expected.

Lance's disbelief had been palpable. Heart-thumping. Hand-sweating. Gut-wrenching. He'd presented a logical solution: more time. It had been rejected, with the failing economy as an excuse. That was when Lance begged. When that failed, he lost his mind.

The moment Ball turned his back to pick up his briefcase, Lance grabbed a baseball bat that had been hanging on the library wall since his high school days and hit the lawyer in the back of the head with the same fervor as when he'd hit the ball over the fence and sealed the county championship during his senior year of high school. That swing had ended the game. This one ended Ball's life. Austin Ball dropped without uttering a sound. Even though he was down, and very obviously dead, Lance continued to swing. By the time he got himself together, nearly every bone in Ball's body was broken, and blood was everywhere.

That was when panic hit.

He dropped the bat beside the body, rolled them up together into the rug on which Ball had dropped and dragged it out of the house and into the rental car Ball had driven out to his property.

Still in a state of hysteria, and fearing someone would drive up at any minute and catch him in such a bloody mess, he ran back inside and began cleaning up all the blood splatter. With one eye on the clock, he tore off all his clothing and threw it into the washing machine, then raced through the house to his bedroom naked and dressed again. Minutes later he was in the rental car, driving on a narrow, single-lane road that led into the woods behind the family home. He needed to hide the body, and though he'd never dug anything deeper than a hole to plant flower bulbs, he was about to dig his first grave.

Now here he was, almost an hour later, battling panic and regret. The palms of his hands were burning. He would definitely have blisters. His back was aching, and his heart was pounding so hard he feared he might have a heart attack and die in the grave he was digging for Austin Ball.

As a gust of wind swirled the loose leaves into an eddy, then sent them flying across the forest floor toward where he was digging, he glanced up at the sky. A storm predicted earlier in the day was almost upon him.

"Son of a bitch," he muttered, and dug a little harder.

It was getting darker. The hurricane in the Gulf was going to miss them, but it had obviously stirred up some rough weather. He had to get Ball's body buried before it started to rain or, with Louisiana's loamy soil and an elevation barely above sea level, the damn thing was likely to float out. He jabbed the point of the shovel back into the earth. Just as he was about to throw out another scoop, he heard what sounded like a gasp, then a scream. The sound was so unexpected that he nearly died on the spot. He pivoted in panic, then stared in disbelief.

The hair rose on the back of Carolina North's neck as she rubbed her finger and thumb together, smearing the droplet that she'd found on the leaves of the forest floor. Her morning walk had just taken a startling turn.

It was blood!

She'd been seeing the small red spots for some time but thought them nothing more than autumn's natural colors. Now the bright red hue had taken on a more sinister meaning.

The next question had to be, was it animal or human?

At twenty-nine and a successful author, the mystery writer in her wanted to know the answer, and the only way she would find out was to follow the trail. She glanced up at the gathering clouds. From the look of the sky, they were in for some bad weather. The side winds from a hurricane were forecast to brush the Louisiana coast sometime today, although the brunt of the storm was predicted to go farther south and west, and hit Galveston, Texas. She was sorry for Galveston, but sincerely happy this one was going to miss them. Still, all kinds of storms could erupt from such turbulent weather. The smart thing to do would be to turn around and head for home before she got soaked, but her conscience wouldn't let her. It could be something as innocent as a hiker like herself who'd been injured and was now wandering the Louisiana woods and bayous in search of help. What kind of a person would she be if she ignored the possibility of helping someone?

She paused long enough to get her bearings, although she wasn't far from the home she shared with her aging parents. If she walked up on an injured animal, which could prove dangerous, she needed to know which way to run to safety.

With a touch of anxiety, Cari moved forward, although the wind from the storm front was getting stronger and the blood trail was almost gone. She was on the verge of turning around and making a run for home when she stumbled into a small clearing. It was a familiar place—a clearing in which she had played countless times as a child.

At first, all she saw was an unfamiliar black car. Then she took a couple of steps to the right and realized there was a man standing in a very deep hole and shoveling out dirt. Within seconds she recognized Lance. He was someone she'd grown up with—a man she'd once been engaged to until she'd caught him in bed with a stripper from Baton Rouge. She watched for a moment, noticing the frantic manner in which he was digging.

What on earth…?

Before she could call out and announce her presence, the wind gusted sharply, blowing back the corner of what she'd first taken to be a pile of rags. When she saw the face and shoulder of a man's bloody body suddenly revealed, she realized she'd found the source of the blood.

And then it hit her.

The man was dead. And the hole Lance was digging was a grave.

Before she thought, she screamed, and for a few, life-altering seconds, Cari had an out-of-body experience as she found herself staring into the eyes of a killer. That it was Lance Morgan, her closest neighbor and childhood friend, seemed impossible.

She heard him shout out her name, and when he started to climb out of the hole, instinct told her to run.

So she did.

Within the space of a heartbeat, she was gone—running toward home as fast as she could go, without looking back. The wind was at her heels now, pushing at her, urging her faster and faster. Leaves were being torn from the trees and swirling around her head in a blizzard of reds and yellows. The wind was rattling the limbs overhead so sharply she kept thinking she was being shot at. Once she stumbled and fell to her knees, but she quickly caught herself and sprang up. With one frantic look over her shoulder to make sure Lance wasn't on her heels, she bolted.

Desperate to notify the authorities before Lance

caught her, she pulled out her cell phone as she ran, intent on calling 911, but she couldn't get a signal. Blaming the lowlands and the oncoming storm, she kept on running, praying for a miracle.

With each passing second, she imagined she could hear Lance's footsteps coming up behind her and feared that—at any moment—she would be caught and overpowered. When a strong gust of wind suddenly sent a dead limb flying from overhead to land on her heels, she pitched forward, certain that she'd been caught. Screaming and kicking, she rolled over on her back, unwilling to die without a fight, only to find herself doing battle with the limb, which had been caught in the hem of her jeans.

"God, help me," Cari muttered, and quickly kicked herself free.

She scrambled to her feet, desperate to get home, never thinking to check for her cell phone, which had slipped from her pocket as she fell.

Lance screamed Cari's name as he leaped out of the half-dug grave, then stumbled and fell over the body in the rug. Once again, Austin Ball had thrown a major kink in his plans. By the time he got up, Cari was out of sight. He dashed into the woods with the shovel in his hand, racing through the thickets and brambles without care or caution for his bare skin. He had to stop her. His life and Morgan's Reach depended on it. But it was with growing horror that he realized she had eluded him, and that she knew these woods as well as he did—maybe better.

Now he was faced with a dilemma. She would get the parish police, of that he was certain. He only had one chance out of this mess and that was to deny everything she said. Which meant he couldn't bury Ball's body here now because she would certainly bring back the authorities to look for it.

Cursing at the top of his lungs, he began running back to where he'd been digging. The wind was tearing at his clothing as he dashed into the clearing. To his horror, the rug had completely blown away from around Ball's body, and the sight of the man lying flat on his back in the middle of a blood-soaked family heirloom was horrifying.

In a panic, he began filling in the hole he'd just dug. The rain would wash away any loose soil and pack the dirt back down, so even if Cari brought the authorities here and dug again, there wouldn't be anything to find.

The first drops of rain were beginning to fall as he threw in the last of the dirt, then propped the shovel against the black rental car. Now that the hole was refilled, he still had to do something with the body. With shaking hands, he rolled the rug back around Ball's corpse, then hefted it over his shoulder and grabbed the shovel. He needed to find another place to hide what he'd done, but that meant going deeper into the forest—farther from his house—closer to the bayous. He didn't have time to get to the swamp-lands and use the gators as a method of getting rid of the body. He had to bury it.

But if he went farther, the car was going to be of no use.

With a muttered curse, he gritted his teeth and headed deeper into the woods, walking with his head down, sometimes staggering against the dead weight of Austin Ball's body and the prevailing winds.

But where to hide it so Cari and the cops couldn't find it? Where could he dig another grave that wouldn't be found? The answer didn't come until he passed a familiar landmark—an ancient cypress stump. His granddad used to tell stories of how the bayou had once come up this far, until they'd built levees and dikes around Bordelaise. The moment he saw the stump, he remembered what lay beyond. The fact that he suddenly had an answer to his problem made his load lighter and his steps easier.

Cari's legs were shaking from exertion and there was a pain in her side, but she couldn't stop. She had no way of knowing how close Lance was behind her, but she kept telling herself that it would all be okay as soon as she got home. Mom and Dad would be there, as well as her cousin, Susan, who'd come down from Baton Rouge only yesterday for a quick overnight visit. There was safety in numbers, and she would call the authorities from there.

The wind was getting stronger and the sky darker as she came out of the trees onto the small rise above her family home. When she saw the barn and the outbuildings, and the familiar sight of the old lowland plantation house that had been built on a stilted foundation, she shuddered with relief.

She'd made it.

Then the first drops of rain hit her in the face. They were hard and cold, and shocked her from her reverie. She started down the slope on the run, fighting a headwind and an ever-darkening sky. In the distance, she could see Tippy, the family dog, tucking tail and running for the barns. The chickens that were usually pecking about the barnyard were noticeably absent.

At that point, it occurred to her that the storm must be a bad one for the animals to all be taking shelter, which made her run that much faster.

It wasn't until she was in the yard and struggling against the wind to get up the steps to the front door that she heard her mother start screaming. The panic in Maggie North's voice made Cari desperate to get inside. She couldn't see the tornado her family had spotted suddenly dipping down out of the clouds on the other side of the house. She couldn't see them all running for the back door as she was trying to get in the front.

Her hand was on the doorknob when it hit. Suddenly the roof was off the house and swirling above her head, then the storm took both it and Cari's scream away. The front door flew off the hinges and into Cari's chest, throwing her backward. The last thing she saw was a splintered piece of lumber impaling her father against a wall.

And then everything went black.

Cari woke up pinned beneath part of the dining room table and a piece of wall, with the rain hammering on her face. She struggled weakly, trying to free herself from the rubble, but movement sharpened her pain, and she passed out.

The next time she opened her eyes, the rain had stopped and she could see patches of blue sky above her. For a few seconds, all she could think was that she shouldn't be able to see the sky from her bed, and then she realized where she was and remembered what had happened. Twice in one day she'd seen a dead man. One she hadn't known. The second one was her father, and she'd had to watch him die.

Pain rolled up and out of her in waves as she began to weep.

"Daddy! Daddy!" she screamed, praying she'd been wrong—begging God to give him back. But no one answered her cries.

It took a long time for her to become aware of the unnatural silence. Even though the storm had passed and the wind had calmed, the absence of any sound of life was frightening. There were no birds chirping—no hens clucking—none of Tippy's playful yips as he tormented the squirrels that lived in the live oaks in the backyard. The only thing she heard was the unsteady thunder of her own heartbeat pounding against her eardrums. In a panic to find the rest of her family, she began pushing against the debris once more, struggling to free herself.

"Mom! Mother! Can you hear me? Are you all right? Where are you?"

The fact that there was no answer made the skin crawl on the back of her neck.

Despite the pain, she had to get free of the debris. Her family needed help. When she raised her head, everything started to spin, and for a few moments she thought the tornado was back. Finally the nausea passed and she managed to sit up. From there, she pushed and kicked her way out from under what turned out to be half of the dining room table, then climbed over broken tree limbs and what was left of their living room sofa before she managed to get completely free. When she could stand without staggering, she began to search, calling out for her mother and Susan with every step.

She found her father first, his body still pinned to the living room wall, leaving him mounted like a butterfly in an entomology display. Horrified, she tried to pull him down. Sobbing with every breath and unable to look at his face, she failed, then tried to budge the huge stake instead and wound up with dozens of splinters in the palms of her hands.

Cari wailed, then dropped to her knees and covered her face, sobbing hysterically. Afraid to look further, but knowing she had no choice, she made herself get up and continue her search. Her mother and Susan had to be there—somewhere. All she had to do was find them.

Her knee was throbbing, and the longer she moved about, the more blood continued to run down her forehead and into her eyes. She already knew there was a cut in the top of her head as long and deep as her finger. She knew she needed to get help, but she couldn't worry about herself until she'd found the rest of her family.

She swiped at the blood with her forearm, then looked around and for the first time realized the complete devastation of what had once been her home. Nothing had been left standing. Everything was gone. The house. The barns. All the outbuildings and even the corral. A few feet away, she found Tippy dead beneath a tree that had fallen on her parents' car. She was struggling against nausea when she spied her own car upside down in the pasture beyond. All of a sudden, sickness bubbled up her throat.

She turned away and leaned down, bracing her hands against her knees to keep from going headfirst onto the ground while she retched and heaved until she was shaking. When the spasms finally passed, she managed to pull herself upright and resume her search.

As was so often the way with tornadoes, she found Susan's car completely untouched and right where she'd parked it yesterday. She opened the door and leaned in. The keys were in the ignition, and her cousin's purse and suitcase had already been loaded.

Cari shuddered on a sob. Susan hadn't wanted to go walking with her and had opted to check her e-mail instead. If she hadn't been waiting for Cari to come back to say goodbye, she might already have been gone.

Cari shut the door of Susan's car, then paused with her hand on the hood and said a brief prayer.

Please, God, help me. I can't find Mom. I can't find Susan. Please let them be all right.

A few minutes later, it was the bottom of a brown leather lace-up shoe sticking out from beneath part of the roof that caught her attention.

"Oh...no, no, no," she moaned, as she recognized the shoe as her mother's.

She dropped to her hands and knees and began moving away debris, finally locating her mother's lifeless body. The look of horror still etched on her face shocked Cari to the core.

"Mommy," Cari whispered, unaware she'd slipped into the name she'd used as a child.

Too sick at heart to weep and with shock pulling at her sanity, she sat for a moment beside the body, just holding her mother's hand, as if it might change the outcome of the storm. Finally she thought of Susan again and pushed herself upright. She had to keep searching. Susan had to be somewhere. Surely God wouldn't take them all. He wouldn't let them all be dead.

When she finally found her cousin, lying flat on her back behind what had once been the smokehouse, she knew she'd been wrong. Susan's face had been crushed beyond recognition.

Too numb to cry, too sick to think, she stood without moving, trying to wrap her mind around everything that had happened and what to do next.

At the same moment it hit her that she was the last living member of her family, she remembered Lance Morgan and why she'd been running for home.

She pivoted quickly as she flashed a swift look toward the road, then felt in her pocket and realized she didn't have a phone. She couldn't call for help. Lance could come driving up at any minute and do to her what he'd done to that man. No one would know the difference. They would just think she'd died in the storm.

Panic hit.

She had to get away.

She needed to get some medical help and figure out what to do next. But she knew Lance well enough to know that he would be behind her at every move.

She could take Susan's car and drive into Bordelaise. Someone there would help her. She could—

She stopped and moaned, blinded by a sudden pain from the deep wound in her head. She needed to regroup first. No need making accusations against Lance that she would never be able to back up. Lance might be a lot of things, but he wasn't stupid. Whatever she said, he would just chalk it up to her head wound. And now that he knew she'd seen him, there was no way he would bury that body where he'd been digging. He would move it, of that she was certain. And until she could figure out where, she needed to keep herself and her accusations under wraps.

She started toward the car when her legs suddenly went out from under her. She fell only a few feet away from Susan's body. It took every ounce of strength she had left to get back on her feet, and as she did, found herself looking down at Susan again.

They'd been born to twin sisters and within a month of each other. They had grown up like sisters, their features so similar that people had often mistaken *them* for twins, as well. They even wore their thick dark hair in the same casual style. At that moment, a thought occurred. It was daring, if not crazy, but it might give her the space and time she needed.

Susan's facial features were forever altered by whatever had killed her. But she was wearing jeans and black shoes like Cari's, as well as a white T-shirt.

The only difference was Cari's dark green, three-quarter-length all-weather coat. If she put the coat on Susan's body and got away before anyone saw her, whoever eventually found the bodies out here would quite naturally assume Susan was Cari. Especially Lance, who'd been the last person to see her alive.

And better yet, even though Susan was known in Bordelaise, no one knew she'd driven over from Baton Rouge to spend the night, so no one would suspect anything. Convinced this was the answer she needed, Cari took off her coat and, without looking at the wreck of Susan's face, knelt down and managed to put it on her by rolling her first one way, then the other.

Shaken and sick at heart, she finally crawled to her feet, then stopped and looked down. As she did, she shuddered. If she didn't know better, she would have thought she was looking at her own dead body.

Suddenly afraid she would be caught before she could get away, she headed for Susan's car as fast as she could go, stumbling once and falling yet again before she managed to get behind the wheel.

Her hands were sore from the splinters, and sticky with the same blood that was all over her clothes, but she couldn't let it matter. With every ounce of strength she had left, she started the car and put it into gear. The only thing she could think of was getting herself to Baton Rouge and, under the guise of her cousin's identity, getting some medical attention. She'd been to Susan's town house countless times and knew the way almost as well as she'd known the way home from the woods.

It wasn't that far.

All she had to do was get there.

Lance had been only vaguely aware of the thunderstorm while he'd been inside the cave burying Austin Ball, but when he got back to where he'd left the rental car, he was shocked by the devastation. Trees were uprooted. Bits and pieces of sheet iron and lumber were scattered about, and the car was nowhere in sight.

At first he'd thought someone must have stolen it. But the farther he ran toward home, the more certain he was that it had become a casualty of what must have been a tornado. He began to panic, fearing Morgan's Reach might have been hit, but when he reached the back of the property just beyond the stables and saw the familiar roofline, he started shaking from relief. There was evidence of damage, but nothing drastic, and nothing that couldn't easily be repaired. Some corrals were down, and there was a portion of roof missing off the barn, but the house seemed intact.

He ran through the mud and then to the back door, taking off his shoes at the stoop before going inside. Too many years of not bringing in mud on his shoes had been drummed into his consciousness to do it now—even if he was the one in charge.

He made a quick run through the house, checking for further damage. The electricity was off, but he still checked the laundry to make sure all the blood had washed out of the clothes he'd tossed in earlier. It had.

Unable to use the dryer, he took the clothes out and spread them over the washer and dryer to air-dry. No time like the present to put his world back in order. Except for a broken windowpane and some missing shingles he'd seen earlier, the house seemed solid, although he couldn't bring himself to do more than glance into the library where he'd committed the murder.

Now that he knew his home and property were in basic order, focus immediately shifted to Carolina North. This situation needed a lot of damage control, and the more time that passed, the harder it would be. He grabbed the keys to his truck and headed out the door, intent on a quick visit to his nearest neighbor.

His heart was pounding as he pulled out of the driveway and started down the blacktop toward the North property. He'd driven this road countless times during his life. With his brother, Joe, on their way to deliver Christmas gifts from one family to the other, then later, when he and Cari had been engaged. He knew and cared for the Norths almost as much as he'd cared for his own parents. And four years ago, when his parents died in a car wreck, Cari and her parents had been the first ones to arrive and the last to leave, long after everyone else was gone.

The closer he got to the turnoff to the North property, the sicker he became. He didn't know what lay ahead of him and wasn't sure if he had the stomach for what needed to be done. It had been one thing to stop a stranger from taking Morgan's Reach. It was another thing altogether to kill someone he knew in order to keep his secret.

Two

Every fear Lance had of facing Cari and her parents came to a halt as he drove up on the scene of devastation.

"Oh my God," he gasped, as he stomped the brake and killed the engine. The urgency of his situation had suddenly changed.

Every structure on the North property was gone.

The house, the barn, even the corrals.

A tree had fallen over on Frank and Maggie's vehicle, and Cari's car was upside down in the pasture beyond. He could see the dead carcasses of some of Frank's cattle, but most of the wreckage the storm had left behind was impossible to identify.

He jumped out of the truck and started toward the debris with his heart in his throat. Would there be survivors? If he found them, how would he be able to tell if Cari had already told them what she'd seen? If they were alive, what was he going to do? Finish them off—or get them to a doctor?

"Hello! Hello! Can anybody hear me?" he yelled, as he frantically started his search. "Mrs. North… Maggie…it's me, Lance! Can you hear me?"

Something shifted in the debris off to his right, then fell with a thud. He jumped, then ran in that direction, thinking someone might be trying to get his attention. But when he got there, his search was futile. No bodies. No survivors.

"Frank! Frank! It's me, Lance. Can you hear me? Are you here?"

His anxiety level was rising as he dashed throughout the rubble. He stumbled over a pile of lumber and shattered drywall, then pulled up short. The leg and shoe sticking out from beneath the rubble were horribly familiar.

"Maggie! Oh my God… Maggie!" he cried, and dropped to his knees.

When he got the debris away and saw her face, frozen in a death mask of terror, he rocked back on his heels. The first thing that went through his mind was the molasses cookies she used to bake for him. His eyes filled with tears. If Cari had already told her, it no longer mattered. Finding her dead meant that was one decision he wouldn't have to make.

He backed away quickly, then stood up, brushing at the mud on his knees as he sidestepped an upturned sofa and more drywall. A few moments later, he found Frank.

"Oh, Jesus," he whispered, then quickly looked away.

He found the family dog within moments of finding Frank, but still no Cari. Just as he was beginning to fear that she hadn't come home after all but was probably already in Bordelaise and talking to the authorities, he saw her.

It was the dark green, all-weather coat she'd been wearing that caught his eye. From this distance, he could tell she wasn't moving, but she wasn't lying in the midst of any debris. What if she was still alive? Could he finish her off and lay the blame on the twister?

His fingers curled into fists. His belly knotted. This was turning into the worst day of his life. He genuinely cared for all of the Norths, but especially Cari. That his life had come down to this was sickening.

He took a deep breath and then started forward. His legs were shaking; his vision blurred. Then he saw her face—or what was left of it—and froze. Still a good fifteen yards away, he dropped to his knees again, this time weeping from the relief of knowing he'd just been given a second chance. The only witness to the fact that he'd committed murder was dead.

After he pulled himself together enough to walk, he stumbled back to his truck and grabbed the cell phone from the seat. He tried to call the parish police but couldn't get a signal. It occurred to him then that the North property might not be the only scene of disaster.

Still shaking, he crawled up into the truck seat and started the engine. When he pulled back onto the main road and turned toward Bordelaise to notify the authorities about what he'd found, he had to remind himself that it was grief he would be expressing and not relief.

Cari drove the thirty miles from the family farm to Baton Rouge on autopilot. She had to stop twice to vomit and guessed she was probably concussed. The blood had dried on her clothes and in her hair, and the palms of her hands were beginning to swell from the splinters under the skin. She could only imagine what she looked like, but she couldn't let that stop her. Getting to safety, then getting medical attention, was paramount. She wouldn't let herself think of what she'd left behind—or that the bodies of her loved ones were lying exposed to the elements. They were beyond help and would have been the first to understand. If she was going to save herself, she needed to get well.

There was money in Susan's purse on the seat beside her. Inside were her driver's license, and insurance and credit cards, as well as a card stating her blood type, which they also shared. Cari should be able to get in and out of a hospital emergency room without complications. The fact that her claims would technically be fraudulent was nothing compared to being tracked down and killed to hide a murder.

When she finally reached the city limits of Baton Rouge, her hands were shaking so hard she could barely hold on to the steering wheel. She didn't see the shocked expressions on the faces of other drivers as they passed her, or of the people at the crosswalks as she stopped for lights. She was too focused on not passing out and keeping the car in the proper lane.

She glanced up at a street sign as she braked for another red light. The words kept blurring and running together, but if she wasn't mistaken, the hospital was just a couple of blocks down on her right. She turned on her signal. Just as the light went green, she felt herself fading.

"God, help me," she whispered, and jammed the shift into Park just before she passed out.

"Susan! Susan Blackwell! Can you hear me? Open your eyes, Susan. You're in a hospital."

Cari moaned. Someone was yelling. Didn't they know enough to speak softer? Her head was killing her.

She could feel someone taking off her clothes, which didn't make sense. It wasn't time for bed.

"Susan? You're in a hospital. My name is Dr. Samuels. Can you tell me what happened to you?"

Images moved through Cari's mind in disjointed flashes. Something red on the leaves on the forest floor. Wind whipping through the trees. *Panic!* Why panic? Running. The sky turning dark. Mother screaming. Oh Lord. Oh Lord. They're gone.

She felt a hand on her shoulder, then heard a woman's voice near her ear. "Susan, my name is Amy Niehues. I'm a nurse. Do you hurt anywhere besides your head? How did you get all these splinters in your hands?"

Cari inhaled slowly. Everything hurt, but she couldn't wrap her mind around the words long enough to answer before she lost consciousness again. The next time she came to, she was aware enough to realize she was in a hospital. A momentary swell of relief rushed through her. She'd made it. She was safe. On the heels of that emotion came the memory of what had happened. The tornado. Her family. Everyone gone.

Breath caught in the back of her throat. She would never hear their voices again. Never feel their arms around her. Never laugh with them. Never have her father walk her down the aisle. She might be a grown woman, but she'd just been orphaned.

Tears welled. A sob burned at the back of her throat. She covered her face with her hands, but the images from the storm were seared into her brain. What started out as a simple sigh of defeat turned into a scream. And once she started screaming, it didn't feel like she could stop.

Amy Niehues came running, as did several of her coworkers. Cari's room quickly filled as they began frantically trying to find the source of her discomfort. They kept asking her if she was in pain. They didn't know, and Cari couldn't tell them, that the pain wasn't fixable. There were no pills or treatments that would make what she was feeling go away. She didn't notice when Amy shot a sedative into her IV, but in a few minutes she closed her eyes and the room fell silent.

A doctor stood at the foot of her bed, studying her chart. He looked at her, then over to the nurse beside him.

"Amy…has anyone been able to locate her parents?"

"They've been dead for several years."

"What about extended family?"

"We're not sure," Amy said. "Someone contacted her place of employment, and we're just waiting for someone to get back to us."

The doctor handed the chart back to the nurse, gave Cari one last glance, then left the room.

Mike Boudreaux was in his office, pacing between the windows and his desk as he spoke to his assistant on the other end of the line.

"It doesn't matter, Kelly. You tell them they have the only offer they're going to get. They can either accept it—and me—or lose it all. I'm not the one who ran that company into the ground, and I'm also not the one who embezzled the entire company retirement fund. I said they could keep all the employees on the present payroll, but…the CEO is out. He didn't know how to keep his own company safe from the accountant who embezzled all their money and ran with it. What happens to *him* is the state of Ohio's problem, but no way in hell am I putting his boss in charge of a company I own."

"Yes, boss. I'll make sure they understand that."

"See that you do," Mike said, then frowned when he heard his housekeeper's footsteps coming down the hall. She was running, and Songee Wister never ran.

Songee burst into his office carrying the house phone. He could tell from the look on her face that something was wrong.

"There's a nurse asking for you," she cried, as she thrust it in his hands. "Something has happened to Miss Susan."

Mike's heart sank as he put the phone to his ear. Susan wasn't just an employee, she was his personal assistant, as well as a very good friend.

"Hello. This is Mike Boudreaux."

"My name is Loretta Sawyer. I'm the public liaison at Baton Rouge General Hospital. Do you have an employee by the name of Susan Blackwell?"

"Yes, she's my personal assistant," he said. "What's happened to her? Is she all right?"

"We're not sure," Loretta said. "She's injured, as if she's been in some kind of accident, although the paramedics who brought her in said there was nothing wrong with her car. It's possible she has been the victim of a crime, but at this point, we just don't know. We're calling you because she has you listed as her emergency contact."

"Yes, yes, I'll be right there," Mike said, then realized he didn't know which location. "Wait! Are you calling from Mid-City hospital, or the Bluebonnet location?"

"Bluebonnet, on Picardy Street," she said.

"Okay, thanks," Mike said, and disconnected. He was already running toward the hall to get his car keys when Songee met him at the door.

"Your keys," she said, as he handed her the phone.

"Thank you, Songee. As always, you're a step ahead of me."

"Is Susan all right?"

"I don't know," he said. "I'll call when I know something. In the meantime, it wouldn't hurt to send up one of your prayers."

"Yes, sir," Songee said. "I'll make it a powerful one…just in case."

She stood and watched until the taillights of his car disappeared down the driveway, then went back inside with praying on her mind.

Physical pain brought a rude awakening. Every heartbeat throbbed throughout her body. Her hands were stiff and bandaged, and for a moment she couldn't remember why. Then the memories flooded back…ugly, mind-numbing memories. Struck again with overwhelming sorrow, tears were already brimming as she opened her eyes.

Then she gasped.

A stranger—a man with dark hair and angry green eyes—was leaning over her bed. His voice was soft, his words accusing.

"I don't know what kind of game you're playing, but you're not Susan Blackwell. Talk now, or I'm calling the police."

Cari's stomach knotted as panic shot through her. She couldn't be outed—not like this. Not—yet.

"You don't understand," she mumbled, and grabbed at his wrist. "Susan and I are cousins. I needed to—"

She heard a swiftly indrawn breath, then the man quickly stepped back. The anger on his face slowly shifted to understanding. He put a hand on her arm, as if to steady her.

"Carolina? Is your name Carolina?"

Cari shuddered on a sob as the tension eased.

"Yes, but how did you—"

"I'm Michael Boudreaux, Susan's boss…and friend. The hospital called me when you were brought in. Susan always said you two looked alike, although it's hard to tell beneath the bruises and bandages."

"Oh, thank God," Cari said. She'd heard Susan talk about him for so long that her panic shifted to hope. Maybe he could help.

Mike frowned.

"What happened, Carolina?"

"Cari...please."

"Cari it is. Why the deceit? Why did you enter the hospital under Susan's name?"

Cari's eyes welled again, but this time, tears rolled. She hadn't planned on telling on herself quite this soon, but Mike Boudreaux's unexpected appearance gave her no choice.

The moment Mike saw the tears, he knew the answer wasn't going to be good.

"Susan's dead. My mother and father are dead. The storm...there was a tornado at our farm."

"Sweet Jesus," Mike muttered, then turned away, overcome by shock.

For a few moments all Cari saw was the stiff set of his shoulders. Panic swept through her. What was he going to do? Would he out her to the world before she had time to protect herself?

Then, all of a sudden, he turned back. His eyes were wet with tears, but his voice was steady as he lightly touched her shoulder and asked, "Is that what happened to you?"

She nodded, then wished she hadn't, because the motion made her sick.

Mike frowned. This wasn't making sense. "How did you get here? Why didn't you go to Bordelaise for medical treatment? That's where you live, right?"

Cari couldn't stop crying. Every time she tried to answer, the words seemed to swell and choke at the back of her throat.

Mike sighed. Obviously this wasn't a good time to push. But something was off. Unless…

"I think I understand," Mike said. "I was told you were found unconscious at a stoplight in Baton Rouge. You were driving Susan's car. Her stuff was in it. They assumed you were her, right? Don't worry. I'll straighten all this out for you."

When he moved, Cari grabbed his wrist, then winced at the pain in her bandaged palms. "No! Don't!" she cried. "You don't understand." She swiped at her tears with the edge of her sheet, then took a breath, trying to calm her thoughts. "Just before the storm hit, I walked up on a neighbor in our woods. He was…he was…oh God…just saying it aloud makes no sense."

"What was he doing?" Mike persisted.

"Digging a grave to bury the dead man wrapped up in the rug beside him."

"What the hell? You witnessed a murder?"

"Not the actual murder. Just the disposal of the body. He started running after me. I lost my phone while I was trying to get away. I just needed to get home. The tornado hit just as I reached the house. I lived through it. My family didn't. It wasn't until I found Susan's body…her injuries were mainly to her…" Cari shuddered, then covered her face with her hands. "Oh God, oh God…to her face." She shivered, then made herself continue. "I knew I had to hide until I figured out what to do, so I put my coat on Susan's body, knowing she would be identified as me, and ran."

Mike swallowed past the knot in his throat. Susan Blackwell had worked for him for seven years. He adored her and depended on her—as a friend and as his personal assistant. To know her life had ended like this was devastating. But his sorrow was obviously not on the same level as Carolina North's losses.

"I'm so sorry," he said, and then turned away and walked toward the windows overlooking the parking lot to gather his own emotions.

Cari's head was pounding. All of a sudden, she knew she was going to be sick—again.

"Mr. Boudreaux… Mike! I think I'm going to throw up," Cari said.

Mike spun and rushed to her side, grabbing the wastebasket and holding it up at the side of the bed as Cari leaned over. She didn't feel his hand on her back or see the empathy on his face. All she knew was that by the time she'd finished, her nurse was in the room, waiting with a fresh washcloth to wash her face.

Cari fell back onto the pillow with a groan. "Oh my God, I am so sorry."

"There's nothing to be sorry for. You're fortunate to still be alive," Mike said.

The nurse checked Cari's IV flow, eyed Mike curiously, then left to get something for Cari's nausea.

Once again, Cari and Mike were alone. He spooned a couple of ice chips into her mouth, then waited for her to chew them. When he thought she could handle the questions, he started talking again.

"Why didn't you go straight to the Bordelaise authorities?"

"And say what? That I saw my neighbor burying a body in the woods?"

"You knew the man?" Mike asked.

"Unfortunately, yes. Lance Morgan. I grew up with him.... His family's land joins ours on two sides. Lance is a lot of things, but stupid isn't one of them. There's no way he buried that body there. Not after I saw him. When I realized he wasn't still chasing me, I knew he'd gone back to move it. He would have buried it somewhere else. By the time I would have gotten to the authorities, it would be my word against his, and I've got a big hole in my head. He'd just claim my story was nothing more than a hallucination from the injury. His parents are dead, but he comes from an old and prominent family. Mine has been around almost as long, but it would just be my word against his. I didn't recognize the dead man, which means he wasn't a local, which means no missing person case to back up my claim. In fact, given our history, Lance could laugh it off and lay it all on our past."

"How so?" Mike asked.

"A couple of years ago we were engaged, until I caught him cheating on me. I called it off. He could claim I was just trying to get back at him for what he did to me."

"Oh."

Cari grimaced. "'Oh' is right. But it wasn't until after the tornado when I found Susan that...*this* occurred to me. No one in Bordelaise knew she'd driven down for the night. And her car was the only one that hadn't been damaged in the tornado. Her face was..." Cari bit her lip, struggling with her composure. "We're the same size. Same color hair and hairstyle. And we'd both been wearing white T-shirts and jeans. Lance had seen me earlier, so when I put my coat on her body, I did it hoping she'd be identified as me. It might have been the wrong thing to do, but I was hurt and needed time to think. Lance had already killed once. He would have no problem getting rid of the only witness to his crime."

"What a mess," Mike muttered.

"You have no idea," Cari said, then closed her eyes. She didn't intend to keep them closed, but a combination of meds and exhaustion soon pulled her under.

Mike watched Carolina drifting in and out of consciousness, and was surprised by the strong connection he felt. Maybe it was because she looked so much like Susan. And maybe it was because of the courage and ingenuity she'd shown in such a dangerous situation.

Courage was something he admired.

Over the years, Michael Boudreaux had become a force to be reckoned with in business, but in his youth, he'd been just another kid on the streets of

Baton Rouge. His grandparents had still been alive, clinging to former glory in their old plantation house outside of the city, while his mother and father held regular jobs. His father had worked for a manufacturing company, while his mother had been a preschool teacher. As the "pretty boy" in his classes, he'd often had to prove his worth with his fists. As a result, he learned the true meaning of courage, and to never be the first one to quit——at anything.

It was that attitude that made him so formidable in his own career. His parents had died within a year of each other while he was in college. His grandparents had passed a couple of years later. He'd inherited the run-down plantation, as well as the row house in the city where he'd grown up, and now he was completely alone in the world.

When he was twenty-two, he sold the little row house for a tidy sum to a company that needed land to expand, then he invested the money. One thing had led to another, until years passed and he had become known as what some might call a corporate shark. He did what he did without apology, but he did it while maintaining his hometown residency in Baton Rouge.

Mike could have lived an opulent lifestyle in any of the country's big cities, with limousines and fine dining, and beautiful women at his beck and call, but he'd chosen not to. He was tall and lean, with black hair and green eyes, and a stubborn streak inherited from his Cajun ancestors. And when he'd made his first million dollars, he'd renovated the old Boudreaux plantation outside of Baton Rouge and had lived there ever since. He traveled all over the world when job and duty called, but his roots ran deep in the Louisiana bayous.

For the past few years, Susan Blackwell had been a large part of his life. Now he had to face that she was gone. Sad for himself, and for the woman before him, he laid a hand on her arm.

Cari stirred as she felt his touch. When she opened her eyes, their gazes locked. Hers was unflinching. And in that moment, Mike made a promise.

"I'll help you through this. I'll make sure you stay safe."

Cari sighed, then bit the inside of her lip to keep from crying. "Then you need to start by calling me Susan."

"Right," Mike said, then stepped back and shoved his hands in his pockets. "For now, just know I've got your back."

A huge weight had suddenly been lifted from Cari's shoulders. "Thank you."

"It's the least I can do…for Susan," Mike said, as his voice broke.

Tears welled again, but Cari blinked them away. "For Susan," she echoed.

At that point the nurse came back and shot a syringe full of something into Cari's IV. A few minutes later, Cari was out.

But Mike wasn't sleeping. He'd made a promise, and he didn't make those lightly. He was already on a mission to find out all he could about Lance Morgan. Finding Morgan's weakness would be the first step in learning the identity of the man he'd murdered, which would also be the first step in making sure Carolina North stayed alive.

By the time Lance reached Bordelaise, it was obvious the tornado's damage was widespread. Houses were missing roofs. Trees were down everywhere, as were a large number of power lines. Even a cell phone tower had been twisted into a tangle of wire and metal, probably the reason he'd been unable to reach 911.

Main Street was a melee of cop cars, ambulances and fire trucks from at least half a dozen neighboring communities. It was obvious that the tornado had been on the ground when it came through town. The courthouse and nearby jail had taken direct hits, as had a grocery store, a lawyer's office and a beauty shop. He didn't know where to go to notify rescue services about the Norths.

Finally, when he'd driven as far as he could go, he parked, then started walking. Then someone called his name.

"Hey! Lance!"

He turned around. It was Lee Tullius, one of the parish police officers, standing by a panel van. Lance started toward him at a jog.

“Thank God you’re here!” Lee said. “We need some able-bodied volunteers to help move residents from the nursing home into the hospital.”

“I’ll be glad to help,” Lance said. “But I came into town to report three deaths.”

Lee paused, then put down the cots he’d been unloading. “Who and where?”

“Out at the Norths. Frank, Maggie and Cari are all dead. I drove over there right after the storm and…”

His voice broke. He didn’t have to fake the tears in his voice and eyes.

Lee knew Lance and Cari had once been a couple, and that they’d grown up together.

“Well, damn. I’m really sorry to hear that,” he said, then gritted his teeth. “This might sound cruel, but right now, we’re trying to focus on the living.”

“But they’re just…they’re lying out in the open. Birds…animals…just anything could get them.”

Lee sighed, picturing the pretty, dark-haired girl he’d known who’d grown up to become a famous writer, then palmed his radio. “Tullius here. Over.”

Vera Samuels, the daytime dispatcher at the police department, picked up. “Go ahead, Lee. Over.”

“Got a report of three dead bodies at the Frank North farm southeast of Bordelaise. Need them picked up ASAP. Over.”

Vera started to cry. “All of them? Over.”

“Ten-four,” Lee said. “We need the bodies retrieved before the animals get to them. Over.”

"Oh my God…I went to school with Cari," Vera said, as she struggled to speak through tears.

"So did I," Lee responded. "Get some people out there, and get them back as fast as possible. I'm afraid they won't be the only ones. Over."

"Ten-four and out," Vera said.

Lee hooked the handheld back onto his belt loop and then looked at Lance.

"Mission accomplished. Now, about the nursing home…"

"Right," Lance said, and started down the street at a lope.

By the time the last residents of the nursing home had been moved to the hospital, Lance was muddy and sick to his stomach. One old fellow, a man named Warren, had died in his arms on the way out of the building. Because the man was wheelchair-bound, Lance had been forced to pick him up and carry him through the debris-strewn hallways. He hadn't known the guy was dead until he went to put him down on a gurney outside to be taken to the hospital.

"This one's gone," the EMT said.

Lance's eyes had widened in disbelief. "That's impossible," he said. "He was talking to me when I picked him up."

"Too much stress and strain," the EMT said. "Don't worry about it. No one's going to blame you."

Maybe not for this one, Lance thought, and once

again, accepted his unbelievable luck that Cari North had perished only minutes after walking up on him in the act of hiding a crime. He shook off the shock and nervously swiped his hands down the front of his shirt.

"He was the last one on that wing," Lance said.

The EMT nodded. "Then he's the last one period," he said. "Report back to the town square. It's where emergency services has set up office. I'm sure someone else could use your help. We also have a missing kid."

"Oh, no, who?" Lance asked.

"J.R. and Katie Earle's little boy, Bobby."

Lance tried to remember what the little boy looked like but couldn't. All he could do was shake his head as he walked away. On the way back downtown, he tried his cell phone again, as he had been doing off and on, checking to see if they'd restored reception. To his relief, the connection bars finally showed up.

After what had happened, he knew his brother, Joe, who lived in Savannah, would be frantic. He wanted to let him know he was okay, and that Morgan's Reach had survived the storm. But before he could punch in the number, his phone suddenly rang.

He saw the caller ID and then bit his lip as emotion swamped him. It was Joe. His voice was thick with tears as he answered.

"Joe, I was just about to call you. I'm okay. I'm okay."

"Thank the Lord," Joe said. "I've been trying to call you for hours."

"The lines have been down all day. I just now was able to get a connection."

"Where were you when the tornado hit? Is the house okay? What about the livestock?"

Lance could hardly admit he'd been burying a dead body.

"I was out, but on the property. By the time it passed and I could get home, I was afraid the house had taken a hit. However, we were lucky. It has some damage, but nothing serious. A few missing shingles, barn's missing a corner of the roof, and there are some windows broken. Otherwise, we were fortunate."

"Thank goodness," Joe said. "What about Bordelaise?"

Lance hesitated and took a deep breath. Telling Joe the news was going to be as difficult as finding the Norths' bodies.

"It got hit pretty bad. A lot of the buildings around the town square are gone or damaged beyond repair. The nursing home was also damaged. The back of the jailhouse was hit. And someone just told me there's a missing child."

"Lord, Lord," Joe whispered. "I can't believe it!"

"That's not all," Lance said.

"What?" Joe asked, the sense that something awful had happened clear in his voice.

"The North property took a direct hit. There isn't a building standing, and… Joe…"

"Yeah?"

"Frank, Maggie and Cari…they're all gone."

"What do you mean, gone? As in they weren't there when it happened?"

"No, Joe. They're dead."

There was a long moment of what was probably stunned silence, then Lance could hear Joe crying.

"It's awful, Joe. I was the one who found them."

"Oh, Lance…I'm so, so sorry," Joe said. "I'll get the first flight out and be there as soon as possible. Don't worry. Whatever happens, we'll get through this together, just like we did when Mom and Dad died."

"Thanks, Joe. If I'm not home when you get here, I'll be in Bordelaise. They need all the help they can get."

"Take care of yourself," Joe said. "You're all I've got."

The line went dead in Lance's ear. He dropped his cell phone in his pocket, then swiped at the tears on his cheeks. There was still so much to be done before the world stopped spinning.

Three

Cari woke just as a nurse walked into her room.

"Good morning, Susan. My name is Tammy Bowen. I'll be your nurse today. Did you sleep well last night?"

"Off and on," Cari said.

Tammy frowned. "You should have asked for something to help you sleep. Rest is important to healing."

"I'll remember that," Cari said. "Right now I need to go to the bathroom." But when she started to sit up, the room started spinning. "Yikes," she said, and grabbed the bed rails to keep from falling.

Tammy quickly moved to her side. "Careful, dear. Let me help you."

Cari gratefully accepted the offer. By the time she came out, the nurse had a sink of warm water waiting for her to wash her face and hands.

The simple act turned out to be more difficult than Cari expected. Between the IV still in her arm and the dizzy spells she kept having, she wound up with almost as much water on the front of her gown as on her face.

"Don't worry about it," Tammy said, as Cari brushed uselessly at the wet streaks on her gown. "I'll get you a dry one after your bath."

"Thank you," Cari said. "I'm sorry to be so helpless."

Tammy smiled as she helped Cari back to bed.

"Honey, if you weren't, you wouldn't be here, remember?"

Cari managed to return the smile. "It's just that I'm usually the one doing the helping."

"So now you know how others feel who need help." Tammy added, "What you need to do is quit worrying and concentrate on getting better."

"You're right," Cari said. "Thank you."

Tammy fussed with the sheets as Cari settled against the pillows. "Hang on, Susan. I'm going to raise the head of your bed a little bit. Your food will be coming soon."

It was the name Susan that reminded Cari of what lay ahead, and with that realization came the pain.

Tammy noticed Cari's change in mood as she turned on the television. "Do you need anything for pain? Doctor left orders. Don't try to be brave and do without. It just slows down your healing."

Cari knew the meds would make her sleepy, but in the grand scheme of things, she supposed sleeping was a better way to pass the time than being awake and crying, which made everything hurt worse.

"I guess," Cari said.

At that point an aide entered, carrying a tray with Cari's breakfast.

"Oh look, breakfast is here," Tammy said with professional cheer. "Eat while it's hot. I'll be right back with your meds."

Cari's stomach lurched as she eyed the food. It certainly didn't look like her mother's cooking. And the moment she thought it, her vision blurred. Trying to focus on something besides the memory of her parents' bodies amid the tornado debris, she reached for the button on the side of her bed and upped the volume on the TV. She scanned several channels until she found local news, then listened absently while poking at the food without eating it.

It wasn't until she heard the word *Bordelaise* that she realized the story was a report on the aftermath of yesterday's storm. She focused in on the video clip, immediately recognizing the town square—or what was left of it—then turning her attention to what the on-site reporter was saying.

"As of 7:00 a.m. this morning, there have been four confirmed deaths from yesterday's tornado. Twenty-nine people have been hospitalized with injuries of varying severity, and one seven-year-old boy is still missing. Authorities have yet to confirm that his absence is due to the storm. The parents have been divorced for almost a year, and at this time, the authorities have not been able to locate the father, which has led to suspicions of family abduction.

"The town itself has been devastated. Court was in session when the courthouse was hit. The nearby jail was also heavily damaged. Four prisoners who had been incarcerated there are still unaccounted for. As you can see from this clip, several farms in the surrounding area were also destroyed. This house, which was southeast of Bordelaise, was leveled, and all three occupants were killed."

Cari shuddered. The footage they were showing from the air was of her home—or what was left of it. Seeing the devastation from this perspective was even more shocking. Part of the smokehouse roof was in the pasture on the far side of her car. She was heartsick, wondering if her parents' bodies had been recovered when this footage had been shot.

Trying hard not to start weeping again, she reached for her orange juice and took a sip. Anything to shift her focus from the overwhelming need to cry. Then the door to her room opened and Mike Boudreaux walked in.

It wasn't the first time she'd noticed how handsome he was, and how well he wore his clothes, which today happened to be khaki-colored slacks and a navy blue polo shirt. She would have guessed that, as a teenager, some might have called him too pretty for a boy. But age had lent a measure of character to his face, honing angles and tightening muscles, and turning him into a very handsome man. Still, what he looked like was the last thing she needed to be thinking about.

Mike didn't know what had preceded his arrival, but he didn't need to look twice to see what was going on. Between the tears in Carolina's eyes, the uneaten food on her tray and what she was watching on television, she was seconds away from a meltdown.

"Good morning," he said, then leaned over the bed and turned off the TV. "How did you sleep? You aren't eating your food, but on second thought, from the looks of your tray, smart move."

Cari's misery shifted to fury when the television screen went dark. How dare he come in and start directing her life? She didn't answer to him. If she wanted to spend the day bawling, it was her right. She was the one who'd lost her whole family. She was the one trying to dodge a killer.

Mike saw the anger spreading over her face and knew hysterics had been averted when she picked up her fork and pointed it at him.

"Thank you so much for stopping by. Don't let the door hit your ass on the way out," she said.

It was all he could do not to grin. She was amazing. Carolina North might be down, but she was definitely not out. She might look like Susan, but she sure didn't act like her. Susan had been a phenomenal assistant, but she never would have stood up to him like this. He watched as Carolina stabbed her fork into the food and took a bite of what were most likely tasteless scrambled eggs, eating as if they were the best thing she'd ever put in her mouth just because he'd implied the food was inedible. She spread jelly on the soggy toast and then ate until it was gone, all the while ignoring his presence.

Satisfied that his ruse had worked, Mike watched her without comment. She might hate his guts, but for the moment, he would gladly bear the brunt of her anger. When she'd finished her meal, he decided to add a new topic.

"The doctor is releasing you today."

The news was not unexpected, but at the same time, it was a little unsettling. Here, Cari felt safe. Once she was out on her own again, there were big decisions to make.

"Good," she said.

"But he doesn't recommend you stay on your own…at least not for the first week. I am issuing an invitation for you to come to my house. I know I ticked you off, but there was a reason behind it." His voice softened. "I'm sorry I was so damn bossy, but do you still feel like crying?"

Cari eyed the man with new appreciation as it began to soak in why he'd been so pushy.

"No, I don't. I guess I should say thank-you, both for your empathy and your offer."

"So…will you accept?" Mike asked.

"At the risk of sounding unappreciative, I really don't have a choice. This is the first time in my life that I've been so completely at the mercy of others. I *will* come stay with you, and I thank you for the offer."

Mike thrust his hand forward.

"Truce?"

Cari clasped it carefully.

He nodded, satisfied that all was going according to plan. "I'm going down to the business office to settle your bill. When I come back we'll—"

"Wait!" Cari said. "You don't need to do that. I have money."

Mike shook his head. "No. Carolina North had money. Susan has money, too, but I don't think you've thought through the legal liabilities of your impersonation. You can't spend Carolina's money, because everyone thinks she's dead, and right now you want them to go on thinking that. You can't spend Susan's money, because that would be theft, as well as fraud."

Cari groaned. "I hadn't thought of it from that standpoint."

Mike gently touched the bandage on the side of her head. "That's because you've got a monumental boo-boo on your thinker."

"A boo-boo on my thinker?"

Mike grinned. "My nearest neighbors have a three-year-old. He's one of my favorite people. I was borrowing some of his vocabulary to cheer you up."

Cari wondered if he knew how sexy he looked

when he grinned, then ignored the thought. "Once again, I find myself thanking you for your generosity and compassion."

"No biggie," Mike said, and handed her a business card. "This has my cell number, in case I'm not here when the doctor makes his rounds and gives you your marching orders. Just call me. I'll come pick you up."

Cari took the card, then glanced up, studying the set of his jaw and the cut of his cheekbones. He looked like a man used to getting his way. Still, she was grateful.

"Thank you, Mike."

"You're welcome, tough stuff."

Cari frowned. "Tough stuff?"

"I can't call you Carolina, for obvious reasons, and I'm not going to call you Susan. I call it like I see it, and you, my lady, are tough with a capital *T*."

Cari blinked. "Was that a compliment or a criticism?"

"In the business world, they call me a corporate shark, because I do what I have to do to make something feasible and profitable, even when it's at others' expense. I don't feel guilty for it. I'm not responsible for the mess the company I'm buying is in. They got there all by themselves. I'm just saving them from financial ruin in a way that works for me, too. You're doing what you have to do to keep yourself safe, and at the same time, you're seeking justice for a man you don't know, all at your own risk. In my book, that makes you damn tough…and quite a woman."

Cari felt her face getting hot, and the look in his eyes made her nervous. "Thanks," she said, and then quickly looked away.

Mike knew he'd said enough. "So…is there anything you need?"

"I don't have any clean clothes. Susan's suitcase was in her car, but I don't know where that is."

"They towed it. I've already gotten it out of the impound yard. It's parked at my house, but I put the suitcase in my car, figuring it would come in handy, so I'll bring you up a change of clothes. And since the key to her apartment was on her key ring, I'll take you by her house after you're released, so you can get some of her things."

Cari shuddered, just thinking of going through Susan's clothes.

Mike noticed her reaction, then winced. "I'm sorry. That was unfeeling of me, to assume you wouldn't mind wearing Susan's belongings. If you'll write down your sizes, I'll go get some new things for you myself."

Tears welled once more, but Cari managed to maintain her emotions. "That's not necessary. Susan wouldn't care, and if the situation were reversed, she would wear mine."

"Okay, but don't hesitate to let me know if you change your mind."

Cari squinted her eyes, as if judging him anew. "Thank you for understanding."

"I'll be waiting for your call," he said, then left.

She shoved aside the tray table with the congealing leftovers, and then nestled down into her pillows as the door closed behind him. It felt as if Mike Boudreaux had taken all the energy in the room with him. Weary from too much thinking and too many meds, she closed her eyes.

Just to rest.

She was still asleep when the doctor came in on rounds.

After a whirlwind of orders she didn't remember, she dressed in the clothes Mike had left at the nurses' station. A short while later, she'd been properly discharged and was down in the lobby, sitting in a wheelchair with an orderly at her side, waiting for her ride.

Her head was throbbing. Every time she moved, something hurt. She was still waiting for her latest pain meds to kick in when she saw Mike drive up.

"There's my ride," she said, pointing to the gleaming black Cadillac just pulling under the breezeway. The orderly began pushing her toward the exit, but Cari's gaze was fixed on the man striding purposefully toward the doors.

He must have run home, because he was dressed now in dark slacks and a white knit shirt. Besides the fact that he was undeniably stunning, he emanated power. Cari couldn't help but wonder why Susan had never mentioned that.

"Ah…ready to go, I see," Mike said, as the orderly pushed her wheelchair through the exit doors and up to his car. "Easy does it," he said gently, helping Cari out of the wheelchair and into the front seat, then proceeding to buckle her in as if she were a child.

"Thank you," she said, as Mike leaned across her to fasten the seat belt.

At the sound of the click, she suddenly flinched.

He frowned. "Damn. Did I hurt you?"

"No. I'm just jumpy, I guess."

"You're allowed," Mike said softly, but instead of pulling back, he gazed straight into her eyes. With less than a foot between them, he carefully eyed the bruises on her skin and the dark shadows under her eyes, and resisted the urge to kiss her.

"You're going to be okay," he said softly.

Cari's gut knotted. He was so close she could have counted his eyelashes. Then she amended the thought. They were too thick to count. The last man she'd been this close to had been Lance, but that was when they'd still been intimate. The thought of Lance killed the surge of interest she'd just felt, as her mood shifted to anxiety.

Lance!

She couldn't help but wonder what the hell he was doing now. Probably privately congratulating himself on the news of her death while playing the part of the grieving friend and ex-lover all over Bordelaise.

Mike gave her another quick glance, then closed the door and circled the car to slide in behind the wheel. "Are you okay?"

She nodded.

"Still up to stopping by Susan's house? And please don't hesitate to say so if you're not. I can easily get some stuff for you later."

"No, no, I'd rather do it myself, if you don't mind."

"Sure thing," Mike said, then put the car in gear and headed for Susan's. Within fifteen minutes, he was pulling into the driveway. "Hang on," he said, as he killed the engine. "I'll help you out."

Cari waited for him once again, grateful for his assistance as he steadied her on the way to the door. The more time passed, the stiffer she was getting. There were bruises all over her body, which left her with nothing but guesses as to what had happened to her during the tornado.

Mike was going through his own set of issues. He steeled himself as he opened the door, knowing Susan would never greet him again with that happy smile. Still, whatever it was he was feeling, it was nothing compared to what must be going through Cari's mind.

When he glanced at her, he knew his instincts had been right. She looked like a lost child. Without thinking, he slid his arm around her shoulders, bracing her for what lay ahead.

"Chin up, tough stuff."

Cari nodded as she gazed around the room. "I haven't been here in a couple of months, but I know where everything is."

"I'm coming with you," Mike said. "No lifting, pushing or pulling for you until you're better. Oh. Wait. I brought one of my suitcases for you to pack up some stuff. I'll go get it out of the car."

Cari moved farther into the living room as Mike ran back out.

The first thing she noticed was the flashing light on Susan's answering machine. Once again, she was reminded of how involved her impersonation was becoming. There must be appointments to cancel, people who would be expecting answers to their calls. She looked for a pen and paper, and then sat down in the desk chair and punched Play.

The first three calls were nothing more than reminders for appointments. But it was the fourth call that left her shaking.

"Miss Blackwell. I'm Hershel Porter, with the parish police in Bordelaise. Lance Morgan gave me your name and number. I need you to call me back at your earliest convenience regarding a matter of extreme importance."

"Oh Lord," Cari said. She knew what was coming. Susan, being the next of kin, was about to be notified of the deaths.

Mike came back in with the suitcase, saw her face and hurried to her.

"What's wrong?"

Cari played back the message without speaking. Midway through, Mike's hand was on her shoulder. By the time the message was over, he knew she had yet another bridge to cross. She was about to become the next of kin—to her own death.

"What are you going to do?" he asked.

"Make the call," she said, then took a deep breath, bracing herself for what was coming.

Mike pulled up a chair and sat down beside her. "I'm here if you need me."

Cari tried to smile but felt too much like weeping to complete the effort. Her hands were shaking as she dialed the number, then waited for the call to go through. When the police picked up, she went another step deeper into her impersonation of Susan by lengthening her drawl and softening her tone.

"This is Susan Blackwell. I'm returning a message from Chief Porter."

"Oh!" the dispatcher said. "One minute, please."

Cari recognized Vera's voice. She wanted nothing more than to weep on her old friend's shoulder. Instead she struggled to maintain composure, waiting for Hershel to come on the line. When she finally heard him, she bit her lip, needing pain to shift her focus from breaking down.

"Miss Blackwell?"

"Yes. I had a message to call you?"

She heard him take a deep breath and knew this

wasn't easy for him. He was a few years older than she was, but, like her, he'd been born and raised in Bordelaise.

"Miss Blackwell, I don't know if you remember me or not. I think we've met several times through the years."

"Yes, I remember you," Cari said. "Please… what's wrong?"

"I'm afraid I have some bad news. The tornado that came through Bordelaise on Sunday hit your aunt and uncle's property. I'm so sorry to tell you, but Frank, Maggie and your cousin were all killed."

Cari's breath caught. Hearing it said aloud—like this—sealed the awful truth. She didn't have to fake the sorrow.

"Oh Lord… Lord," she said softly.

"They were at the farm when the tornado hit. Their bodies have been taken to Sumner's Funeral Home here in Bordelaise. The funeral director has been notified and is expecting your call. Again, I'm so sorry for your loss."

Cari's voice was shaking. She felt like she was going to throw up. "They're all the family I had left."

"I know. I'm so sorry."

Cari started to cry.

"Would you like the number to the funeral home?" Porter asked.

"Yes…no…yes, I guess."

All the while Cari was saying the words, the

weight of her reality was hitting anew. By the time she got the number, she was sobbing. She disconnected, then collapsed.

"I can't do this. I can't. I need to see my mother. My daddy. Susan… I can't bury them long distance. I have to be there."

Mike ached for her. This was, in truth, a hell of a mess. "Don't worry. We'll figure something out," he said, then handed her his handkerchief. "Are you going to call the funeral home now?"

Cari wiped her eyes, blew her nose, then took a deep breath. "Not yet. I need to think a few minutes. I think I'll go pack first. Maybe by the time I'm finished, I'll be able to face talking to someone else."

"What can I do?" Mike asked.

She pointed to the suitcase. "Carry that into the bedroom for me, I guess."

"Absolutely," he said, and followed her down the hall.

Cari started into Susan's bedroom, then hesitated, once again, staggered by the enormity of what she was about to do. But all it took was remembering Lance and the dead man, and she knew she had no choice. She set her jaw, then strode across the room to the closet as Mike put the suitcase on the bed.

"Let me know when you're through and I'll carry it to the car for you," he said, then left her on her own.

Cari stared at the closet door for a few more moments, then took a deep breath and reached for the knob. The moment she opened the closet, the scent of lavender hit her like a slap in the face. She shuddered. Lavender. A scent she'd always associated with Susan. Now it would be hers—at least for a time.

Gritting her teeth, she quickly sorted through the clothes on the hangers, choosing several outfits, then carrying them to the bed. She packed quickly, anxious to be gone before her emotions caught up with her again. By the time she'd filled the suitcase, she also had underwear, shoes and sleepwear, along with an assortment of Susan's makeup. Besides being the same height and size, they shared the same skin tone and hair color, so whatever she used would pass, although the lipstick colors were more subdued than what she would have worn.

She fastened the suitcase and started to drag it off the bed, then remembered the doctor's orders and stopped. Healing was what she had to do first. Undoing the rest of this mess would come later.

As she started down the hall, the sound of her footsteps on the hardwood floors alerted Mike. He came to meet her, his expression wreathed in concern.

"How you doing, *cher?*"

The tenderness in his voice was nearly her undoing. "Not as well as I'd like," Cari said. "The suitcase is on the bed. Thank you for carrying it for me."

"Yeah, sure," he said, leaving her to make her way into the living room.

Suddenly anxious to be out of this house and away

from her cousin's ghost, she went back to the desk and eased down in the chair. There was still the matter of calling Sumner's Funeral Home, but while she'd been packing, she had come up with a plan.

Her head was pounding, and there was a bitter taste in her mouth as she picked up the phone. "God. I need this day to be over," she muttered, and made another call to Bordelaise.

Her call was answered promptly, and once again, she recognized the voice. Sarah Beth Spellman had worked for Sumner's for as long as Cari could remember, which meant she needed to be careful not to give herself away.

"Sumner's Funeral Home, Sarah Beth Spellman speaking."

"This is Susan Blackwell. I've been told the North family…my family members…were taken there."

"Yes, they're here," Sarah Beth said. "And, honey…I just want you to know I'm so sorry."

Cari pinched the bridge of her nose and closed her eyes, trying not to say too much, or somehow give herself away, but Sarah Beth's sympathy was getting to her. It was even more difficult to talk to her than it had been talking to Hershel Porter.

"Thank you," Cari said shakily.

Sarah Beth continued. "We all know you're the only surviving family member, so the lawyer for the family has had us wait until you were notified to see if you wanted to be the one to make funeral arrangements."

"I do…. I just have a couple of problems right now," Cari said.

"You just name a day and time when you want to come in and make arrangements. We'll do everything we can to make this as easy as possible for you."

Cari took a deep breath. *Lord help me make this work.* "I'm grateful for your offer, but I'm going to have to make an unusual request of you."

"We'll be honored to do anything we can," Sarah Beth said.

"I suffered a serious accident a couple of days ago. I just got out of the hospital this morning, and at the moment I'm unable to travel. Not being able to make arrangements in person is devastating to me, but I have no choice. Would it be asking too much if you would—"

At that moment Cari caught a glimpse of a framed photo of herself and Susan, taken last Christmas in front of her mom and dad's Christmas tree, and came undone. With her focus gone, she was unable to stop the harsh, ugly sobs tearing up her throat.

"I'm sorry… I can't… I—"

Suddenly the phone was taken out of her hands. She was vaguely aware of Mike's deep, steady voice, explaining who he was to Sarah Beth and making decisions she couldn't make for herself. Heartsick to the depths of her soul, she pushed herself up from the chair and stumbled into the kitchen.

She got a glass from the cabinet and thrust it under the faucet, letting it fill, then overflow, unable to stop weeping long enough to take a drink. Suddenly

Mike's arms were around her, and then he was taking the glass out of her hands and pulling her hard against his chest. She didn't know he was crying with her, but it wouldn't have mattered.

"Go ahead and cry, *cher*...cry," he said softly. "Let it all go. I know.... I know.... It hurts like hell, and you and I both know it's not fair. I'm sorry. I'm just so, so sorry."

Cari's hands were fisted, her anger only slightly less than her sorrow. She tried to push away, but he wouldn't let her go. Finally she collapsed against him as she screamed, "God...oh God...all I keep wanting to ask is why? Why did they all have to die? Why didn't I die with them? How can a life go from happy to over that fast?"

"But your life isn't over," Mike said. "I don't know why this happened the way it did, but you owe it to yourself and to your family not to waste what you've been given. Live for yourself, and for them."

Cari knew he was right, and she held on to Mike as if he were her lifeline, leaning on his strength because all of hers was gone. She cried until her eyes were swollen and it hurt to breathe. And with the last of her tears, her legs went out from under her and the room began to spin.

Mike grabbed her just as she went limp. "We've been here too long," he muttered, and carried her into the living room, out the door and back into his car. He cupped her cheek briefly. "I'll be right back," he promised, then closed the door.

Cari leaned against the headrest and closed her eyes, wanting this all to be nothing but a nightmare. A hell on earth that would go away just as soon as she opened her eyes. But when she did, all she saw was Mike coming out of the house with a suitcase full of her cousin's clothes. Their gazes met.

Her heart thudded hard against her chest.

Oh, sweet Jesus. He's been crying, too.

It was then that she remembered that he, too, had a reason to grieve.

Susan.

Had their relationship been more than boss and employee?

Had he loved her?

Four

Mike felt a huge sense of loss as he drove away from Susan's house, knowing it might be the last time he would ever have a reason to be there. Her death closed a door on a big part of his life. He didn't want to think about telling everyone down at the office what had happened, or how awkward it was going to be to have to try to replace her. How did one replace a best friend and the best damn employee he'd ever had?

He glanced at Cari as he braked for a red light, then quickly looked away. He had to admit, his first impression of her had certainly done a one-eighty. Waiting for her to wake up in the hospital, he'd been certain she was some con artist who'd stolen Susan's identity. Part of the reason he hadn't immediately seen the resemblance to Susan was that he wasn't expecting it, but there was also the fact that whatever hadn't been bruised on her face and neck had been bandaged. Never in a million years would he have guessed the staggering truth, or that he would find himself so enmeshed in her deception.

Cari had no idea what was going through Mike's head, and if she had, she wouldn't have cared. Dealing with her own misery was overwhelming everything else. Her head was pounding so hard she felt numb, and while the bandages had been removed from her hands before she left the hospital, they were still stinging. It felt as if every bone in her body ached. Added to that, talking to the parish police and passing herself off as Susan, then doing it again with Sarah Beth Spellman, had been draining. That reminded her of the phone call she'd been unable to finish. The least she could do was let Mike know she appreciated his backup.

"Mike…?"

"Yes?"

"Thank you for helping me with the call to the funeral home. I thought I could pull it off. Obviously I was wrong."

"No problem," he said softly. "It was the least I could do, and I should tell you that the lady said for you not to worry, that she'd treat them as if they were her own family. She knows their clothing was destroyed in the storm, so she's going to shop for them on her own. We set a time for the services, too. And there was one more thing."

"What?"

"They won't be opening Susan's casket. I assume it's because of her…of the injuries."

Cari nodded, as she remembered once again how Susan had looked, and how limp and heavy her body had been as she'd struggled to put on the coat. Then her thoughts went straight to the burial. Another step in the finality of loss. Oh my God. Her parents interred in the family mausoleum. Susan so horribly disfigured that she wasn't even presentable. This couldn't be real.

She turned away to stare out the window, unable to talk anymore.

Mike could see the information was hurting her, but the details had to be said.

"They'll hold services on Thursday at 11:00 a.m. Today is Tuesday. The lady said there's so much cleanup still going on that waiting an extra day would be better…that everyone knew and loved you and your family, and would want to attend."

Cari leaned back and closed her eyes, unable to think about it anymore.

Instinctively Mike reached for her hand, then stopped. He had to keep reminding himself that she wasn't Susan. Unfortunately this was his housekeeper's afternoon off. There wasn't going to be anyone to temper the tension between them. Still, he'd offered his help in Susan's honor, and he wasn't going to go back on his word.

"Hang in there," Mike said. "We're almost home."

* * *

The sun was setting as Lance pulled up to his house and parked. He was exhausted, both mentally and physically, but after witnessing all the devastation, never more grateful to be alive. It did not occur to him to feel guilty that he'd taken someone else's life or had been willing to end three others to keep the secret. He'd been indulged all his life, and still expected the world to revolve around him and his needs.

His gaze swept the storm-tossed area as he walked toward the veranda. There were things here to be cleaned up as well, but most of it involved downed tree limbs, some missing shingles and a corner off the barn roof.

The only thing that had been pressing was the broken windowpanes inside Morgan's Reach, and those had been dealt with while he'd been in Bordelaise. Jim Bob Greeley had come out and replaced the glass while Lance had been in town. The rest of the repairs could be dealt with as time permitted.

He bent down and lifted the doormat, retrieving the key he'd given Jim Bob to use, grunting slightly as he straightened up to unlock the door. Remembering that there were four prisoners from the jail who were still missing, he turned around and locked the door behind him as he went inside. It did not occur to him that he was no better than they were—maybe worse. The men who'd been jailed had been arrested for drug trafficking. Lance had committed murder. Yet he'd already justified his act as necessary and moved on, just as he hoped those prisoners had done.

His steps were dragging as he walked through the house, taking off his clothing as he went. By the time he got to his bathroom, he was nude. The power was back on, which was good. He couldn't wait to get into a hot shower and then some clean clothes. He turned on the water, waiting until it ran warm as he grabbed a bottle of shampoo. Just as he was about to get into the shower, his phone began to ring. He started to ignore it, then remembered Joe was on his way here, and stepped back into the bedroom and checked caller ID.

When he saw the name Dominic Martinelli, his heart dropped. The Chicago loan shark. The nightmare of losing the family home was once again looming on the horizon. In typical Lance fashion, whatever he couldn't handle, he ignored. He let the answering machine pick up and strode back into the bathroom.

But the seed of worry had been replanted.

Lance showered, then dressed in sweats and a T-shirt and made his way into the kitchen. As he entered the room, he remembered the broken windows and gave the repair job a closer look. Jim Bob had done well. He saw a broom and a mop in the corner of the kitchen, and realized the repairman had not only swept up the glass, but mopped, as well. It was satisfying to know he had such thoughtful friends.

The light was blinking on the answering machine. When he checked and saw the only call was from

Martinelli, he deleted it without listening. Indignation grew as he checked for leftovers. Surely the chinchy bastard knew they'd suffered a terrible storm here in Bordelaise. Martinelli should have had the decency to wait a few days before dunning him for money.

Lance wouldn't let himself think of what kind of repercussions Austin Ball's absence would have back in Chicago, but he knew what he was going to avow. He planned to say he'd never seen the man, so if Ball had planned to visit Bordelaise on Sunday, then it had been a poor decision, because he must have perished in the tornado. The rental car truly *had* been blown away. If it was found, he would have to explain his fingerprints, but other than a phone call Ball had made from Chicago, there was no firm way of tying Lance to the guy, much less to his absence.

The longer he thought about it, the better it sounded. This tornado was still working for him all the way. Not only had it removed the only witness to his crime, but it had also given him support for the claim he intended to make—that he'd never seen Austin Ball.

Just as he was about to sit down to some reheated jambalaya, he heard the front door open. His heart leaped. The only other person who had a key to the house was Joe. He turned off the heat under the pan and hurried into the living room.

Joe Morgan was still in shock from the news Lance had given him. He couldn't believe his oldest and dearest friends were all dead—and so horribly. He had been anxious on the short flight from Savannah to Baton Rouge—eager to get home just to see for himself that Lance and Morgan's Reach were okay. He'd rented a car at the airport in Baton Rouge and started driving toward Bordelaise, needing to see the devastation for himself.

Driving through Bordelaise and seeing his old hometown in such turmoil had been worse than he'd imagined. He'd stopped at Sumner's Funeral Home, thinking he might be able to see the North family, only to learn they weren't ready for viewing.

Sarah Beth Spellman hadn't wasted any time passing on the newest gossip regarding the family, either. According to Sarah Beth, Cari's cousin, Susan, had been in some kind of accident and just been released from the hospital. There was a question as to whether she would even be well enough to travel to the funeral, which would be held this Thursday.

She'd also passed on the news about four prisoners who'd been in the jail and were still missing, as well as the ongoing search for Katie Earle's seven-year-old son, Bobby. She warned him to tell Lance to be sure and keep their doors locked, just in case the prisoners were still alive and on the run. Joe could only imagine Katie Earle's horror, not knowing if her child had been killed in the storm or, as the authorities suspected, kidnapped by her ex. Then Sarah

Beth had added the news that old man Warren, who'd been in the nursing home for years, had died during the evacuation after the storm, making that four people they had to bury this week.

By the time Joe left Bordelaise, he was sick to his stomach. It didn't get any better when he drove past the North property on his way home. The grand old house that had been there for over a hundred and seventy-five years was gone, as were all the outbuildings. He thought of Lance finding the bodies and wondered how he was holding up.

There had been a time when they'd all believed Cari North would be a part of their family and Joe had been almost as upset with Lance for cheating on her as Cari had been. But blood had turned out to be thicker than water—and infidelity. Ultimately he and Lance had to stick together, no matter what.

When he finally turned down the long driveway toward their house, he felt an overwhelming sense of relief. Even though the arched trees lining the driveway were missing some of their limbs and leaves, Morgan's Reach was still there—in all her aging glory.

"Thank you, God," Joe said softly, and parked next to his brother's car.

He got out with a sense of urgency, anxious to see Lance's face and make sure for himself that his younger brother was truly in one piece. He grabbed his suitcase and headed up the steps to the front door.

Lance met him in the foyer just as he walked inside. Joe dropped the suitcase and opened his arms. Lance walked into them with a smile as they hugged.

“Thank the Lord that you and the place were spared,” Joe said, as he clapped Lance on the back. “I can’t believe what a mess Bordelaise is.”

“I know,” Lance said. “I was there almost all day helping with cleanup and rescue.”

Joe grabbed Lance by the shoulders and looked him square in the face.

“Are you okay?”

“Yeah,” Lance said.

“I can’t imagine how awful it was for you, finding the Norths.”

Lance looked away, afraid the relief he was feeling would be evident. Luckily Joe mistook his behavior for sorrow.

“I’m heartsick about the whole thing,” Joe muttered. “God. Poor Frank and Maggie. And Cari…so damn young.” He shook his head. “What a horrible way to die.”

Lance nodded, then sighed and quickly changed the subject, aware Joe would think he didn’t want to talk about it due to grief.

“Your room is waiting for you. Wash up, and then come on into the kitchen. I reheated some jambalaya,” Lance said.

“You cooked?” Joe asked.

Lance smiled wryly. “Takeout from in town.”

"Hope it's some of Mama Lou's from the Crab Shack."

"It is," Lance said.

"Give me five," Joe said, grabbed his suitcase and headed for his old room.

A few minutes later, they were both at the kitchen table and, like old times, sharing food and memories, as people so often do when there's a death in the family.

"How long can you stay?" Lance asked, as he spooned some rice into his bowl.

"At least until after the funeral, which is this Thursday, by the way. I thought I'd help you start cleaning up around here, too."

"That would be great. Jim Bob Greeley was out today and repaired the broken panes in the kitchen windows. I think there are a few missing shingles on the roof and a corner of the barn roof rolled back, but that's just a matter of nailing the sheet iron back down."

"I'll do the shingles and nail down the sheet iron," Joe offered. "I know you don't like heights."

"You've got that right," Lance said, and took a big bite of his food. It didn't seem strange to him that he was sharing a cozy meal with his brother as if nothing untoward had happened. In his mind, all he'd done was what he'd had to do to save the family home.

Right in the middle of the meal, the phone began to ring. Without thinking, he got up and answered it.

"Hello?"

"So...Mr. Morgan, you're finally home."

The moment Lance heard Martinelli's voice, he knew he'd made a mistake. How was he going to talk to the man without letting Joe know what he'd gotten them into? All he could do was play it by ear.

"Yes. Just," Lance said. "I've been in town all day, helping with search and rescue."

"Oh? Has someone gone missing?" Martinelli asked.

Lance frowned. "Don't you watch the news? Hell yes, someone went missing, and some are dead, too. We were hit straight-on by a tornado day before yesterday. Four people are dead...one of them a woman I used to be engaged to...as well as her parents. We also have a little boy we can't find, along with four prisoners from the jailhouse."

There was a moment of silence, then he actually heard a hint of sympathy in Martinelli's voice. It was what he'd hoped for.

"Sorry to hear it," Martinelli said. "I didn't know."

"Yes, well...you can understand how upset we all are. I'm sorry if I sounded a little short, but it's been hell."

"Yeah...sure...say, why don't I give you a call in a day or two?"

"Fine," Lance said. "That would be most considerate of you."

"No problem," Martinelli said. "Oh...say... have you talked to Austin Ball, yet?"

Lance's heart skipped a beat. "Who?"

"Austin Ball…he's one of my lawyers."

"No, I haven't heard from him. When was he going to call?"

"He flew out to see you on Sunday."

"He came out here? Really? Well, that was the day the tornado hit, and it was pretty crazy around here. Maybe he changed his mind."

"Okay. He'll probably call in soon. Sorry for your loss. We'll talk later."

"Yeah, later," Lance said, and hung up.

Reprieve.

He turned to Joe, who was frowning.

"Who was that?" Joe asked.

"Oh…just a business call. No big deal."

Joe wasn't satisfied. Lance had a habit of getting himself into trouble—trouble that Joe usually had to rectify.

"Are you sure?" Joe asked.

"Absolutely," Lance said. "Do you want dessert? I think there's some coconut cake."

Joe shrugged off the worry. "Yeah, sure. Sounds good."

The moment passed.

Night fell.

Lance Morgan slept like a baby, secure in the knowledge that his big brother was asleep in the room across the hall, and that, once again, he'd dodged a bullet. Somehow, someway, he would use the sympathy he'd heard in Martinelli's voice and convince the man to give him more time.

Cari had been given what amounted to a suite on the second floor of the Boudreaux mansion, but she wasn't in the frame of mind to appreciate the beauty of her accommodations. The sitting room was bright and airy, with a massive white mantel over a fireplace centered in the middle of one wall. The furniture was upholstered in off-whites and creamy yellows, while accessories and knickknacks in varying shades of blue gave the room a personal feel.

The bedroom just off the sitting area was a reverse of the first. Pale blue sheers at the windows, a royal blue spread on the bed, with bits of yellow and white interspersed on shelves and tabletops.

The adjoining bathroom was stark by contrast—white walls, floor tiles, fixtures and curtains. The single bit of color was a whimsy of art. A tiny school of clown fish made of hand-blown glass had been mounted on the wall in perfect formation, as if they were swimming in a snowy sea.

She'd turned down Mike's offer of food so that she could rest. All she really knew and cared about was that the bed she'd crawled into was cool and the sheets were soft. She also knew there were many doors and walls—and a man named Mike Boudreaux—standing between her and the danger of being discovered. For now, it was enough.

Downstairs, Mike went about the business of his life, explaining to those at the office that Susan was out of town. It wasn't exactly a lie. She was in Bordelaise. He just hadn't mentioned she was dead and wasn't coming back. Like Cari, a part of him clung to the misapprehension that if it wasn't said aloud, then it might not be the truth.

The responsibility he felt for Carolina North was wrapped up in his friendship with Susan and the knowledge that the woman was in serious trouble. He wasn't sure how she was going to go about alerting the authorities to the man she claimed was a murderer, but all that could wait. Right now, she needed to hide and heal. Providing her with those small comforts was the least he could do. That, and find out all he could about a man named Lance Morgan. He'd already availed himself of the services of his security chief, Aaron Lake, and now Aaron was on the job, checking into Lance Morgan's background.

Cari woke herself up screaming in the night.

Mike was in her room even before she could sit up and turn on the lights.

"Hey, hey," Mike said, as he slid onto the side of her bed and clasped one of her hands. "You're okay, *cher.* You're okay." Then he leaned over and switched on the lamp beside her bed.

"Oh my God," Cari muttered, as she struggled to a sitting position. "The storm… I was…"

She shuddered, then shoved the hair away from her face. "I was dreaming."

"I know," Mike said. "Hang on. I'll get you some water."

Cari swung her legs off the side of the bed, disoriented. "Do you know where my pain pills are?"

"On the table beside the lamp," he called out.

Cari looked, found them behind the clock and shook out two pills, then downed them with the water Mike handed her.

"Thanks," she said, as she set the glass aside. "I'm sorry I woke you."

Mike wanted to touch her, to hold and assure her she wasn't alone. But it wasn't the truth. Just because she was under his roof, that didn't mean anything. She was alone, in every way that counted. Still, she looked so beaten and so lost, and his frustration came out in his voice, making it seem too abrupt.

"You don't need to apologize for something that's not your fault."

Cari blinked. She didn't understand the anger in his voice, but at three in the morning, according to the clock, she wasn't in the mood to investigate.

"Then thank you for the water and the concern," she said shortly and got up from the bed, stumbled, then stiffly moved past him on her way to the bathroom.

The firm click of the door and the chill tone in her voice shamed Mike. It wasn't her fault he hadn't been able to sleep. Every time he closed his eyes, he kept remembering the countless times he'd taken Susan for granted. He might be mad at himself, but that didn't give him the right to take it out on Carolina.

She came out a couple of minutes later and appeared surprised he was still there.

"I don't need to be tucked back in."

"I'm sorry," he said. "I was curt with you, and you didn't deserve it. Truth is, I'm mad at myself."

Cari frowned as she settled down on the side of the bed. "Why?"

Mike shrugged, then sat down beside her. "Mostly for taking Susan for granted."

Cari's shoulders slumped. "I know what you mean. The other morning I went out for a walk. Weather permitting, I've done the same thing every day for as long as I can remember. Only on Sunday, everything was off. Like I'd stumbled into another dimension or something. I walk up on a man I've known all my life, and he's burying a body. I get back to the farm to tell my parents just as a tornado wipes them and everything we own from the face of the earth. I took my world and the safety of familiarity for granted."

Mike slid his hand over hers and turned it palm up, looking down at the cuts and bruises, then up at her face. The scratches there were shallow. The nurses had removed most of her facial bandages before he'd checked her out, but the bruises were blatant, and the staples in her head an ugly reminder of how close she'd come to dying.

"My mother used to say there was a reason for everything, but that we weren't always meant to understand it. I guess this would be one of those times," he said.

Cari's voice shook. "I guess."

The sound hurt his heart, but he knew sympathy was the last thing she needed.

"Think you can get back to sleep?"

"Maybe."

Mike stood up, then pulled back the covers. "Crawl in."

The offer was unexpected and oddly touching. "I can do it," she said.

"I know," he said, waiting as she gingerly scooted back beneath the covers. As soon as she'd settled, he straightened the spread, then leaned down to turn off the lamp.

Cari grabbed his arm. "Leave it on. Please?"

Mike frowned. The fear of a nightmare rerun was there on her face. The thought crossed his mind to lie down beside her—just as a friendly gesture to remind her she wasn't alone. But then instinct told him to get out. He had a feeling that it would be far too easy to cross a line with this woman, and this was neither the time nor place.

"I'm just across the hall," he said. "Call out if you need me."

Cari nodded, then turned her back on him and rolled up in a ball.

He sighed. Nothing like a little body language to let you know what was really going on. She'd just made herself as small a target as possible. He just wasn't sure how effective it was going to be against bad dreams, but it was enough to change his mind. Instead of leaving, he quietly moved to a white over-stuffed chair nearby, eased himself down into the cushions and crossed his legs.

Cari shifted slightly beneath the covers, unaware of the man who sat sentry at the foot of her bed.

When her body finally went limp and the covers ceased moving, Mike knew she'd fallen back to sleep. He could have left then—*should* have left then. The pain pills would likely carry her through until morning. But there was something so vulnerable about the slight bump she made beneath the covers that he couldn't bring himself to abandon her.

So he sat.

An hour had passed, when she suddenly turned from one side to the other with a muffled moan, then threw off her covers. Immediately he was on his feet. He pulled the sheet and blanket back up over her shoulders, then paused, studying her face, feature by feature, and her wounds, bruise by bruise.

Now that he knew who she was, he was surprised that he hadn't immediately seen the resemblance to Susan, because it was truly amazing.

Even through the bruises, he could see that the shapes of their faces and mouths were identical. Susan's eyes hadn't been quite as round, but everything else was so alike that he knew when she was healed, he would have been hard-pressed to tell them apart.

Suddenly Cari sighed and then spoke, but the words were so soft, he didn't understand what she'd said.

The last thing he wanted was for her to wake up and find him standing over her like some crazy stalker. He started to back away when a tear slid out from under her lashes, puddled in the hollow under her eye for just a moment, then slipped down her cheek.

"Daddy…Daddy," she said softly, and then sobbed.

"Ah, God," Mike whispered. "Poor baby."

Suddenly she gasped, and Mike knew she must be reliving the entire horror of the storm. Without thinking, he slid onto the mattress and took her hand.

"Shh, shh, it's okay, *cher,* it's okay."

She shuddered, but the pain pills had taken her far enough down that she didn't wake up. It was the death grip she had on Mike's hand that told him how frightening her dream must have been. She was holding on to his fingers so tight that her knuckles had gone white.

At that point, Mike forgot decorum. Without letting go, he carefully moved over her, then behind her. With the covers as a barrier, he spooned his body up against hers and pulled her close.

Within seconds, all the tension in her body seemed to dissipate. Unfortunately he was now within inches of her head wound. He could have counted the staples, but he couldn't bear to look. Instead he closed his eyes and concentrated on the slow, steady rhythm of her heartbeat.

He didn't know when he fell asleep, but he woke up just as dawn was breaking. Sometime during the night, Cari had turned to face him. Now he could feel the occasional exhalation of her breath against his chest—warm and soft.

Her eyelids fluttered. She was near to waking, and the last thing she needed was to find him in her bed. Slowly he eased his arm out from under the pillow above her head, then scooted off the bed. He paused for a moment, reluctant to leave her, but unwilling to think about why.

Somewhere downstairs, a phone began to ring. It had to be the dedicated line to the phone in his office, because none of the home phones were ringing.

He gave her a last thoughtful look, then made a quick exit.

The next time Cari woke up, sunlight was coming through the sheer fabric of the bedroom curtains. It took her a couple of moments to reorient herself as to where she was and why, and once she did, the sick feeling in the pit of her stomach returned.

Oh God. My family is dead, my world is destroyed, and the man I once thought I would marry is a murderer.

She started to kick off the covers, then winced. Motion resurrected all the dormant aches and pains.

"Have mercy," Cari muttered, as she eased herself out of bed and headed for the bathroom.

Within minutes, she was in the shower, using the warm jets of water to ease her knotted muscles. As she was drying off, she stopped in front of the full-length mirror on the back of the door to study her reflection. She had dozens of bruises in varying sizes all over her body. Besides the scrapes and cuts, there was the bald patch where her hair had been shaved so her head could be stapled.

"Basically, Carolina, you're such a wreck not even Mom and Dad would know you," she muttered, and turned away.

But within seconds, what she'd said triggered a notion that turned into an idea, then grew into a full-blown plan. She turned back around to look at herself in the mirror again, then pulled her long hair away from her face and squinted her eyes, turning first one way, then another.

The longer she stood there, the more certain she became that she'd just figured out a way to get herself to Bordelaise for the funerals. She tossed her towel aside and hurried into the bedroom.

A few minutes later she was in the hall and heading for the stairs, following the smell of bacon and freshly brewed coffee.

Songee entered the breakfast room carrying the plate of fried eggs she'd made for Mike's breakfast and slid it in front of him.

"Um, I'm glad you're back, because as always, you outdid yourself," Mike said, as he laid his newspaper aside and reached for the biscuits and bacon.

Songee Wister was barely five feet tall, but at fifty-one, easily a force of nature. The crisp pink dress and equally crisp white apron she was wearing were great foils for her café-au-lait skin. Her hair, once dark and curly, now a salt-and-pepper shade, was worn in dozens of tight little braids, then pulled back at her nape. She'd worked for Mike for more than fifteen years and considered the old mansion hers to run.

"Mr. Mike, will your lady also want some eggs to go with my biscuits and bacon?"

Mike slid a trio of bacon slices onto his plate, then reached for a biscuit and began to slather it with butter.

"I don't know, Songee. We'll ask her when she comes down."

"Ask me what?" Cari asked, as she entered the breakfast room.

Songee turned around, then gasped. "Saints alive! She looks like—"

"Easy, Songee. I already told you, she's Susan's cousin, remember?

"Carolina, this is Songee. She runs this house and keeps me in line."

Cari swallowed past the knot in her throat, wondering how long the pain of loss would last. Everyone always said she and Susan looked like sisters, if not twins. But that wouldn't be happening anymore.

"I'm pleased to meet you, Songee," Cari said.

Songee nodded. "I'm sorry, miss. You just took me by surprise. I have many cousins, but don't any of them look like my twin."

"No need to apologize," Cari said. "Our mothers were twins. We were born within a month of each other, and we grew up together, which accounts for some of the same mannerisms, as well."

Then she glanced at Mike, who pointed to the chair to his right. "Sit," he said. "Songee will make you some eggs to go with these fine biscuits and bacon. Just tell her how you want them cooked and how many."

Cari felt as if she would choke if she ate anything, but she also knew she needed her strength for what lay ahead.

"Maybe I'll have one fried egg, well done, please."

Songee smiled. "Yes, miss," she said, and got the coffeepot from the sideboard and poured some coffee in Cari's cup. "Sugar and cream are on the table. I'll be right back with your egg," she said, and left the room.

Cari sat down, then put her hands in her lap.

"What did you tell her?" she asked.

Mike put down his fork, then leaned back. "The truth."

Cari's eyes widened. "Do you think—"

"Don't worry. She'll keep your secrets, just like she keeps all of mine."

Cari hesitated, then leaned forward. "I have a plan."

Once again, Mike was struck by how different Carolina and Susan really were. Susan was the kind who always waited for instructions. Carolina had yet to wait for much of anything.

"I'm listening," he said.

"I need to get to a hairstylist. Can you recommend a salon?"

Mike frowned. This wasn't what he'd expected. Getting her hair styled seemed out of place considering everything else that had happened.

"Yes, but can I ask why?"

Even though he saw a sudden film of tears in her eyes, her chin jutted.

"Because I'm going back to Bordelaise for the funeral. I will not stand by and hide while others bury Mother and Daddy…and Susan."

Mike frowned. "What about the killer? I thought you wanted him to think you were dead?"

"He'll see Susan because he's expecting to see

Susan. And I need to get to the hair salon because Susan is about to get a makeover."

Mike's eyes widened with newfound respect. Damn, but she was something.

"As soon as breakfast is over, I'll have Songee find you a stylist."

"Thank you," Cari said, then took a list out of the pocket of her gray slacks and handed it to him. "While they're working on me, I would appreciate it if you could get these items for me. I think you'll be able to find all of them at any good pharmacy."

Mike eyed the list curiously. "Bandages. Gauze pads. Surgical tape. A sling." Then he frowned. "A sling?"

"Susan had an accident, remember?"

A slow smile spread across Mike's face. "Oh, yeah…I get it. With enough bandages, the obvious similarities to you and Susan would be expected, but at the same time, disguised." Then he pointed to her head. "What about the staples in your head?"

"The hair is already gone from there. The rest is about to be shortened dramatically."

Mike eyed her thoughtfully, picturing the way everything she was talking about would change her looks. "You know what? You just might pull this off."

"Not might. Will," Cari said. "And when we get to Bordelaise, you're going to have to force yourself to call me Susan, whether you like it or not."

"I know," he said, and looked away.

"I know this is hard for you, too. Susan talked about you all the time." Cari hesitated, then added, "Even though she always denied it, I always thought there was more than a working relationship between you."

"A lot of people thought that," Mike said. "Truth was, she was one of my best friends. I admired her. I depended on her. But romance never clicked."

Cari frowned, thinking of her broken engagement to Lance. "Love is a pretty fickle emotion. Sometimes it works, sometimes it doesn't, and for a whole host of reasons."

Before anything more could be said, Songee returned with Cari's food.

"Eat up while it's still warm," she said. "Anything else you two might be needing?"

Mike eyed Cari, who shook her head. "We're good, Songee, but thanks."

The woman nodded briefly and bustled out of the room, leaving them on their own again.

Cari was staring down at her food, wondering if she was going to be able to swallow it, when Mike leaned forward and added a piece of bacon and a hot buttered biscuit to her plate.

"You don't want to hurt Songee's feelings, now do you?"

Cari sighed. "No."

"I find it much easier to get along if I do as she says," Mike said softly, then picked up her fork and handed it to her.

Cari looked at the fork, then up at Mike. There was so much compassion on his face it was almost her undoing. She took the fork, then looked away. By the time she got herself under control, he was reaching for his third biscuit.

Five

Cari sat motionless in her chair at the salon, watching as her long, dark hair fell to the floor in swatches. The stylist Mike brought her to was not only cautious regarding her injuries, but highly skilled. Somehow she'd managed to create a perky style of spikes and wisps that almost concealed the missing hair. She was working a styling product through the wisps as Mike came striding back into the salon.

Cari could tell by the look on his face that her transformation was drastic.

"Wow," he said. "Talk about changing your appearance! I don't think you're going to have much to worry about come Thursday."

She nodded. "Good. Did you get the stuff on my list?"

"Yes, ma'am."

"Thank you," she said.

"You're very welcome," Mike said, as he pulled out his wallet and paid the stylist.

Cari eyed the money changing hands, making a mental note of yet another thing she was going to owe him. One day she would have her life back, and then she could repay him. Then her conscience demanded she amend the thought. She might be able to give back the money she owed, but she would never be able to repay Mike Boudreaux for his willingness to trust a total stranger.

"Are you ready?" he asked, as he slipped his hand under her elbow.

"As ready as I'm ever going to be," she said.

A short while later, they were home.

Marcey Ball was bordering on hysterical. She'd called her husband's cell phone so many times that the batteries in her own cell had gone dead. It wasn't like Austin not to call home. She was six weeks away from the delivery of their first child, and no one was more excited about being a first-time father than Austin.

He'd left home yesterday for a day trip to Louisiana and hadn't been heard from since. The last time she'd talked to him had been right before he'd boarded the plane to Baton Rouge. He had not checked in at the office or with Mr. Martinelli. She didn't want to admit that something terrible must have happened, but in her mind, there was no other explanation.

So it was with shaking hands that she finally made a call to the Chicago Police. When her call was answered, it took every ounce of guts she had left to say, "I need to speak to someone in Missing Persons."

"One moment, please," the operator said.

Marcey started to shake. Making this call was a final confirmation of the fact he'd gone missing. *God, oh God, help me find him.* She was on the verge of tears when her call was answered.

"Missing Persons… Detective Smith speaking."

Marcey flinched. She hadn't been prepared to hear a female voice. It took her a moment to pull herself together.

Sandy Smith frowned. She was already up to her eyes with paperwork and in no mood for hang ups. She grabbed a handful of napkins and blotted a spill of coffee from her desk as she repeated herself. "Hello? Detective Smith."

Marcey took a deep breath. "I'm sorry. I wasn't— Sorry. I need to start over."

Sandy tossed the napkins in the trash and reached for a pen and paper. "That's okay, ma'am. Let's start by you giving me your name."

"Oh. Yes. Uh… My name is Marcey Ball." Then she relayed her address and phone number. "I called because my husband is missing."

"What's his name, Mrs. Ball?"

"Austin Ball. He's a lawyer…a partner, actually, in a firm downtown."

Sandy frowned. "Are you referring to Meacham and Ball?"

"Yes."

Instinct told the detective this might be more than the marital fight gone bad that usually led to someone taking off for a few days. Meacham and Ball's choice of clients would never make the social register, even though they were some of the wealthiest in the city.

"Has he checked in with his office?"

"No. They haven't heard from him, either. I think I was the last to talk to him."

"When was that?" Sandy asked, making notes as they talked.

"Yesterday. He was at O'Hare, getting ready to board a plane for Baton Rouge, Louisiana."

"Was this on business?" Sandy asked.

"Yes, but I don't know details. His partner, Paul Meacham, can fill you in on that. Austin never talked business at home. You know…client privacy and all that."

"Yes. Okay, Mrs. Ball. I'll do some checking and see what I can find out, okay?"

Marcey shivered. "It's something bad," she said.

Sandy frowned. "Why do you say that?"

"Because I'm six weeks away from delivering our first child. My husband is so excited. He always calls me…at least three times a day. He was supposed to go with me to my doctor appointment this morning.

I went alone. Whatever has kept him from calling me has to be bad."

"I see. Well, let's don't borrow trouble. Let me do some checking, and then I'll get back to you."

"Yes. Thank you."

"I'll be in touch," Sandy said, then hung up.

She looked down at the notes on her desk, then picked up the phone again. First things first. Check the airport and see if a man named Austin Ball really got on a plane to Baton Rouge, then go from there.

The cleanup at Bordelaise was slow but steady. By Wednesday evening, power had been restored to the town. Debris removal was a work in progress. The main concerns revolved around the child who was still missing, and the lack of information regarding the four missing prisoners. It was as if they'd all disappeared off the face of the earth. Gossip had turned into dire predictions, and the tentative assumption was that the prisoners had perished in the tornado and their bodies had yet to be found. The little boy, though... People from three neighboring parishes had been searching the area around Bordelaise and even into the swampland for signs of Bobby Earle. Searchers with bloodhounds, even a National Guard helicopter, had joined the effort, but all to no avail. Katie Earle had been hospitalized, bordering on a nervous breakdown, and they were still looking for her estranged husband, J. R. Earle.

It was the impending services for Frank, Maggie

and Cari North that finally brought the town together again. With the absence of a family to help bury the Norths, and the uncertainty of Susan Blackwell being able to travel after her own accident, the members of Frank and Maggie's church had stepped in.

A potluck dinner was to be held after the upcoming service, and the compassion that would have been offered to surviving family members had shifted to Lance, since he'd once been engaged to Cari.

Lance liked being the object of concern and had begun to believe that he was invincible. Whatever had happened was in the past. He was convinced that his troubles were over.

Joe was putting the finishing touches on a corned beef sandwich when the phone began to ring. He licked the mustard off his thumb and then answered absently, thinking it would probably be Lance. It was Lance's bad luck that Martinelli mistook Joe's Southern drawl as his.

"Hello," he said.

"Good afternoon, Mr. Morgan. It's Dominic Martinelli again. I think it's time we resume our conversation from the other day regarding the lack of payment on your outstanding loan."

Joe was about to explain who he was, and then he heard the word "loan." His stomach dropped, and it was all he could do to keep breathing.

"Um…I, uh…" he stammered.

Martinelli took the hesitation as more of the same he'd been getting from Lance for the past six months.

"Look, Morgan. Business is business. You've defaulted on a loan. I'm calling it in."

Joe felt the room beginning to spin. "Calling it in?"

"Yes. I had the papers calling in your collateral drawn up and sent one of my lawyers to deliver them the other day. Remember, I asked you if you'd seen Austin Ball? You said you had not. So you can expect another visitor before the weekend."

Joe panicked. What the hell had Lance used for collateral? To his knowledge, the only thing of value he had left was—

Oh God.

"Mr.…uh, Dominic…there's something you need to know. I'm not Lance. I'm his older brother, Joe."

"Ah…my bad," Martinelli said. "Have your brother call me as soon as he gets home. I've given him all the time I can. I'm sure you understand."

"Wait!" Joe said. "I need to ask. What did Lance use for collateral, and how much did you lend him?"

"Why, the property, of course…for a quarter mil, with a deuce still outstanding."

Joe staggered backward, then dropped into the nearest chair.

"Jesus," Joe whispered. "Morgan's Reach? He mortgaged Morgan's Reach?"

"Yeah."

"And two hundred thousand is still unpaid?"

"Yeah. It's not like I want to do this, but business is business."

"This property has been in our family since the late seventeen hundreds."

"Yeah, that's what he said," Martinelli said.

"I'm half owner, and I knew nothing of this."

Martinelli's demeanor shifted from affable to firm. "Then you've got a beef with your brother, not me. You've got thirty days to vacate."

"Oh God, wait, wait," Joe muttered. "Give me a couple of days to liquidate some assets and the money will be in your hands."

"Are you serious?" Martinelli asked.

"As a heart attack," Joe muttered.

"I'll give you a week," Martinelli said.

"Thank you," Joe said. "Oh…wait. I need a number where I can reach you."

"Your brother has my number," Martinelli said.

Joe's demeanor shifted, too, from shock to fury. "Yes, and I've got *his*. Since he's not in the habit of telling the truth and I'm the one who's going to cough up the money, then I want your number."

"Yeah, sure. Whatever," Martinelli said, and rattled it off. "I'll be expecting to hear from you in a week," he said.

"Yes," Joe said, and hung up.

He stared at the sandwich he'd just made, then got up and walked outside and off the veranda, past the pile of downed limbs he'd been gathering and all the way to the family cemetery. The old wrought-iron gate squeaked in protest as he opened it and walked inside.

The mausoleums dated all the way from 1798 up to those of their parents, who'd died in an accident in 2005. He walked among the little stone houses with the interred bones of his ancestors while anger built. When he got to his parents' mausoleum, he stopped, then shoved his hands in his pockets and stared at the names carved into the side.

"It's your fault, you know. From the day he was born, he could do no wrong. You excused him at every turn in his life. Not once was he ever held accountable for anything. You paid off the windows he broke one Halloween. You paid off the judge to make the drunk driving charges go away. You paid off the girl he got pregnant in high school. And ever since you've been gone, I've followed suit, like a damned lemming, paying off his bad checks and buying him out of one fix after another…but no more."

Joe pivoted angrily, striding past the tombstones and mausoleums, then paused and turned, as if someone had just called his name.

"No more!" he shouted, and slammed the gate behind him as he left.

Lance was whistling as he got out of his car and headed toward the veranda. Joe came out to meet him as he started up the steps.

"Hey, brother, how's it going?" Lance asked, and

started into the house when Joe grabbed him by the arm and spun him around. Lance frowned. "Hey! What's wrong with you? That hurts."

Joe was so furious he could hardly speak. "You better be glad it's just your arm, because I am struggling with an overwhelming urge to wring your goddamned neck."

Lance's voice deepened angrily. "What the—"

"Does the name Martinelli ring a bell?" Joe asked.

Lance's stomach lurched. "Oh shit."

"Yeah. It definitely hit the fan while you were gone," Joe said, then grabbed Lance by the shoulders and literally shook him. "What in hell were you thinking? Morgan's Reach has been in our family for over two hundred years. It has survived hurricanes, an outbreak of malaria that killed every male ancestor but one, a civil war, a depression, good times and bad, and now you come along and mortgage it—illegally, I might add, because I own half of it—to some Yankee and let it default? Jesus Christ, Lance! Have you lost your mind?"

Lance shrugged off his brother's anger. It wasn't the first time Joe had been pissed at him. At least now it was out in the open.

"I needed some capital. If it hadn't been for the hurricane ruining the last crop, I would have been fine."

Joe stared at Lance as if he were a stranger. Even now, his brother was blaming something besides himself for his problems.

"You have been nothing but a class-A fuckup your entire life," Joe snapped. "The only thing about you that has changed is your age."

Rage shifted through Lance so fast it made him shake, but he couldn't argue with the truth. He just didn't have to like it.

"Calm down. I'll figure something out," he said.

"I already did that," Joe said. "The money will be paid. But you, little brother, have just lost your birthright. The only way I'm buying you out of this mess is if you sign over your half of Morgan's Reach to me."

Lance felt as if someone had cut the earth out from under him. "No! Hell no!" he cried. "I'm the one who loves the land. I'm the one who chose to live on it and work it. You wanted the city. You left it for Savannah, remember?"

"Yes, I remember. And I also remember how many times I've bought you out of messes since Mom and Dad died. This was the final straw. You might live here, but it's still half mine, and you mortgaged it illegally. How much do you want to bet if records were searched, I would find my name forged to something?"

Lance looked away, unable to meet his brother's gaze.

"Damn you!" Joe shouted. "You did, didn't you? And you still think you deserve another pass? Well, guess what? No more. I'll pay Martinelli, but you will sign over your rights to me first. If you don't, I'll start by pressing charges against you for forgery and go from there."

"You wouldn't!" Lance cried.

Joe's whole body was shaking. "Try me," he whispered.

Lance cursed beneath his breath, then strode past his brother and into the house.

Cari couldn't quit looking at her reflection in the bathroom mirror. The haircut had so changed her appearance that she hardly recognized herself. Without the curtain of dark hair framing her face, her eyes looked even larger and her cheekbones more pronounced. And her wound was barely noticeable. The bruises on her face and neck were beginning to fade into lighter shades of purples and greens. Wearing Susan's clothes only added to the confusion. Satisfied that she'd done all she could to disguise herself before going back to Bordelaise tomorrow, she made her way downstairs.

Songee was carrying an arrangement of fresh flowers into the foyer as Cari came down. She paused and looked up, then nodded approvingly at Cari's transformation.

"Mmm-hmm...you are a woman to be reckoned with, aren't you, missy?"

Cari's smile was little more than a shift of the muscles. "So you think this will work?"

Songee placed the bouquet on the hall table, then put her hands on her hips and gave Cari her full attention.

"Well, you sure don't look like the same woman I saw yesterday," she said.

"Good."

Songee shrugged, thankful she wasn't in Cari North's shoes. "I'm thinkin' you're puttin' yourself in some danger by going to that funeral tomorrow."

A muscle jerked in Cari's jaw. "I'm burying my family tomorrow. Danger will have to wait."

Songee nodded approvingly. "You're gonna be all right."

Cari sighed. "I don't feel like anything is ever going to be all right again."

Songee's dark eyes softened with understanding. "I know, honey, I know. I buried my man and my only child more than twenty years ago. Wanted to die with them and was mad as all get out at God for leaving me behind."

Suddenly Cari felt humbled. She'd been so wrapped up in her misery she'd forgotten the world did not just revolve around her.

"I'm so sorry," she said.

Songee shrugged. "Shoot, honey. It wasn't your fault. It wasn't anyone's fault, really. The house was old. It caught on fire while I was at work. They died. I didn't. What you have to remember is that God still has a plan for you or you wouldn't be standing here talkin' to me right now."

Cari's shoulders slumped. "I guess."

"No. You don't guess nothin'. You're a smart

woman. You know what you gotta do. Just get your head wrapped around it and do it. In the meantime, come on into the kitchen with me. I just took a pecan pie out of the oven. Mr. Mike does like my pecan pies."

"Thanks, Songee, but I'm not all that hungry."

"That's no excuse," Songee said, then headed for the kitchen. She paused in the doorway then turned around. "Well…you comin' or not? Mr. Mike won't be back for a couple of hours. I'll make sure we leave some for him."

Cari sighed. Time had to pass somehow. She might as well pass it with Songee and a piece of pie.

Mike's morning at the office had been awkward and full of discord. He had wasted half an hour looking for information that Susan would have been able to give him in minutes, which only aggravated his sadness and sense of loss. Finally he'd found what he needed and the conference call had gone as planned. Now he was on his way home, but with an unusual sense of anticipation.

He even found himself accelerating as he pulled into his driveway. He loved his home. He loved coming home. But this was the first time he'd had someone besides the housekeeper waiting for his arrival. Even though the situation was full of despair, he was becoming more and more intrigued by his unexpected guest.

He drove around to the back of the property and

parked under the shade of a live oak, unloaded two sacks of potting soil and carried them to the shed, then headed for the back door.

It was the sound of laughter that Mike first heard as he walked up on the porch. In the short time they'd known each other, he'd seen Carolina North run through a gamut of emotions, none of which had been joy. A shiver ran through him as he listened, and he suddenly wished he'd been the one to make her laugh. Choosing not to decipher why he'd thought that, he grabbed the doorknob and entered just as Cari laughed again.

The door swung shut behind him.

At the sound, Cari turned, still wearing the smile.

Breath caught in the back of Mike's throat. Not once in the seven years he'd known Susan Blackwell had he ever had an urge to take her to bed. He would have felt a little easier if he could say the same about Carolina, but that was no longer the case.

"Speak of the devil," Songee said, as she got a dessert plate from the cabinet.

Mike grinned. "So, Songee, since you were obviously talking about me, I deserve to know what beans you just spilled."

His housekeeper smiled. "I was just tellin' Miss Cari about the night the skunk came into the kitchen through the dog door."

Mike chuckled. "You notice I no longer have a dog—or a dog door."

Cari shuddered sympathetically. "I can only imagine how long it took for the smell to go away."

Mike squinted slightly, then looked at Songee. "I'd guess it was at least a month, right?"

Songee rolled her eyes. "Seemed longer to me," she muttered.

Cari laughed again, and then almost immediately felt guilty. How could she be laughing when everything was so awful? She ducked her head and looked away.

Mike sighed. How quickly joy could end.

"I made pie," Songee said.

"Could I talk you out of a piece?"

Songee snorted softly. "You know you got a silver tongue when it comes to gettin' what you want."

Mike winked at Cari, trying to tease her back into the conversation. "Don't listen to her. She's totally in charge of this house, and of me, too."

"The pie was wonderful," Cari said.

Mike pretended indignation. "You mean to tell me you two have already cut it?"

"Oh, stop your fussin' and grab a fork."

"Yes, ma'am," Mike said, and slid into a chair on the opposite side of the table from Cari.

He eyed the shadows in her eyes and wished she would smile again. Just once.

"I'm really liking that haircut," he said.

She tucked a stray lock behind one ear and then ran her fingers through the sides, trying to fill the awkward moment and ignore the glitter in his eyes.

"Thanks. It's definitely different."

"Wasn't that the point?" he said, then looked up at Songee as she slid a piece of pie in front of him. "Thank you very much."

Songee smiled. "You're very welcome."

"Yum," Mike said, as he dug into the pie.

Cari sat quietly, remembering how she and her parents had shared moments like this and wondering if she would ever know that kind of joy again.

"So, do you have everything you need before we head to Bordelaise tomorrow?" Mike asked.

Cari hesitated.

He looked up. "What?"

"I might need to go back to Susan's. I didn't bring anything that would be proper for the services."

Mike swallowed the bite he was chewing, then said, "I could take you back there to see if there's anything that would work…or we could go for something completely new."

Not having to go back to Susan's would be a blessing.

"Something new, please," Cari said softly.

Mike nodded. "Yeah, I vote for that, too. If you're up to it, I'll take you into Baton Rouge just as soon as I finish my pie."

"That would be great," Cari said. "I'm just going to go change my shoes."

"I'll be ready when you are," Mike said.

Cari left the kitchen, unaware that Mike was watching every step she took.

Songee saw him and smiled to herself as she turned away. Out of sorrow, sometimes comes joy. Maybe this was going to be one of those times.

Detective Sandy Smith was beginning to believe she had a tiger by the tail. According to the information she'd been able to gather, on Sunday morning Austin Ball had boarded a plane at 6:00 a.m. in Chicago, bound for Baton Rouge, Louisiana. His office verified that he'd rented a car at the Baton Rouge airport later that morning, because the information had come through from his corporate credit card. But that seemed to have become Austin Ball's last act. No one had heard from him since.

Sandy might not have been so suspicious about his fate except that he'd been on business for Dominic Martinelli. Even though Martinelli appeared to operate his businesses on the up-and-up, the Chicago P.D. had long suspected he was into a lot more than met the eye.

She had a call in to Martinelli and was waiting to see what he had to say before she called Marcey Ball, but she was beginning to believe Mrs. Ball had reason for concern. According to everyone Sandy had talked to, Austin Ball had been impatiently awaiting the day he would become a father. It didn't seem likely that all that would change overnight. Additionally his reputation as a lawyer was on the line. Again, something he wasn't likely to ignore.

Her gut feeling was that this wouldn't have a positive outcome, but she'd been mistaken before. She thought of Marcey Ball, only weeks from delivering her first child, and hoped this was one of those times.

Six

Cari was sitting in the dressing room of the boutique where Mike had taken her, wearing nothing but her bra and panties and trying to gather her emotions. There were a half-dozen rejected black dresses hanging on the hook, and she was beginning to think it wasn't the dresses that were wrong so much as the reason for wearing one.

The first one she'd tried on had been too big. The second one, too sexy for the occasion. Then she discarded the other four, one after the other, without a specific reason other than that they just didn't feel right. Exhausted from the whole affair, she'd turned down the last one the salesclerk brought to the dressing room without even looking at it, then locked the door and broke into tears.

Now her head was throbbing, and once again, her eyes were red and swollen. If only this were a nightmare from which she could wake, not the living, breathing hell it had become.

When she heard a knock on the door, she expected it to be the attendant, back with yet another dress, and was startled to hear Mike's voice, instead. His voice was gruff, but the delivery was tender.

"Hey, tough stuff, please tell me you're not crying."

Cari blew her nose. The truth was obvious.

Mike winced, then leaned his forehead against the door, wishing there was something he could do for her other than pay for a black dress.

"I'm fine…just waiting for the lady to bring back some other styles," Cari said.

"Uh-huh," Mike said. "Do you need my handkerchief?"

She looked down at the shreds of tissue in her fingers and sighed. There was no need to pretend.

"Yes, please."

"Coming over," Mike said, then reached over the partition and dropped the handkerchief into the dressing area.

"Thank you," Cari said as she caught it, then promptly blew her nose again.

"Do you mind if I have a go at choosing a dress?" he asked.

A little surprised by the offer, she agreed. "Knock yourself out," she said, and listened as his footsteps faded away.

She leaned her head against the wall and closed

her eyes while she waited, and as she did, suddenly realized she had yet to address a whole other facet of her life.

Her agent.

Her publisher.

The manuscript she'd mailed off the day before the tornado.

They would all think she was dead.

She was beginning to see the full scope of the tangled web she continued to weave. At least, if she ever managed to undo this mess, she would have one hell of a story to tell.

When she heard Mike's footsteps again, accompanied by the clerk's shorter strides, she quickly stood up.

"I'm back," Mike said. "Are you decent?"

She caught a glimpse of herself in the mirror and grimaced. "No."

"Ah, the images that just shot through my mind," he drawled.

Cari laughed before she thought. God, but he was good for her soul.

"Just give them to the clerk. I promise your wait is almost over," Cari said.

"Waiting for you is my pleasure," Mike said softly, then handed the dresses to the clerk, who looked enthralled by the fact that she was only inches away from *Baton Rouge Magazine*'s most eligible bachelor.

For Cari, the gentle rumble of his voice edged yet another tiny bit of sorrow to the side. By the time she was zipping up the first dress he'd chosen, she had her first positive reaction.

It was a perfect fit. Not too short. Not too revealing, but still stylish. And the knit fabric was so soft against her battered body. She turned and looked at herself in the mirror.

How had he known?

Her lower lip trembled.

"Mike?"

"Yes?"

Impulsively she flattened the palm of her hand against the door, as if reaching out to touch him.

"I wasn't sure you'd still be out there," she said.

Unaware he was mimicking her action, he flattened his hand against the door, wishing he could touch her.

"I made you a promise, Carolina. I'm here for as long as you need me."

"I really like this one," Cari said.

"Show me," Mike said.

Cari's heart began to pound. What was the matter with her? All she was going to do was open the door, not go to bed with the man. And the moment that thought went through her mind, she shoved it aside. This was nothing but momentary weakness from her grief. Nothing but a need to feel something besides pain. It would go away.

Surely it would go away.

The lock clicked as she turned the doorknob.

Mike's heart skipped a beat. What in hell was

wrong with him? This wasn't an occasion for contemplating sex. She was in mourning.

Then she opened the door, and all the breath went out of his body as he saw her framed in the doorway, wearing that dress like a second skin.

"What do you think?" she asked.

Mike's nostrils flared. The words came out before he thought.

"You don't want to know."

Cari's eyes widened. "Is it that bad?"

"Not from where I'm standing," he muttered, then pulled himself together. "Sorry. That was uncalled for. Let me try that again. I think the dress is perfect for the occasion, and it looks good on you."

Cari's pulse skipped a beat. Had he just made a pass? "I really like this one, so there's no need trying on the other one you brought."

"Ditto," Mike drawled.

Cari eyed him curiously.

"Look. I've already stuck my foot in my mouth," he said. "I'm just playing it safe by keeping the rest of my opinions to myself."

A little embarrassed, Cari stepped back. "I'll get dressed now," she said, and closed the door between them.

It wasn't until Mike heard the lock that he realized he'd been holding his breath.

"Holy..." Mike shoved a hand through his hair and walked away before he let his mind wander into forbidden territory and picture Carolina North naked behind that damned door.

By the time Cari came out with the dress over her arm, Mike had himself together and was all smiles, charming the salesclerk as he handed her his credit card.

"How are you fixed for shoes?" Mike asked, as the clerk rang up the purchase.

"I have a pair of Susan's I can wear, but I do need some sunglasses."

"Oh. We have some right over there," the clerk said, pointing to a display of accessories near the front of the store.

"Okay, thanks," Cari said, and headed for the table.

Choosing a pair with large lenses that would cover more of her features, she quickly handed them over to the clerk.

"Will there be anything else?" the woman asked.

Cari shook her head.

Mike frowned. "Yes, actually there will be," he said, and headed for a shelf displaying small clutch purses. He scanned them briefly, choosing one with clean lines and a small gold clasp, then paused at a jewelry display.

"That's enough," Cari said, but Mike wasn't listening.

Finally he chose a small cameo on a silver chain and brought it back, as well.

When he laid the stuff down on the counter, Cari

couldn't help but gasp. The cameo was exquisite—and it was black.

"My grandmother had one like this, only it was a brooch," Mike said. "I never saw her without it. Didn't know for years that she'd bought it to wear at Granddad's funeral and had worn it in honor of him ever since. I think they call it mourning jewelry. Hope you approve." Then he glanced at Cari, taking note of the fierce glint in her eyes and added, "She would have liked you."

"Thank you," Cari said.

"You're very welcome," he said softly, then slid an arm across her shoulders and gave her a gentle hug.

Cari leaned into his strength, telling herself it was only because she was tired from all the stress, but the truth was far more involved. She liked being around this man. She admired his patience, and the fact that he seemed to understand without asking when she had reached the limit of her endurance.

He also qualified as a hunk, but that totally didn't count.

She inhaled quietly, then added one silent addendum to the list of reasons why Mike Boudreaux was special. He smelled good—really, really good.

Mike signed the credit card slip, pocketed the copy, then picked up their purchases and offered Cari his elbow.

She slid her hand in the crook, and let him lead her out of the boutique and to the car. The butter-soft leather of the Cadillac's seats was warm from the sunshine coming through the windows, soothing her achy muscles as she sat down. She buckled her seat belt as Mike put the purchases in the back, then got into the car.

"How are you feeling?" he asked.

"I'm okay," she said.

"Not too sore? Not feeling sick in any way?"

"No. I took a pain pill before we left, why?"

"I already told Songee we wouldn't be home for lunch, so we can either grab a quick bite at one of the local restaurants or pick something up at a drive-thru and take it home to eat. It's your call."

"If there's a place nearby, I think I'd like some soup," Cari said.

Mike smiled approvingly. "Good call, and I know just the spot."

Within a few minutes they were pulling into the parking lot of a chic little sandwich shop called Croissant.

"I went to high school with the owner," Mike said. "I think you'll be able to find something tasty here."

"Sounds good," Cari said.

Mike parked and then helped her out of the car. As they started into the shop, he slipped his hand beneath her elbow.

Cari couldn't help but notice the perfect manners and constant consideration. She could almost hear her mother's voice saying, "Someone raised him right." A quick shaft of pain shot through her as she realized she would never hear her mother's voice again, but then she checked herself. There was no need to dwell on the depths of her loss. Life without her family would be a rude enough reminder.

The aroma that greeted them as they entered the shop quickly changed her focus. The comforting smell of freshly baked bread melding with the scents of cheese and spices made her hungry. The dining area was more than half full, adding a low rumble of conversation, as well as the occasional clink of china and flatware. Before they could seat themselves, a great big man came bursting out of the kitchens with his arms outstretched and a happy smile on his face.

"Mike! Susan! Long time no see!"

The moment Cari realized he thought she was Susan, she panicked. Any second he would figure out it was a ruse, and then questions would follow. And then…

Mike saw the look on her face and gave her hand a quick squeeze.

"Easy," Mike said softly. "Let it ride."

Then he shifted the focus by stepping in front of her just before the burly giant enveloped him in a hug.

"Welcome! Welcome!" the man said.

Mike quickly backed out of the hug before his ribs cracked.

"Good to see you, Maurice! How is the family?"

"Growing," Maurice said. "Polly is expecting twins."

Mike thumped him on the shoulder. "Great to hear. What will that make…four?"

"Five," Maurice countered, then immediately turned to Cari, eyeing her hair and face with an appreciative smile, while politely ignoring all the bruises. "I like the new look."

"Thank you," she said.

"Sit! Sit!" Maurice said, waving toward the tables. "I have a new lobster salad you need to try…and a corn chowder so good it will make you cry. I need to get back to the kitchen, but I'll send a waitress right over."

"Thanks," Mike said, and quickly seated Cari as his old friend left. He slid into the seat opposite her, then lowered his voice. "Hang with me, tough stuff. Maurice didn't know Susan well, so he won't notice anything."

Cari nodded briefly, then picked up a menu and began reading, needing time to let the panic subside. She made her choice, then kept reading so she wouldn't have to talk. It was one thing that she'd been mistaken for Susan in the hospital, but it was a bit different to intentionally impersonate her out in the world. Obviously she hadn't been as well prepared as she thought. Her heart was still thumping, and she had to keep swallowing past the lump in her throat to keep from crying.

"See anything you like?" Mike asked.

She looked up, and the first thing that went

through her mind was *yes, you,* then she quickly looked away, horrified by the wayward thought.

"The lobster bisque?"

"Great choice," Mike said, then smiled at the little waitress who arrived with an elegantly appointed tray bearing a white-and-gold teapot with two matching bone-china cups.

"Hi, ya'll. My name is Melanie. May I pour you some tea? It's lemon chai today. Really yummy."

"Yes, please," Mike said, and handed Cari the first cup, then took the second one for himself. "Sugar or cream?" he asked.

"No, thank you," Cari said, then lifted the cup to her lips and took a small sip. The flavor was as perfect as the place itself, and she soon began to relax.

"Have you decided what you'd like to order?" Melanie asked.

"She would like the lobster bisque, and I'll have some of Maurice's lobster salad on a croissant and a bowl of that corn chowder."

"Coming up," Melanie said, and hurried away to turn in the order.

"It's going to be okay," Mike said.

Looking into Mike Boudreaux's eyes, Cari could almost believe him. But there was so much to be done.

"I don't know how," she said. "For sure not now, and not tomorrow. The last thing I want to do is show up in Bordelaise, but I have to do this for my parents…and Susan. Once that's behind me, I can focus on finding out who Lance killed and where he hid the body so I can have my life back."

"First things first, which means we eat the wonderful lunch we just ordered. Then I take you back to the house, where you will try to get some rest."

When she started to argue, Mike held up a finger. "Doctor's orders."

Cari smiled. It wasn't much as smiles went, but Mike would take it.

"That's better," he said. "You're a very beautiful woman, especially when you smile."

A kind of longing shifted within, and before Cari thought, she felt the need to put a mental wall between them.

"Was that something you used to tell Susan?"

Mike frowned. "I told you before, there wasn't anything like that between us." Then he added, "And just for the record, when I look at you, I don't see Susan. I see Carolina."

She shouldn't have felt relieved. After all, the whole ruse she was trying to pull depended on people believing she was her cousin. But it was getting more and more difficult to ignore a growing attraction to this man. The last thing she wanted was to fall for someone whose first attraction to her hinged upon her resemblance to someone else.

"Ah…lunch is served," he said, giving her a quick heads-up that the waitress was returning.

Cari leaned back in her chair and fiddled with the

napkin in her lap while Melanie unloaded her tray, serving Cari's food, then Mike's.

"Is there anything else I can get for you?" she asked.

"We're good for now," Mike said. "However…if Maurice made his fabulous crème brûlée today, we might be ordering dessert."

"You know he did," Melanie said. "Enjoy your food. I'll bring you a fresh pot of tea."

Then the doorbell jingled as a group of six walked in, and Melanie shifted into higher gear.

Cari's first spoonful of soup was tentative, making sure it wasn't too hot to eat. It wasn't. The creamy soup was smooth and rich, with bits of lobster in every bite.

"Good?" Mike asked.

"Amazing," she said. "Thank you for bringing me here."

"Entirely my pleasure," Mike said softly.

And just for the rest of the meal, Cari let herself pretend that was the truth.

Mike coaxed and charmed her into eating the entire bowl of soup, even buttering a croissant for her from the bread basket. By the time she was finished, he'd already ordered them some of Maurice's famous crème brûlée he'd mentioned earlier.

"I don't think I can eat any more," Cari said, as Melanie served the desserts.

"Just take a bite," Mike urged.

So she did, breaking the sugar crust with the bowl

of her spoon, then scooping up a small bite. It didn't take long for her reaction.

"Mmm," she said, her eyes widening. "That's amazing."

"So you're telling me there won't be any leftovers for me to clean up?"

She just smiled and took another bite.

Pleased, Mike beamed as he dug into his own dessert and soon finished it off. By the time Cari was done, Melanie was bringing back Mike's credit card and receipt.

Maurice stuck his head out of the kitchen long enough to call out, "Don't be a stranger," then wave as he went back to work.

A short while later, they were on their way home. With her stomach full and the worst of her pain momentarily abated from the pain pill she'd taken earlier, she leaned back and closed her eyes. She didn't intend to sleep, but the Cadillac was such an elegant ride, and she was exhausted.

Mike knew the moment she went to sleep, because her lips parted softly and the tension in her body eased. He felt no guilt in looking his fill when he braked for a red light. She was in his car—staying in his house—momentarily living under his protection. Surely it was all right to check her welfare. Surely.

The light turned green, and he accelerated slowly, making sure not to rouse her. His heart hurt for all she'd lost, and he couldn't help but be concerned for her safety. Hopefully Aaron Lake would come up with some information on Lance Morgan that would lead to answers to help Cari's situation.

By the time he reached home, Cari was sound asleep. He parked under the portico, then killed the engine. Almost immediately, he was struck by the near-silence of her breathing, followed by the thought of what it would be like to wake up to that sound every morning.

Startled that he'd actually toyed with the notion of Carolina North being a permanent fixture in his life, he yanked the keys out of the ignition and opened his door.

The jingle of keys, coupled with the click of the lock, woke Cari. She sat up with a jerk, then winced as sore muscles protested the sudden movement.

"Oh! We're here! Why didn't you wake me?"

Mike wasn't about to tell her that he'd been playing "what-if" with their lives without her knowledge or permission.

"I was just about to," he said. "How are you feeling?"

"Good," Cari said. "That nap wasn't long, but it was refreshing. And again, I'm indebted to you for the shopping and the lunch." Then her expression dimmed. "I am so dreading tomorrow."

Mike reached for her hand, then threaded his fingers through hers. "I know, *cher.* Just remember, you won't be there alone."

The familiar endearment touched her more than she would have believed. "Yet one more way in which I've indebted myself."

"You owe me nothing," Mike said, then gave her fingers a quick squeeze. "Now we take your purchases inside. I still advise a longer rest, but if you're not inclined to head up to your room, the veranda in back is wonderful this time of day."

He got out, then helped her out of the car before gathering up their purchases and leading the way into the house. Songee met them in the foyer.

"So…I see your trip was a success. Give them to me. I'll make sure everything is pressed for you."

"Thank you," Cari said, as Songee took the sacks and left them on their own. Cari eyed the French doors in the library, just visible from the foyer. "Can I go through there to get to the back of the house?"

"Absolutely," Mike said. "Just don't overdo it today, because tomorrow is going to be difficult, both physically and emotionally."

"I know," Cari said. "I just want to get some air…sit in the sunshine…maybe plot a new book while I'm at it."

Mike eyed her curiously. "That's right. You write mysteries, don't you? I'd forgotten Susan mentioning that."

"Yes, or at least I *did*. Lord knows what the news of my death is going to do to my readership," she muttered, and then walked away.

Mike started to go after her, then thought better of it and let her go. Time would solve some of her problems, but not all of them. He headed for his office to check in with Aaron Lake, hoping he might have news about Lance Morgan.

A huge green parrot took flight from a trio of live oaks, shrieking his disapproval at Cari's unexpected arrival as she walked out onto the veranda. She eyed him absently, too locked into her troubles to appreciate his presence or beauty. She paused for a moment to get her bearings, then headed for a grouping of white wicker chairs with green cushions, sitting around a small white wicker table. At least she could wallow in comfort.

She hadn't been seated more than a few minutes before Songee came out with a pitcher of iced sweet tea and a pair of glasses.

"Just in case," she said as she filled one glass for Cari, then left as quietly as she'd come.

Cari took a sip of the tea, then set it down. As generous as Mike and his housekeeper were to her, it wasn't going to fix what was wrong. She leaned back in the chair, staring across the perfectly manicured lawn without actually seeing it. Her head was spinning with what-ifs and maybes, trying to think of where Lance would hide a dead man. He couldn't have gone far before the tornado hit. But he could have taken cover and buried it afterward.

For all she knew, he'd loaded it back up in the car and driven it into the bayous. If he took it to where the gators could get at it…fat chance it would ever be found.

As she thought, it occurred to her that the car she'd seen in the woods had not belonged to Lance, which meant it most likely belonged to the dead man. She wished now that she'd seen the tag, or taken note of the make and model. But the only thing that had registered was that it was black and she thought it was a rental.

Even though she'd only gotten a glimpse of the dead man's face, she was almost certain she'd never seen him before. She hadn't been able to see much else because of the rug he'd been wrapped in. She knew the rug had come from the library in Morgan's Reach, but unless they found both it and the body, she couldn't think of a way to tie Lance to the death.

"Hi, lady! How come you gots bwuses on you face?"

Surprised she was no longer alone, Cari turned around. When she saw that a little redheaded boy had taken residence in a chair on the other side of the table, she smiled. He was leaning back with his feet crossed at the ankles and his arms resting on the arms of the chair as if he'd decided to hold court. There was a slight frown knitting his brow, and he didn't appear as if he was in any hurry to leave. Then she remembered Mike mentioning that his neighbors had a three-year-old boy. Obviously one of the neighbors had come calling.

"I had an accident," Cari said. "My name is…my name is Cari. What's yours?"

"Daniel Elliot Miller the Twoed."

Cari stifled a grin. "Oh, so your daddy's name is Daniel, too?"

"No. Him's Daniel One. I's Daniel Two."

Cari laughed out loud.

"Ah…there you are," Mike said, as he came around the corner of the house. "Daniel, your momma is looking for you."

The little boy frowned. "You tell her I's fine, Uncle Mike. Me and the wady are havin' a visit."

Mike saw the grin on Cari's face and realized this was better medicine than anything a doctor could prescribe.

"Okay. I'll do that," he said. "But don't go anywhere else before coming in to tell your momma, okay?"

Daniel nodded. "All wight, Uncle Mike."

Mike glanced at Cari. "Are you doing okay?"

She nodded.

But apparently her visitor wasn't okay. He held up one little finger to get Mike's attention. "Hey, Uncle Mike?"

Mike grinned. "Yeah?"

"Um, uh, would you pwease tell Miss Songee I's here? I's pwetty sure her'll be wantin' to bwing me some cookies."

Cari laughed again, then looked at Mike. "Would you tell Songee to add a cookie for me?"

Mike's grin kept getting bigger. "You got it," he said, and left with a bounce in his step.

Daniel shifted his attention back to Cari. "Is you Uncle Mike's gwul-fwend?"

Cari's smile slipped a little. "No. He's just helping take care of me until I get well."

Daniel eyed the bruises on her face and arms again, then nodded.

"One time he gived me a SpongeBob Band-Aid for my knee."

Cari couldn't take her eyes off his little face. He was seriously adorable.

"Then I'm in the right place to get well, aren't I?" she said.

Daniel nodded, then folded his legs up beneath him and proceeded to explain why his cat, Roger, couldn't make babies.

By the time Songee came out carrying a plate with four round, fat gingerbread cookies sprinkled with sparkling sugar crystals, Cari was enchanted.

"There's my little man," Songee said.

Daniel threw back his head and cackled with laughter. "I's not no wittle man, Songee. I's only fwee."

Songee saw the joy on Cari's face and knew something wonderful was happening. Carolina didn't know it yet, but this was the first day that would count toward healing her broken heart.

"He's something, isn't he, miss?"

"I think I'm in love," Cari said softly.

Mike came out with Daniel's parents just as the words left Cari's mouth. There was a brief moment of shock, followed by a serious moment of jealousy before he realized how nuts it was, being jealous of a kid.

Fortunately Daniel's father shifted the subject.

"Tell the nice lady goodbye, Daniel. We're ready to go."

"Her name is Cawi, and I hasn't had my cookies yet."

Mike had already explained a bit about Cari's situation to his friends, but he was surprised she had used her real name. But then he realized how unlikely it was that a three-year-old living in another city would give her away.

"Cari, I want you to meet Dan and Nora Miller. Dan is a lawyer," he added.

Cari stood up. "Your son is an absolute delight," she said.

"Anybody wants a cookie?"

Cari looked down. Daniel had decided to slip into the role of host and was offering her a cookie.

"Why, thank you. I believe I will," she said, and took one from the plate.

Daniel watched her every move, right down to the moment she took her first bite, but whatever he was thinking, he kept to himself. He chose a cookie, then set the plate aside, and began to eat.

"How about me?" Mike asked.

Daniel sighed as he eyed the plate. "You can have

one, Uncle Mike, but somebody betta tell Songee to bwing mo-uh, cause we's gonna wun out."

Cari laughed again, and at that moment Mike felt as if a door had just opened into another facet of his life. He didn't know how it was going to pan out, or if she would even be willing, but he made a silent vow to himself that he was going to have a relationship with this woman or die trying.

Seven

Daniel eyed the cookie still left on the plate as his parents said their goodbyes. Cari saw the wistful look on his face and quickly wrapped it up in a napkin and handed it to him.

"You can save it for later," she said.

The smile on the little redhead's face was more than rewarding, proving the power of a cookie as the perfect attitude adjuster.

"What do you say?" his mother coached.

"Good cookie?" Daniel said.

Cari bit her lip to keep from laughing as his mother tried again.

"No. Thank you very much."

"You welcome," he countered.

All the adults burst into laughter, which prompted Daniel to follow suit. He wasn't sure what was so funny, but it was easy to be happy with a cookie in your hand.

Cari was still smiling as she watched them walk away.

"He's something else, isn't he?" Mike said.

"He made me laugh," Cari said.

"He makes everyone laugh," Mike added, then slid his arm around her shoulders. "Laughter is healing, *cher,*" he said softly.

It took all her willpower not to turn around and hide her face against his chest. It would be too easy to quit and let everything fall on Mike's shoulders, but she couldn't. She owed it to her family to see this through.

"I think I'll go in and call the funeral home...make sure everything is all set for tomorrow," she said.

"Want me to call?" Mike asked.

Cari hesitated, then shook her head. "I want to say yes, but I can't keep letting you solve all my problems. I can do it, but thank you for asking."

As he watched her walk away, Mike felt like calling her back—to tell her he *wanted* to solve her problems. But that would only lead to her asking why, which would lead to more questions for which he did not have answers.

Yet.

His cell phone rang just as he started into the house. He stopped, glanced at the caller ID, saw it was Aaron, then quickly answered.

"Tell me you have news," Mike said.

Aaron was used to his boss's impatience. "I have

information, and I think you're going to like it. Well, not like it, but—"

"Tell me," Mike demanded.

"A few days ago, Lance Morgan was basically bankrupt. Today, he's suddenly solvent. He has a brother named Joe who just liquidated a butt load of stocks and bonds to the tune of more than two hundred thousand dollars, but it didn't go into his bank account."

"So he bankrolled his brother. That's not an answer."

"That's just it," Aaron said. "He didn't give it to his brother. At least, not the bulk of it. It took some digging, but it seems Joe Morgan sent it to a shady guy up in Chicago named Dominic Martinelli—on his brother's behalf."

"Lance Morgan owed this man money?"

"Yes. Martinelli has quite a reputation. Among other things, he's something of a loan shark."

Mike began to pace the veranda as he absorbed the news.

"So...Lance owed a Chicago loan shark a bunch of money, but his brother came through for him. I still don't—"

"Lance had mortgaged the family estate, worth more than a million dollars, and which has been in the family about two hundred years. I'd say the possibility of losing that might cause a man to do something drastic."

"I guess," Mike said. "But it still doesn't make

sense. It doesn't explain why Lance had a reason to commit murder. If he needed money, all he had to do was ask the brother…what's his name again?"

"Joe."

"Right, Joe. But it doesn't matter—Lance didn't kill Martinelli."

"But what if Martinelli sent someone out to see Lance and *that's* who Lance killed?"

"But why would he kill someone connected to Martinelli when that wouldn't do anything to stop the property from being seized?"

"I can't say exactly what went on in the man's mind," Aaron answered. "But I do know Lance isn't exactly a knight in shining armor. It didn't take a lot of digging to find out his family has been buying him out of trouble for years. A serious drunk driving incident in his younger days that somehow went away. In high school, a pregnant girlfriend whose family suddenly came into a lot of money and moved away. You get the picture."

"Okay, I see where you're going with this. Lance Morgan doesn't think before he acts. So let's find out if someone connected to Martinelli has gone missing. If not, then we can rule out that angle and look elsewhere."

"I'll get right on it," Aaron said and disconnected.

Mike dropped his cell phone back into his pocket, then went to find Cari. He wanted to know how much she knew about Lance Morgan's life and lifestyle. He found her in the library, still on the phone. He could tell by the look on her face, she was struggling to control her emotions.

Cari had dreaded making the call for so many reasons, not the least of which was that Sarah Beth Spellman was an old friend. She couldn't help but wonder what had gone through Sarah Beth's mind when "Cari's" body had been brought in to be embalmed, then seeing the facial damage and being in on the decision to have a closed casket. It was all too gruesome to consider, and yet consider it she must.

So she'd dialed the number, bracing herself to hear her friend's familiar voice.

"Sumner's Funeral Home. Sarah Beth Spellman speaking."

"Ms. Spellman, this is Susan Blackwell."

"Oh. Yes, Ms. Blackwell. Please call me Sarah Beth, will you?"

"Yes, thank you," Cari said. "I called to tell you that I will be attending the services tomorrow. I'm healing more quickly than expected."

"That is certainly good news," Sarah Beth said. "Will you be needing any special assistance? We can have a wheelchair available. It won't be a problem at all."

"I won't be needing any special assistance, but thank you for asking."

"You're very welcome." Then she added, "Susan, please know that you have our sympathies."

Cari shuddered, then swallowed back tears. "Thank you."

"Oh. I almost forgot," Sarah Beth said. "The Ladies Aid has organized a dinner at the church after the services. As you know, your loved ones had so many friends in the area. Everyone has been invited to come, and I hope you will, too. People will want to make sure you don't feel alone."

Cari's voice broke. "That's so very kind."

"So we'll see you at the church tomorrow at 11:00 a.m. And...just so you know. If you want some private time in the viewing room, we won't be moving the caskets until about 10:30," Sarah Beth said.

Cari was rattled by the thought of having to see her parents' bodies. It would be the ultimate demonstration of facing the truth of what happened. She didn't know Sarah Beth had disconnected or that Mike had come into the room until she looked up and caught him watching her. Startled, she heard the dial tone for the first time, then hung up the phone and stood to face him.

"You okay?" he asked.

"Not really."

"If you have some time, I want to talk to you."

"Right now, time is about all I do have."

"Good. Let's go back outside, okay? I think there's still some iced tea."

He opened the door for her, then followed her out. As soon as she sat back down, he joined her.

"What's up?" Cari asked.

"I've had my security chief, Aaron Lake, doing a little investigating into Lance Morgan's affairs. Thought it might help us figure out who got murdered."

Cari scooted to the edge of the chair. "What did you find out?"

"Nothing definite but something pretty indicative," Mike said. "That's what I want to talk to you about. How much do you know about his business?"

"He lives on a place called Morgan's Reach and raises soybeans and peanuts, which are pretty big cash crops in the South, on about six hundred acres of bottom land. They used to raise horses on the other five hundred acres, but they got rid of the last ones soon after his parents died. The horses were his father's pet project, but after he was gone, neither of the boys wanted anything to do with them."

"So if you had to make a guess, how stable would you say he was financially?"

"Why…I guess I would think they were pretty well-set. It was certainly the case when his parents were alive. Why?"

"Up until a day or so ago, Lance Morgan has been teetering on the verge of bankruptcy."

Cari sat all the way back in her chair. Her shock was evident. "You're kidding me."

"No."

“How? And what changed?” she asked.

“It seems his brother liquidated a lot of stocks and bonds to the tune of two hundred thousand dollars plus, and bought him out of trouble.”

Cari’s shoulders slumped. “Poor Joe,” she muttered. “Still picking up after little brother’s messes. At least Joe must have made Lance’s banker happy.”

“Oh…Lance didn’t owe the bank.”

Cari frowned. “Then who in the world would he borrow money from?”

“A loan shark in Chicago.”

“Why would someone like that advance money on a crop?”

“It gets better,” Mike said. “He didn’t borrow against his crop. He mortgaged Morgan’s Reach.”

Cari gasped. “Oh. My. God.” Suddenly she was out of the chair and on her feet. “All of a sudden things are beginning to make sense. Now that I know what was at stake, I wouldn’t put anything past him.”

“You’re saying he would kill to make sure he didn’t lose the family home?”

Cari turned, her eyes afire with emotion. “Without hesitation. That place has belonged to the Morgans for…I don’t know…something like two hundred years or more. So…do we know where the loan shark is?”

“Yes. He’s safe and sound in Chicago.”

“Drat,” Cari muttered. “I was thinking he might have been the dead man I saw.”

“Aaron is still checking on some things.”

Cari started pacing again. "Wait. You said Lance was bankrupt up until a day or so ago."

"Yes."

"And now he's not."

"Right."

"So Joe coughed up some operating money, as well as paying off the loan. But do we know when the loan was going to be called in?"

Mike frowned. "I didn't ask. But that's definitely a good point. Wait a minute. I'll call Aaron." As soon as Aaron answered, he said, "Hey, Aaron. Cari had a good question. Do we know when Lance Morgan's loan came due?"

"Yes. It was actually six months *over*due."

"Hang on," Mike said, and then turned to Cari. "It was six months overdue."

Cari nodded. "So the loan shark was most likely planning to take Morgan's Reach."

Mike started grinning. "I like the way your mind works," he said, and then put the phone back to his ear. "Aaron. Check and see if foreclosure papers had been filed, will you? And while you're at it, find out the name of Martinelli's lawyer."

"You got it," Aaron said. "Anything else?"

"Not at this time," Mike said, and disconnected, then turned to Cari. "You have a good head for business."

Cari smiled wryly. "It's not so much business sense as it is methodical nitpicking. I think that's why I can do mysteries. I like the way a mystery unfolds. You know…foreshadowing…laying false clues…more than one suspect. The truths that are revealed in subtle increments."

Mike watched the life come back in her eyes as she talked about her writing. It was obvious how much she loved it. And since he'd checked and found out she was regularly on all the bestseller lists, it was also obvious she was good at it. He made a mental note to pick up one of her books. Then it dawned on him that her own personal library must have been destroyed in the tornado. In fact, everything she would have used to work with must be gone. He couldn't imagine losing his office: the records, the open files. It would be devastating.

As soon as they got past the funeral, he would contact her publisher and see what he could do to replace the copies of her published works. Then he caught himself. He couldn't do that without giving away the fact that she wasn't dead after all. Still, it was something he could do down the road.

"So we're agreed Lance Morgan isn't exactly a candidate for man of the year," he said.

Cari rolled her eyes. "As far as I'm concerned, he's not even worth calling a man. He's a big spoiled brat who doesn't know the meaning of responsibility. I feel sorry for Joe. He's a good man. Conscientious to a fault, but like his parents, he has this bad habit of bailing Lance out of one mess after the other."

"We'll figure it out," Mike said. "I promise."

A wave of exhaustion swept through Cari as she nodded. "I know, and again, you can't know how much I appreciate you honoring Susan by helping me."

"It isn't all for Susan. You're pretty worthwhile yourself, you know." Then, before she could argue, he wrapped his arms around her and pulled her close. "Just between friends…okay?"

If he hadn't added that last bit, she might have backed out of his arms, but now she was caught. If she moved, she came across as making a big to-do out of a simple hug, and he was definitely strong enough to lean on. She made herself relax, then hesitantly wrapped her arms around his waist and hugged him back.

Oh God…this feels better than good, Cari thought, then closed her eyes, inhaling the subtle scent of his aftershave.

As she did, the steady, rock-hard thump of his heart skipped a beat. She couldn't help but wonder if he was as affected by the hug as she was, then immediately told herself she was crazy. They hadn't known each other a week. She was just suffering from the aftereffects of traumatic loss and wanted to be consoled. That was all this was.

All it *could* be.

Ill at ease from her jumbled emotions, Cari let go of him and stepped back.

"Thank you," she said, primly, as if he'd just served her a slice of turkey, not taken her in his arms.

Mike felt the chill of her withdrawal and wished things could be different. So she didn't want him touching her. He understood.

Sort of.

"You're welcome," he said. "Hope I didn't offend you."

"I'm not offended. I think I'm just tired. Maybe I'll go take that nap after all." And before Mike could comment, she flashed him a brief smile and walked into the house.

Mike shoved his hands in his pockets, then turned and walked off the veranda and out into the yard.

Chicago P.D. was in an uproar. A bomb threat had been called in to the courthouse right in the middle of a trial. The fact that the defendant was a known member of a Japanese crime organization probably had everything to do with the threat. That the threat was valid had yet to be proven. All they knew was that clearing the courthouse in a timely fashion and getting the bomb squad inside were the first two orders of business.

Off-duty officers and detectives from every division were called to the scene to help with evacuation and crowd control, which was why Detective Sandy Smith wasn't at her desk when the call from the law firm of Meacham and Ball finally came. The receptionist who took the call simply wrote down the message and left it with a half dozen others for Missing Persons.

It wasn't until the next morning that Sandy Smith got back to her desk, and even longer before she shuffled through the stack of messages to find the one from the law office.

"Damn," she muttered, and picked up the phone to return the call.

"Meacham and Ball," the receptionist answered.

"Detective Smith returning Paul Meacham's call from yesterday."

"One moment, please," the receptionist said.

The call was answered a second time, this time by Meacham's private secretary, and once again Sandy had to explain herself and the call. Yet again she was put on hold, but this time not for long.

"Detective Smith. Paul Meacham here."

Sandy had the open file on Austin Ball's disappearance in front of her and picked up a pen to make notes.

"Thank you for getting back to me, Mr. Meacham. I won't take up much of your time, but Austin Ball's wife, Marcey, has turned in a missing person's report on her husband. I don't suppose you've had any recent contact with him, have you?"

"No. We haven't. And I must tell you that we're all terribly concerned. This isn't like Austin."

"So I've been told," Sandy said. "If you would bear with me for a few minutes, I have some questions."

"Anything I can do to help," Paul said.

"I understand Austin Ball was on business for the firm when he flew to Baton Rouge, Louisiana. Is that true?"

"Yes."

"Could you please tell me who the client was?"

"I'm sorry?"

"The client. Whoever Austin was representing."

"I'm sorry. We're very careful with attorney-client privilege here."

"It wouldn't be breaking that privilege to tell me who the client was."

There was a moment of silence, then she heard a sigh. "I suppose you're right. Still, you understand that this isn't information we would want bandied about."

"No bandying. Just answer the question, please."

"Dominic Martinelli."

Sandy straightened. Aha! No wonder they wanted this kept quiet.

"Could you elaborate? Anything you could tell me that would help us locate Mr. Ball? I know you're as concerned as Marcey is. I mean…she's expecting their first child. She's afraid she's going to be a widow before she's a mother."

It was the baby angle that got him. "I don't know details, but I do know that Austin had filed foreclosure papers on behalf of Mr. Martinelli. I believe that would be public record."

Sandy grinned. "Yes, sir. You're right. I know I could

look it up, but I'd like to get Marcey some answers as soon as possible. Would you happen to remember the name of the person Martinelli was foreclosing on?"

"I don't remember, but I can get that for you. Please hold."

This time she didn't mind being put on hold. And again, it wasn't for long.

"Detective?"

"Yes, I'm here," Sandy said.

"Lance Morgan, of Bordelaise, Louisiana, had defaulted on a quarter-million-dollar loan. He was six months in arrears when the papers were filed, and Austin's reason for flying to Bordelaise was to present foreclosure papers to Morgan on Mr. Martinelli's behalf."

Sandy was writing furiously as Meacham talked.

"That's really all I know, Detective, other than the fact that he rented a car from Hertz. He picked it up in Baton Rouge, but no one seems to know anything after that. Oh…we do know that the car was never returned. And, to my knowledge, hasn't been found abandoned or anything like that."

Sandy dotted her last *i* and crossed her last *t* and leaned back. "This is very helpful, Mr. Meacham. Thank you."

"Yes, well…please keep us informed," he said. "We think the world of Austin and hope there is some logical explanation for all this."

"Definitely," Sandy said and disconnected. She was

even more convinced that something had happened to Austin Ball. Anyone doing business with Martinelli automatically put themselves in a precarious situation.

Next order of business would be to contact the authorities in Bordelaise and see if they had any information on the missing man. She called information, got the number, then settled in for the call.

Vera Samuels's job as day dispatcher in Bordelaise had always been busy, often hectic. But never had the parish P.D. been as hassled as they had been since the tornado. There was the ongoing investigation into Bobby Earle's disappearance from the church where he and his mother had gone for services, and the four prisoners who'd disappeared from the jail after the tornado had hit it. Some thought all five of them were dead and it was just a matter of finally finding the bodies, but Chief Porter wasn't one of them. There were too many clues pointing to the child having been abducted out on the church playground before the tornado ever hit. As for the missing prisoners, he was on the fence.

And then there were the funerals. They'd already buried old Mr. Warren from the nursing home, and the North family funerals were tomorrow. She was heartsick and worn-out as she answered the phone.

"Bordelaise Police Department."

"Detective Sandy Smith, here. Chicago P.D. May I speak to your chief, please?"

"I'm sorry, Detective Smith, but he's not in at

the moment. If you'll leave your number, I'll have him call you."

Sandy stifled a sigh. She hated playing phone tag. "Yeah, sure," she said, and rattled off the number and extension, then added, "Mind if I ask you something? I—"

Vera eyed the cruiser pulling up outside. When she realized it was the chief, she interrupted.

"Detective Smith, I believe Chief Porter just drove up. If you don't mind waiting, you can talk to him right now."

"That would be great," Sandy said. "I'll hold."

Vera got up from the desk and went to the door, anxious to catch the chief before he was diverted by someone outside.

"Chief? There's a call for you on line one. Some detective from the Chicago Police Department."

Hershel Porter frowned. "I don't wanna talk to anyone from Chicago. I got my own set of problems down here. I don't need any of theirs."

"Sorry," Vera said. "She's on hold."

"She?"

Vera grinned. "Oh. Didn't I tell you? It's a female detective."

Hershel strode past Vera and into his office.

She watched him pick up on line one and was about to do a little eavesdropping when the phone began ringing again.

"Drat," she muttered, and picked up the call while the chief dealt with his.

"Chief Porter speaking."

Sandy Smith shifted into gear. "Detective Sandy Smith, Chicago P.D."

"What can I do for you, Detective?" Hershel asked.

"I'm working a missing person's case and have reason to believe my guy was last seen heading in your direction."

Hershel sighed. "We got ourselves a whole lot of missing people down here right now," he said.

Sandy frowned. "I'm sorry?"

"We got hit by a tornado a few days back. Four dead…so far. A kid and four prisoners still missing."

"Oh my God," Sandy muttered, as her thoughts began to shift into a whole other scenario. This could explain what happened to Austin Ball. "Sorry to hear that," she added.

"Yeah, thanks," Hershel said. "So tell me about your case."

"Got a lawyer named Austin Ball who caught a flight out of Chicago last Sunday."

"That would be the day the tornado hit," Hershel said.

Sandy frowned. "Damn." Then she scanned her notes before asking, "Do you know a man named Lance Morgan?"

"Why yes. Youngest son of a fine old family. Known him all his life."

"Well, the son of that fine family owes almost a quarter of a million dollars to a loan shark here in Chicago. He's six months in arrears and has defaulted on the loan. The loan shark filed foreclosure papers, and my missing person was sent to Bordelaise to present them to Mr. Morgan."

"The hell you say," Hershel said. "Are you sure? The Morgans are what we down here call well-heeled."

"Obviously not anymore, or he would have paid back the money. We know that Ball landed in Baton Rouge and picked up a rental car. Then…nothing. It's as if he dropped off the face of the earth."

"Maybe he just walked away from a stressful job or something."

"We don't think so. He was six weeks away from becoming a father for the first time. Crazy about his wife. No financial problems."

"I see where you're coming from," Hershel said. "Real sorry to tell you we haven't come across any unidentified bodies or unaccounted for cars. However, if you'll fax me your particulars, I'll have my deputies be on the lookout."

"I'd appreciate it," Sandy said. "What's your fax number?" she asked, then wrote it down. "I'll be in touch," she added.

Hershel frowned as he hung up the phone. Just what they needed—another missing person.

Eight

Now that the day of the funeral had finally dawned, Cari was experiencing a new wave of panic. She'd downed a piece of toast and some hot tea just because of Mike's and Songee's concern, but she felt as if her meal could come up at any moment.

It didn't seem possible that the two people who'd given her life were about to spend eternity in matching caskets in the family mausoleum at the Bordelaise Cemetery. And Susan, who'd spent half her life stressing about how she looked, was being buried without a viewing due to the horrific damage to her face. There was a huge part of Cari's consciousness that had yet to fully grasp the enormity of what forever meant. She kept trying to convince herself that they weren't so much dead as just gone, and that she would see them again one day in the heaven she believed existed. And while the true scope of their absence had yet to sink in, she knew after today, all that would change.

Over an hour had passed since she'd gone to her room to dress, and she was still fiddling with the details of her appearance. She had dressed with the precision of a toreador readying for the moment when he would come face-to-face with his nemesis, putting on one garment at a time, then pausing to study the look, making sure it would coordinate with her plan of deception.

While the bullfighter's nemesis was El Toro, Cari's nemesis was, in theory, the entire town of Bordelaise, but most especially Lance Morgan. She had to make sure that when they first saw her, they were only seeing her resemblance to Cari North and nothing more.

Finally she was finished, confident that she'd done all she could to hide her identity. Besides her new short, tousled hairstyle, so unlike the one Carolina North always wore, she had a narrow bandage across one cheek and a smaller one on the opposite side of her chin. She'd used a tiny butterfly bandage at the beginning of one eyebrow and was wearing a sling on her right arm.

Susan had worn makeup, but sparingly, and never in the same shades as Cari. Conscious of her need to stay in character, Cari had used only a little rose-colored lip gloss, which seemed a good choice in deference to all the bandages supposedly covering healing wounds.

The black dress that Mike had picked out for her

clung to her curves, but the neutral color took away any hint of impropriety. She had the new bag under her arm, the oversize sunglasses inside, and was carrying the jet cameo necklace he'd given her. With one last glance at her disguise, she headed for the door. If the day and the reason hadn't been so sad, she could almost have convinced herself she was going to a costume party.

She was on her way down the hall when she heard a door open behind her. She turned just as Mike came out of his bedroom and, for a moment, was stunned by his appearance. The black suit he was wearing made him look taller than ever, and the pristine white of his shirt highlighted the slight olive cast of his skin. She watched his expression change as he came closer, and for a moment she wondered what had sparked the sudden glitter in his eyes.

Mike was nervous about today. There was a knot in the pit of his stomach, not only because he was going to Susan's funeral, but also because he was abetting Cari in a serious deception.

He wasn't so sure she was going to be able to pull it off, but he understood her need to try. It was the last thing she could do for her family, and he knew from his own experience that it was a natural step in the process of healing. There was also a part of him that wanted to see Lance Morgan face-to-face. Without identifying all the reasons why, he needed to know who was threatening Carolina North's safety. He wasn't ready to admit that he might be falling for her, and she had too many demons to face to be dealing with anything else.

As he walked out of his bedroom suite, he saw her just ahead of him. He was about to call out her name when she paused and turned around, and he was struck once again by how much he was attracted to her.

"Oh good, there you are. I need help with this necklace," Cari said.

"Sure thing," Mike said, then waited as Cari turned her back to him. He put the necklace over her head, then got sidetracked by the delicate curve of her neck and missed the clasp. "Drat," he muttered. "Sorry. Here we go again."

Cari felt the warmth of his breath on the back of her neck and suddenly shivered. She had the strangest urge to turn, walk into his arms and never let go.

Unaware of Cari's wayward thoughts, Mike managed to fasten the necklace. "There we are," he said, then added, "I don't know if it's the proper thing to say on such a sad day, but you look beautiful."

Cari's heart skipped. "My father always said, 'You can never compliment a woman too much,' so… thank you."

Mike cupped the side of her cheek with one hand, then traced the curve with his thumb. "I'm sorry I never met your parents. Susan talked about them…and you…often."

"After her mother and dad passed away, we were all the family she had left," Cari said, then her chin quivered. "I was an only child, as was she. We always swore we'd have bunches of kids so they could grow up together."

"I'm so sorry," Mike said. Then, because he couldn't bear the sadness in her eyes, he changed the subject. "Come on, tough stuff. We'd better get going."

"Right," she said, and headed for the stairs.

A few minutes later they were in the car and on their way to Bordelaise.

Hershel Porter was topping off his second cup of morning coffee when Vera came into his office.

"Chief, Toby Warren is in the outer office. Says he needs to talk to you."

Hershel set down his cup and followed Vera out into the lobby.

"Hey, Toby. How's it going?" Hershel asked.

Toby was a quiet, unassuming thirtysomething bachelor who tended to keep to himself. But from the expression on his face, he had obviously been shaken out of his normal demeanor.

"Chief! I was out looking for a fox that had carried off one of my best hens this morning when I found something on the backside of Morgan's Reach that I think you need to see."

"What is it?" Hershel asked.

"A car."

Hershel frowned. "And what's so special about this car?"

"It's up a tree. In fact, it's pretty much up a half-dozen trees. I'm guessing the tornado dropped it there. I couldn't tell if there was anybody in it or not, but I could see the tag, and I think it's one of them cars you rent."

Immediately Hershel thought of the call he'd gotten from that Chicago detective about the lawyer who'd rented a car in Baton Rouge right before he'd gone missing.

Shit. I do not want to start my day by finding another dead man.

Still, it was, as his wife sarcastically said, why he got paid the big bucks.

"You say it's on Morgan property?" Hershel asked.

"Yep."

"Can you show me?"

"Yep."

Hershel pointed to a nearby chair. "There's doughnuts and coffee. Help yourself, then have a seat. It'll take me a few minutes to round up some men, and I want to let Lance Morgan know we need to get on his property."

Toby headed for the food as Hershel began issuing orders.

"Vera, call Morgan's Reach for me and put it through to my office. Then get on the radio. Tell Lee Tullius to get a couple of off-duty deputies ASAP and meet me at the fire station. Then call the fire chief and tell him we're gonna be needing help from his rescue unit."

"Yes, sir," she said, as Hershel headed for his office.

Hershel glanced at the coffee he'd abandoned, then told himself he needed to cut back anyway as his phone began to ring. He picked up the receiver.

"Chief. Joe Morgan on line one for you."

"Thanks, Vera," he said, and pressed the button. "Joe. Hershel Porter here. Is Lance around?"

Automatically Joe's stomach knotted. The only time the police chief ever called was when Lance was in trouble.

"No. He's outside somewhere. Do you want me to find him and have him call you back?"

"That won't be necessary," Hershel said. "I can give you the information just as easily. We need permission to come on your property. We just received a report of a vehicle that got picked up by the tornado and wound up in the trees on the back side of your property. Seeing as how we still have some missing people, we're going to have to retrieve the car."

"Good Lord," Joe muttered. "I sure hope no one was in it."

"You and me both," Hershel said. "We just received a report from the Chicago police that some lawyer who was coming to Morgan's Reach the day of the storm never returned home. His wife filed a missing person's report, so we have to check this out. Anyway, I just wanted to let you know that we'll be coming on the property."

Joe figured the lawyer must have been coming on Martinelli's behalf, but the problem with the loan shark was behind them, and when he realized Porter's request had nothing to do with Lance, his anxiety eased. "No problem," he said. "Thanks for calling."

Joe hung up, then glanced at the clock. He wanted to shower before Lance got back and used up all the hot water. He was still in the shower when Lance came back, and by the time he got out and got dressed, it was time for them to leave for Bordelaise. Joe gave his tie one last tug, then went across the hall to his brother's bedroom.

Lance was straightening his own tie as Joe appeared in the doorway.

"It's time to go," Joe said.

"I'm ready," Lance said, as he tucked a clean handkerchief in his pocket. "How do I look?" he asked.

Joe frowned. He was still so pissed at Lance for what he'd done, he didn't feel like being cordial.

"Too damn happy to be going to a funeral," he muttered, and turned on his heel and walked away.

Lance frowned. He hated it when Joe was pissed at him, but what was done was done. It wasn't like he could take it back.

"How long are you going to rub this in?" Lance grumbled, as he followed Joe down the hall and out of the house.

Joe spun. "*Rub it in?* Don't be glib with me, you son of a bitch. This last stunt you pulled wiped out everything I had in the way of savings."

"Yeah, well, you're now the sole owner of Morgan's Reach, so stop bitching."

Joe's fingers curled into fists. He'd never wanted to hit anyone as badly as he wanted to hit his own brother now. But he couldn't. Because he was afraid that if he started, he would never stop.

"By the way, seeing as it's technically mine now, what happened to Grandma Ellie's rug that was in the library? I better not hear that you went and sold or pawned it."

"It's being repaired," Lance muttered, knowing there would come a day down the road when he would have to come up with a better answer.

"We'll see, won't we? If it doesn't show back up, I'll know that's just one more lie you've told. And… just for the record, you're pathetic," Joe said. "You don't care what happens to anyone else as long as you get your way. You've been forewarned. This was the end for me. The next time you screw up…and we all know that day will come…you're on your own. Don't waste your money calling me, because I am through with you. Now get in the car and try not to piss me off on the way into town."

For once Lance was speechless. He'd never seen Joe so angry. Wisely he kept quiet as he opened the car door, though he couldn't hide the long-suffering expression on his face. Joe might be mad at him, but he would get over it. He always did. Besides, today was a sad business, and he had an image to project. He'd once been Cari North's fiancé. All eyes would be on him in his time of grief.

Somewhere in the distance, a hound bayed. Joe frowned, then looked over the top of the car toward Lance.

"Sounds like someone's hunting," he said.

Lance frowned. The sound was too close to the house for his peace of mind. The last thing he needed was for some damned hunter and his dog to find Austin Ball's body.

"They better not be hunting on my property," Lance muttered.

"You no longer own any property," Joe reminded him, and slid behind the wheel.

"Bastard," Lance muttered, and then got into the passenger side and buckled up without looking at his brother again.

Joe pulled out of the driveway and onto the highway that led toward Bordelaise without further comment. Today was the day he paid his respects to dear friends. He had the rest of his life to be pissed at Lance. But they hadn't gone far before Lance flew into a panic that Joe didn't understand.

"Oh hell!" Lance cried, as they passed a trio of parish police cruisers parked on the side of the road. Suddenly the baying hound took on a new and deadly connotation. What if they had bloodhounds? What if Austin Ball's body had already been found? "What could the police possibly be doing on my—on Morgan's Reach?"

Joe glanced at the cars, as well as the uniformed officers, then shrugged. "They're after a wrecked vehicle that got left by the tornado," he said. "I understand someone is still missing."

Lance felt his breakfast backing up in his throat. "What the hell do you mean? Who's missing? They can't just stomp all over the place like that without letting me know."

"Well, actually, yes, they can," Joe said. "And they did call. I told them it was fine."

Lance felt as if the ground had just been yanked out from under him. "What the fuck! Why would you do something like that?" he shrieked.

Joe glanced over at his brother, then returned his attention to driving as he slowed down to take the curve in the road.

"Why wouldn't I?" Joe asked. "What could it possibly matter? There aren't any cattle or horses that might get loose, and the soybean and peanut crops are all on the other side of the property."

Lance didn't know what to say. "Well…because… I…because, oh, hell. What did they say, anyway?"

"That they're following up on a missing person's report made in Chicago. The man—some lawyer—was supposedly on his way to Morgan's Reach. Anyway, no one's heard from him since, but someone spotted a car on our property, so they're checking it out." Then he looked back at his brother and added, "Why would a lawyer from Chicago be coming to see you? Was he working for Martinelli?"

Lance suddenly needed to take a piss. "Why would I know anything about it?"

"Because I think it's more than a coincidence that you owed money to a man from Chicago, and that the man who was on his way here was a lawyer and also from Chicago."

Lance felt sick, but he hadn't come this far to lose everything, so he forced himself to calm down. "I didn't see anybody from Chicago. If he was driving around during the storm, the tornado most likely got him along with everything else," Lance muttered, then quickly changed the subject. "Are we going to stop by the funeral home before the cemetery?"

"I see no reason. We've already been there once," Joe said.

But Lance needed a complete change of conversation and remained insistent. "Sara Beth told me Susan is going to come to the funeral after all. I thought if we got there soon enough, we might be able to talk to her alone. Considering the fact that we've known her as long as we've known the Norths, and she's just lost every member of her family, it seems like the proper thing to do."

Joe's antagonism toward his brother subsided

slightly. "Oh. I didn't know. I guess we should at least stop by, then."

Lance nodded, then wisely kept his mouth shut the rest of the way into town, even though his thoughts were churning. Crap. Crap. Crap. Just when he thought he was in the clear, another hitch appeared.

Mike and Cari had been traveling for the better part of an hour when she happened to look up and realize they were approaching the turnoff to her family home. At that point she leaned forward in the seat. Seeing so many once-beautiful trees with their tops missing, and others completely uprooted, as well as dead animals and debris in the pasture, slammed her with a host of terrible memories. The closer they got, the more anxious she became, until the turnoff appeared and the hair suddenly rose on the back of her neck.

Mike sensed the sudden tension in her body and thought she was getting sick, or possibly was in pain.

"Carolina...*cher*...are you all right? If you're hurting, I brought your pain pills."

But pills wouldn't cure the pain in Cari's heart. "That's where I used to live," she said, pointing to the side road. "The house was there, where all that debris is now."

"Oh. Hell. I'm sorry," he said.

Overwhelmed by a sudden wash of sorrow, she

swallowed past the lump in her throat and closed her eyes, willing herself not to cry.

"One step at a time, Carolina. And remember, you're not here alone."

"And you don't know how much I appreciate that," she whispered.

"Hey…it's okay. Besides, I—"

"I know. You're doing it for Susan," she mumbled.

Mike opened his mouth to remind her it wasn't just for Susan, then changed his mind. Whatever she needed to believe to get through this was fine with him. He glanced at his watch. They had made good time. Over an hour yet before the services started. Plenty of time to get her to the funeral home.

"How much farther to Bordelaise?" he asked.

"About five miles," Cari said.

Mike nodded with satisfaction, then frowned and pointed out the window. "There's an awful lot of damage through here, as well," he said, eyeing the fences still down and the broken trees in the pastures they were passing.

Cari glanced out the window, then gasped. He was right. The devastation was everywhere.

"Oh, no," she said, pointing to what was left of a house off to their left. "That was the Barber place. The house and barn are gone. God. I hope they'd already left for church."

"That's right. The tornado hit on Sunday morning, didn't it?"

Cari nodded, then bit her lip and looked away.

A short while later they entered the city limits of Bordelaise. To Cari's horror, it was evident her hometown had not escaped the tornado's wrath.

"Oh, no. The back of the jail is gone. And the courthouse...the roof. Oh. Oh. And the beauty shop... So much damage. So much history just gone."

"It looks pretty bad," Mike agreed. "But for every place that got hit, there are two that are still standing. See. The barber shop...and the supermarket. And the flower shop. Looks like they lost a plate glass window, but nothing else. They're still open for business. I know this looks bad. But people are resilient. They will rebuild."

"If they're still alive," Cari said, and then clenched her hands and thrust them into her lap, as if bracing herself for whatever was coming next.

"Where's the funeral home?" he asked.

She pointed. "See that stop sign up ahead? Turn left, then it's two blocks down."

"Got it," he said, and followed her directions all the way to Sumner's Funeral Home.

He parked in front and then killed the engine. "Are you ready for this?"

Cari had started to shake. The knowledge of what lay ahead was overwhelming her.

"I feel like I'm going to throw up."

"If you start to panic, just say my name," he said. "I'll be beside you all the way."

Cari shifted the sling on her shoulder, then reached for her bag and put on the sunglasses. "Don't forget. You need to call me Susan."

"I won't forget. Now sit tight. I'll come around and help you out."

"I can get myself—"

"Your arm is in a sling. You have bandages all over the place and staples in your head. At least pretend you're handicapped, tough stuff."

"Oh. Yes. Right," she said, then waited for Mike.

A few moments later they walked inside, with Cari leaning on Mike's arm. She thought she'd braced herself to face Sarah Beth, but when she saw her old friend, there was a moment when she wanted to turn and run. Then Sarah Beth saw her, and it was too late to escape.

"Oh. Miss Blackwell, you did make it." She started to shake Cari's hand, then saw the sling and clasped her hands in front of her instead. "You're just in time for the final viewing. This way, please. We've put the family together in one room. And once again, please accept my sympathies for your loss."

Cari couldn't speak for the horror that lay ahead. Then she felt Mike's hand at the small of her back, and looked up and caught his gaze. At that moment everything faded but the task at hand. She took a deep breath, then leaned into his strength as she followed Sarah Beth down a hallway and into the first room on their right.

It went without saying that Cari's heart was pounding so hard she could barely breathe. The last time she'd seen them had been brutal. And yet when she walked into that small, quiet room and saw all the flowers, and then the three caskets lined against the wall, she went weak—but with an odd sense of relief.

The trauma that had been done to her parents had been skillfully hidden. The clothing Sarah Beth had chosen for them to wear was perfect. Her mother's dress was blue, which had been her favorite color. The gray suit they'd dressed her father in was unfamiliar, but the expression of peace on his face was not.

When she realized she'd been holding her breath, she slowly exhaled, and with that, came tears.

"Oh Lord, help me through this," she whispered, and moved forward, drawn like a magnet by the need to touch her loved ones one last time.

Mike stood back, giving her privacy, while aching for the vastness of her loss. As he waited, he couldn't help but notice the closed casket at the end of the row.

That would be Susan. Such an ignominious end to a good and gentle woman.

Goodbye, dear friend. You will be missed in so very many ways.

Then his gaze turned to Cari, and just in time. He leaped forward and caught her just as her knees gave way. Within seconds, she was holding her sunglasses and stammering through tears.

"I d-don't know what h-happened. I started to—"

"It doesn't matter," Mike said, and then turned her around and wrapped her in his arms. "I am sorry…so sorry," he said softly.

His sympathy was Cari's undoing. Silent tears turned to harsh, ugly sobs, ripping up her throat and shattering the silence with her grief.

"I know, I know," he whispered, as he rocked her where they stood.

Cari cried until her head was throbbing and her eyes were all but swollen shut. Ironically her red and swollen features added to her disguise when Joe and Lance Morgan walked into the room.

Mike saw the men enter and was about to ask them to wait until Cari was ready to leave, when one of them suddenly rushed forward.

"Susan! Sweetheart! We're so sorry for your loss."

Mike heard Cari gasp, then saw her tense. Before he could think what to do, she had turned to face the visitors, her sunglasses still in her hand.

"Lance. Joe. Thank you for coming," she said.

Ah, Mike thought, as he narrowed in on the younger of the pair. He felt Cari's nervousness and pulled her a little closer.

Lance took one look at Susan, then stopped suddenly, as if he'd run into an invisible wall.

Mike watched the shock spread across the man's face and for a moment thought the whole ruse had failed before it started. Then Lance started rambling, and Mike realized she'd pulled it off.

“My God, Suze! Sarah Beth said you’d been in an accident, but I had no idea it was so serious. Are you okay? Is there anything we can do for you? Here, let me help you—”

The moment Lance reached for her, Cari flinched and held up her hand. “No!” Then she realized how strange that might seem and managed to stammer an awkward explanation. “I mean, Mike…uh, my boss, Michael Boudreaux, is helping me, but thank you.”

Joe reached out, gently touching Cari’s shoulder. The compassion on his face was nearly her undoing.

“Susan, it’s been too long, and this is a terrible place for a reunion. You know how sorry we are. We loved Cari and your parents like they were our family, too.”

Lance, however, had moved from consoling her to being impressed by her boss’s presence.

“Say, are you Michael Boudreaux of Baton Rouge?”

Mike looked a bit taken aback. “Yes, I’m from Baton Rouge.”

Lance grabbed his hand and shook it. “I’ve read a lot about your business ventures, and I’m a great admirer of your business acumen. If you ever have an opening—”

“Lance, for God’s sake! This is not the time or place,” Joe said, then glanced back at Cari. “Sorry, Susan, but you know Lance.”

Cari did know Lance—all too well. Still, she chose to ignore his gaffe.

"Thank you for your sympathy," she said, then turned to Mike. "What time is it?"

He got the hint that she wanted them gone and quickly glanced at his watch. "A little after ten-thirty. The service starts at eleven."

"I need to freshen up," Cari said.

"Certainly. Lean on my arm," Mike said.

Cari nodded, then glanced at the Morgans one last time. "I hope I'll see you both at the dinner afterward?"

"Absolutely," Lance said. "After all, we were almost family."

Cari tried not to glare. "I remember," she said sharply.

Lance looked taken aback, as if puzzled by Susan's emotional reaction. Then he realized Cari had probably told her everything about his faux pas with the stripper. He still thought she'd made a big deal out of nothing, but it was all water under the bridge.

"We'll see you later," he said, then added, "Joe, we'd better head to the church, too, or we won't be able to get a seat…unless Susan wants us to wait and sit with her. After all, we were like family."

Mike saw the look on Cari's face and knew it was time to intervene. "She'll see you later at the dinner, okay?"

"Sure," Joe said, and grabbed his brother's arm. "Come on, Lance. We've intruded enough as it is."

Cari waited until the sound of their footsteps had faded, then went limp against Mike.

"Oh my Lord," she muttered. "For a moment there, I thought it was over before it had started."

Mike slid a hand down to the small of her back. "You're doing it," he said softly. "If he bought it, they all will."

She turned back to the caskets. "Mike?"

"Yes?"

"If you don't mind, I would like to be alone for a few minutes."

"Absolutely," he said. "I'll make sure no one else comes in."

Cari nodded. She heard him walking away, but her focus had already shifted as she went back to her parents. She stopped at her father's casket first and reached for his hand.

"I hate this," she whispered, as her voice broke. "It isn't fair, Daddy. I took you for granted, didn't I? You were always there to fix whatever went wrong in my life. Who's going to walk me down the aisle when I get married? Who's going to teach my children how to bait a hook like you taught me?"

She choked, then swiped at the tears running down her face as she moved to her mother. God love Sarah Beth, but she'd even gone so far as to get some small gold loops for her mother's pierced ears, knowing Maggie North was never without earrings and would want something formal to match her dress.

"And you, Mom. You weren't just my mother, you were my best friend. No matter what happened to me, you always had a way to make it better. I can't believe I'll never hear you laugh at those crazy Road Runner cartoons again. That I'll never walk into a kitchen on Thanksgiving and smell your cornbread dressing baking in the oven again." Cari's shoulders slumped as her voice slipped to a fragile whisper. "Without you and Daddy and Susan, I have nothing left. No roots—no sense of direction—no family."

She moved toward the closed casket, then laid her hand on the highly polished surface of the white metal. "You don't know it, Susie Q, but right now, you're sort of saving my life. I love you like the sister I never had, and I'm going to miss you like crazy."

Cari grabbed a handful of tissues from a box on the table and blotted her tears, then took a deep breath before exhaling on a sigh. "I'm not sure how all this works, but wherever you've gone, don't forget to save me a place."

Then she turned and walked away without looking back. She knew she would have to sit through a long, endless viewing at the church after the service, but this was the one that had mattered. As she stepped out of the room, Sarah Beth and two men from the funeral home entered.

"I'm sorry," Sarah Beth said, "but they're going to have to take the caskets to the church, now. The limousine for you is ready. If you'll follow me, I'll show you."

Cari was still trying to pull herself together when Mike suddenly appeared.

"You're doing great," he said quietly, as he gave her a hug. "The ladies' room is over here. I'll wait for you in the hall."

Once again, he'd thought of everything. By the time Cari came out, she'd washed away the tracks of her tears and reapplied her lip gloss.

"Where's your car?" Cari asked, as Mike helped her into the limousine.

"One of the employees is driving it to the church for me. We'll ride in the limo to the church, then to the cemetery, then back to the church for the dinner, but the car will be on-site for when we're ready to leave, okay?"

Mike slid into the seat beside her, then took her hand and held it all the way to the church. Without talking.

Just as a reminder that she wasn't alone after all.

Nine

The funeral was a blur.

From the time Cari sat down in the pew to the beginning of the last song, she was aware of little save the three caskets at the altar. She kept wanting to scream—to demand someone stop this nightmare—to please let her wake up and find this had all been a bad dream. But it wasn't happening.

Once she heard the minister mention her name, and as he did, someone in the congregation behind her began to weep—loudly. She knew it was a woman, but had no idea who. It was an odd thing to be sitting at one's own funeral—to hear the litany of her life and accomplishments read aloud and know that people wept for her passing, which led to the thought of wondering what they would do when the news finally came out that she wasn't dead after all, and that she'd let an entire town bury another in her place.

There was a part of her that felt sick all over again,

just thinking about the ramifications of what she'd done. Still, if she had it to do over, she didn't think she would change a thing. She still needed to find out who Lance had murdered and what he had done with the body. Then she would be able to resurrect herself and get on with life.

When it came time for the viewing and her parents' caskets were opened, Cari couldn't bring herself to look at them again and hid behind the wide frame of her sunglasses. But it soon became apparent that nearly every living person left in Bordelaise had come to the services. The line of people filing by the caskets seemed endless, and she constantly felt the eyes of the entire town upon her. Surely someone was going to stop at any moment and recognize her—call her out for the pretender that she was. But it didn't happen.

All she kept thinking was that the room was too hot. As the mourners moved past, there were a couple of times she thought she might faint. Shortly thereafter, as if someone had read her mind, the ceiling fans came on. While they cooled the air, they unfortunately also stirred the scents of the funeral flowers into a sickly-sweet conglomeration. Now her stomach roiled with nausea.

Cari took a slow, deep breath, trying to calm the sick feeling. Suddenly Mike's hand was on her knee. She looked up. The sympathy on his face was her undoing. Her vision blurred, and she leaned back and closed her eyes, willing herself not to break into ugly sobs.

And again he seemed to sense her needs. When he handed her his handkerchief, she took it gladly and held it to her nose. The fresh scent of clean cotton shifted her focus from the too-sweet aroma of flowers, and her stomach settled.

Later, they headed for the cemetery. The service there was short—little more than a prayer—but this time when people filed past the caskets they stopped to shake her hand, or mutter a "so sorry for your loss" before quickly moving on. To her horror, she recognized someone from her publishing company. It was the first time she realized how far the news had traveled. She could just imagine the headlines. Best-selling author Carolina North, dead at twenty-nine. A promising career over before it had barely begun.

Then, all of a sudden, Mike's voice was in her ear.

"Come, *cher*…it's time to go back to the church." He had her on her feet and was leading her away before she knew what was happening. By the time he had her seated inside the limo, she was shaking.

"I don't know if I can get through the dinner," Cari said.

He frowned. Her eyes were too bright, her face too pale. She was in shock and just didn't know it.

"We don't have to stay," he said, as the driver began the trip back into Bordelaise.

Cari leaned back, then closed her eyes, savoring the momentary quiet.

"I think I have to," she finally answered. "At least

until after they serve the meal. Everyone has gone to so much trouble."

Mike took her hand, but he didn't answer. It wasn't his decision. All he knew was he wasn't abandoning her.

Cari threaded her fingers through his and held on as if he were her only lifeline to sanity.

She still had the meal to get through, and at least one more face-to-face with Joe and Lance. But the way she figured it, if they hadn't seen through her disguise before, they wouldn't now.

When they arrived at the church, Mike escorted her inside. Within seconds, she was swept away to a seat of honor and plied with all manner of food and drink, as if filling her stomach would somehow fill the emptiness left by her family's passing.

There was an empty chair to her right, which became the "visitor's chair." No sooner would she get a bite into her mouth than someone would slide into the chair to express their regrets. She had no recourse but to listen to the mourners regaling her with their memories of her parents and of her. It was the first time she realized how many of her classmates took pride in having grown up with someone who'd become a successful author. She kept thinking, if they only knew, it was she who felt blessed to have so many good friends.

The people came and went as she picked at her food—never staying long—never overstepping the boundaries of propriety. And always she was aware of Mike's quiet presence at her side and was thankful for the times he jumped into the conversation just in time to save her from losing her fragile composure.

The dinner was all but over before Cari noticed Police Chief Hershel Porter's sudden arrival. She saw him pause in the doorway, as if searching the crowd. When he saw her, he headed straight for her.

"Miss Blackwell, I just wanted to come pay my respects. Your family were real good friends of mine. They're going to be sorely missed."

"Thank you," Cari said, then introduced Mike. "Chief, this is Michael Boudreaux of Baton Rouge. Mike…Hershel Porter, parish police chief."

Hershel smiled as he shook Mike's hand. "Nice to meet you. It's kind of you to see after Miss Blackwell, today."

"It has been my honor," Mike said, and realized that he meant it. "I know how difficult this is for her. I lost my own parents a few years back." Then he walked a few feet away, to give the two of them some privacy.

"Yeah, sometimes life just hauls off and hits us square in the face, doesn't it?" Hershel said, then patted Cari on the shoulder. "Anything we can do for you, you just ask."

"Thank you," she said, then added, "I had no idea how badly Bordelaise had been hit until we arrived today."

Hershel grimaced. "Yeah. It's been a tough go. We've still got some people missing."

"Oh, no," Cari said. "I had no idea. Who?" Then she felt obligated to add, lest he think it odd she would inquire about people in a town where she didn't live, "I've spent so many summers here, and I know a lot of people."

"I remember," Hershel said. "Well, we still can't find Katie Earle's little boy, Bobby. They were at church. The kids were outside on the playground when the tornado siren went off. No one has seen him since they began ushering them inside to get to the church basement. Katie said the little guy was real scared of thunder and lightning, so it makes no sense that he wouldn't have gone in with the others. We're just not sure if his absence is due to the tornado or a parental abduction. Katie and her husband, J.R., have been separated for a couple of months, and we haven't been able to locate him, either. We also had four prisoners in the jail when it was hit, and they're still unaccounted for."

Cari knew Katie and J.R. well, and she didn't think J.R. would do anything like abducting his own son and scaring Katie like this. Then she remembered what Lance had done and realized she would never have thought that possible, either. She couldn't even envision how terrifying it must be not to know where your child was. As for the missing prisoners, it was daunting to think they might be on the loose and still in the neighborhood.

"I do remember the Earles. I can only imagine how frightened Katie is. When you next speak to her, tell her I'll keep her in my prayers."

Hershel Porter nodded. "Yes, ma'am, I'll be glad to. Now, I've bothered you long enough. Besides, I need to find Lance and Joe Morgan. Are they still here?"

"Yes, I believe so," Cari said. "At least they were earlier."

"We got a man from Chicago who's gone missing, too. The last his people heard from him, he was on his way to Morgan's Reach. We just found a black rental car in a stand of trees out on the back side of their property. It's the same make and model he was driving. As soon as we verify the tag number, we'll be one step closer to figuring out what happened to him, although it's sure looking like the fellow was a victim of the storm, too."

Cari's heart started to pound. That was the car she'd seen at the makeshift grave site. It belonged to the dead man she'd seen—she was sure of it. The urge to tell Chief Porter what she knew was overwhelming. But after all the lies, and without a body to back up her story, she knew what would happen.

"How awful," she muttered instead.

"Yeah, well, I better go find the Morgans. You take care now, you hear?"

Cari nodded, but the moment Hershel left, she went looking for Mike.

"Mike. The police chief just told me that they

found a rental car on Morgan's Reach that had been damaged by the storm. I'll bet anything it belongs to the dead man."

Mike frowned. "Why didn't you tell him? They already know someone is missing."

"Think about it, Mike. I've just buried my parents. I've laid out this elaborate scheme to hide my identity. If I start spouting off about seeing Lance with a dead man without a body to back up my story, they'll think I'm off my rocker!"

"I didn't think about it like that," he said, and then lowered his voice so they couldn't be overheard. "I have an idea. As soon as the doctor releases you, how about we come back down here, say…on the pretext of cleaning up at your farm? I own a pretty nice self-contained motor home. We can live in it out on the property while we see what we can find. I even know someone who owns a cadaver dog. If we don't find anything within a day or so, I can give him a call."

"You would do that…for me?"

"That and a lot more," he said softly.

The underlying promise of a relationship kept popping up in Cari's mind, although she told herself to forget it. He was way out of her league, so she quickly changed the subject.

"A cadaver dog? Is that like a bloodhound?"

"Sort of," Mike said. "But these dogs are trained to find bodies…like in natural disasters. They used them in New Orleans after Hurricane Katrina, and after earthquakes…even in New York City after 9-11. The dogs home in on the odor of decay."

"Even if they're buried?"

"So I'm told," he said.

Cari sighed. "Once more, I will be indebted to you."

Mike eyed her pale cheeks and shadowed eyes, and then slipped a hand beneath her elbow. "Here, *cher*…I think you need to sit down."

He settled her back into her chair, but he was still concerned. She'd shed her sunglasses for the time being. Her eyes were red-rimmed and teary, and she looked like she had a headache. She still held a wad of tissues in one hand; she'd used them off and on for the past hour to wipe her nose, and whatever makeup she'd had on was gone. The sling she was wearing had slipped sideways. If she didn't have a crick in her neck yet, she was going to. He wanted to wrap his arms around her and carry her off into some quiet place where nothing could ever hurt her again. He wanted to kiss her and make love—

He sighed.

"For the record, you don't owe me anything," he said softly, and scooted a glass of iced tea closer to her hand.

As he'd hoped, she reached for it and took a drink, and the moment passed.

Finally there was a lull in the number of people coming to pay their respects. Mike noticed that, while she hadn't eaten more than a few bites, her glass was empty.

"I'm going to get you some more iced tea," Mike said, and got up.

"Nothing to eat," Cari whispered. "It will come up. I swear."

He frowned, but he didn't argue. "I'll be right back," he promised, and strode off toward one of the tables that had been set up for drinks.

"Finally! A moment to have you to myself," Lance said, and slid right into the seat Mike had just vacated, then set a dessert plate with a cinnamon roll in front of her. "I know how you love sweets, so I brought you a bite of dessert."

Cari flinched. She might have known he wasn't through playing the grieving ex-fiancé. She'd seen him working the room, garnering sympathy as if it was his due. But when he slid an arm around her shoulders and gave her a hug, she jerked, then pulled away.

"Don't touch me," she snapped, then made herself remember to slow down her speech to fit Susan's normal rhythm.

Lance frowned. "Damn, Susie, I'm just trying to offer my sympathies."

"Look at me, Lance! I hurt. Everywhere. And you just squeezed all the hurts together," she fired back, and as she said it, she realized she was telling the truth.

Lance's antagonism quickly faded. "Oh. Sorry. I

wasn't thinking," he muttered, then picked up a fork and cut off a bite of cinnamon roll. "Here. Try a bite. It's delicious."

Cari turned away from the fork he held to her lips. "I'm allergic to cinnamon," she muttered.

"Oh. Sorry," Lance said, and pushed the roll away. Then he leaned closer. "I thought the reason you pushed me away was because you were pissed at me."

Cari cast a sideways glance at him, then frowned. "Why would you think something like that?"

He shrugged. "You know…Cari and I used to be engaged. I figured she…well, you know…we broke it off."

"Get real, Lance. I'm bruised, not stupid. I know all about it. Cari dumped you for cheating on her."

"It was a mistake," Lance said. "One I'll regret for the rest of my life. But that's the past. You and I need to stick together now."

Cari knew she probably looked as dumbfounded as she felt, but she couldn't help it. What the hell was Lance playing at? Was he honestly trying to pick her up? At a funeral? Oh. My. God.

"Why would you think something like that?" she asked.

Lance reached for her hand. "Because we're both on our own now. Our parents are gone. Like me, you're alone in the world."

"You aren't alone. You have Joe."

Lance shrugged. "But he doesn't count. I mean…

he lives in Savannah. I live on my own here at Morgan's Reach. When you're healed up a little more, why don't you drive down? Spend…the weekend? It would do us both some good."

Cari stifled a snort. He *was* trying to hit on her. Suddenly she got it. He'd gotten himself into hot water with the loan shark. He was looking for a way to branch out and maybe recoup some of his losses, even though Joe had bailed him out this time. Her family's land wasn't as vast as the Morgans', but it was some of the richest farmland in the parish.

"Go away, Lance," Cari said, and leaned back and closed her eyes.

"But—"

"You heard the lady. Make yourself scarce."

Cari's heart leaped. Mike was back and, once again, fighting her battles. If he wasn't careful, he was likely to make himself so useful she wasn't going to want to give him up.

Lance thought about arguing, but there was a glint in Michael Boudreaux's eyes that warned him otherwise. Still, he wasn't going to leave Susan without a toe in the door to her inheritance. Joe might own Morgan's Reach now, but there was still all of Frank North's fallow bottomland. If he played his cards right, he might become a landowner once again, as the husband of the North heir.

Mike could see Lance waffling about obeying.

Despite his business acumen and his boardroom skills, there was just enough of his days on the street and his Cajun father's hot temper in him to make him dangerous. While he would have liked to punch the man square in the face, he opted for making him nervous, instead.

"Have you seen the police chief?" Mike asked. "He was looking for you a little while ago."

Lance looked like someone had just shoved a broomstick up his ass. He cast a nervous glance around the room, then left Cari with a parting shot.

"I'll call you when you're feeling better," he said, and made himself scarce.

Mike was still frowning as he slid the glass of iced tea in front of her.

"Are you okay?" he asked.

Cari stifled a grin. "That was absolutely brilliant. You just scared Lance Morgan out of a year of his miserable life."

"I'd like to do more than scare him," Mike muttered, then sat down beside her.

"You and me both," Cari said. "You will not believe what he just did. He made a pass. An honest to God pass at me…and at the family funeral. I swear, that man has no conscience whatsoever."

"Besides being beautiful, you have something he covets."

She was still trying to get over the fact that Mike had called her beautiful when she asked, "Like what?"

"Land. You're the sole heir to land that abuts Morgan's Reach, right?"

Cari sighed. Mike had come to the same conclusion she had. "Yes, and you're absolutely right on. He would think like that. Little does he know, but we've already had this dance."

Mike glanced at the dark circles under her eyes and knew she was in serious need of some rest.

"Don't you think you've stayed long enough to please your hosts?" Mike asked.

"Yes, but I need to thank the ladies of the church for the dinner. Give me a couple of minutes to say my goodbyes and I'll be ready to leave."

"Here," Mike said, and slipped a hundred-dollar bill in her hand. "Since Susan isn't an 'official' member of the church, I think a donation for their charity toward you is in order."

Cari sighed, then reached out and laid the palm of her hand on Mike's chest.

"Did anyone ever tell you what a good man you are?" she asked softly, then walked away before he could answer.

They left within minutes, and before they'd reached the city limits, Cari had fallen asleep.

Mike made himself focus on driving, but it wasn't easy. He snuck quick looks at her several times on the way back to Baton Rouge, telling himself it was just to make sure she wasn't getting a crick in her neck, or that the sun wasn't shining in her eyes. But the truth was, it was getting more and more difficult to deny his growing feelings.

Lance bolted from the church, carrying a box of desserts that one of the women had handed him as he'd taken his leave. He needed to find Joe and get home before Hershel Porter found him. But when he searched the parking lot, he soon realized it was too late. His brother was already head-to-head with the chief beside their car.

"Son of a bitch," Lance muttered. "I do not need this."

At least there was no way anyone could put Ball in his house, although he couldn't deny his own connection to the man's boss. He still believed that the tornado had been God's way of cleaning the slate for him, and that all he had to do was live a virtuous life to pay for it. He was perfectly willing to comply. He just needed people to back off and butt out.

For that to happen, he had a part to play, and he told himself no one could do it better. He made a mental shift from aggravation to concern, combed his fingers through his hair because he knew the tousled look added to his boyish charm, and strode toward the two men with purpose in every step.

"Joe. Here you are. I've been looking all over for you. I need to get home and tend to the animals." Then he smiled at the chief. "Chief. It was kind of you to come pay your respects."

Hershel Porter responded as Lance had expected, right down to the nod and handshake before taking off his uniform hat and scratching his head.

"So, you know we were out on your property today."

Lance cupped the box of desserts against his belly as he leaned against the car. He looked like he was settling in for a friendly visit.

"Yes, Joe said you'd called."

"Here's the deal," Hershel said. "We got a report from the Chicago Police Department about a man named Austin Ball who went missing on his way to Morgan's Reach."

Lance frowned. "Joe mentioned something about that, although I don't believe I know anyone by that name. Did they say what he was doing down here?"

"He was on business for a man named Dominic Martinelli."

"Oh! I do know Mr. Martinelli."

"As we learned," Hershel said. He wondered how Lance Morgan had managed to go through the family fortune in such a short time, but when he saw the angry look on Joe Morgan's face, he kept his comments to himself. "At any rate, when he didn't come home, his wife filed a missing person's report."

Lance hoped he was nodding in all the appropriate places. He wouldn't look at Joe. No, he *couldn't* look at Joe. Joe had always known when he was lying.

"But why were you looking for him at Morgan's Reach, if he never arrived?"

"Well, that's not exactly true," Hershel said.

Lance's heart skipped a beat. Before he could think what to say next, Joe filled in the blanks.

"That car they found on the back side of the place, the one that got dumped in a tree by the tornado… they think it's Mr. Ball's rental car."

Lance straightened immediately, hoping the look on his face showed concern and not shock.

"Do they think he got caught by the storm?"

"Well, we don't know anything for sure," Hershel said. "There wasn't a body in the car, so it's hard to say for sure what happened. But this is one step closer to the truth for his wife. She's about to give birth to their first child. It's all a damned shame."

"How awful for her," Lance said, and then glanced at Joe. "Do we need to cut a fence or something to give the wrecker access to the vehicle?"

Joe shrugged and glanced at Hershel. "I don't know. I didn't ask."

Lance smiled at Hershel, as if excusing his brother for his lack of manners. "I'm sorry if you've been inconvenienced. Joe isn't used to dealing with such matters. Is there any way we can be of service?"

"No. No. We're already through. We were able to tow it out, but we did have to cut down a couple of the trees it had been caught in to get to it."

Lance nodded approvingly. "Well, that's fine, then. So…if there's nothing else we can do for you, I really need to get home."

"The Chicago detective mentioned Morgan's Reach was being foreclosed on," Hershel added.

Joe interrupted. "That's not true. Money was owed, but it's been paid in full."

Hershel didn't bother to hide his disgust. It figured Joe would bail Lance out, just like their father had done before him.

"Well, that's good to hear," he said, then settled his hat back on his head. "Just touching base to let you know what we found."

"Understood," Lance said, and then jingled the car keys to let Hershel know that the conversation was over. To his relief, the chief took the hint.

"If I have any further questions, I'll be in touch."

"That's fine," Lance said. "Joe? You ready?"

"Yeah, sure," Joe said, and got in on the passenger side, while Lance slid behind the wheel.

"I had a text message from the office," Joe said, as Lance started up the car. "I need to be back in Savannah early in the morning, so as soon as we get back to Morgan's Reach, I'm going to pack. There's a late flight going out of Baton Rouge tonight. It'll get me back to Savannah around midnight. Not ideal, but it is what it is."

"Sure, no problem," Lance said.

Joe frowned. "That's not exactly true. This whole trip home has been a problem. In fact, it's been a nightmare in more ways than you can imagine. Yes, we've just buried our best friends. But then there's you. You've disappointed me a thousand times in our lives, but this last stunt was the worst. And talk about embarrassment… Even the police chief knew what you'd done. My God, Lance, do you even care?"

"It's over. Just shut up, will you?" Lance muttered.

But Joe wasn't through. "No, you're the one who needs to shut up…and listen. Morgan's Reach is safe now. But you're not. There's operating money in the account, enough to keep the place up and running, but nothing more. You want more money, get a job. And don't forget what I told you. I have bailed your ass out of trouble for the last fucking time."

"Yeah, yeah," Lance said, as he sped out of Bordelaise. As far as he was concerned, Joe couldn't be gone fast enough.

Detective Sandy Smith had been nursing a toothache all day and was in a terrible mood. She'd been unable to get an appointment with her dentist until tomorrow morning, and while the dentist had offered to prescribe something, she couldn't take drugs on the job, even painkillers for a very real pain, and she was neck-deep in paperwork so taking the day off wasn't an option. All she could do was tough it out.

It was five minutes to seven when she printed out the last report she'd been working on and slipped it in the file. She pulled her purse from the bottom drawer of her desk and slung the strap across her shoulder. Thank God she was off tomorrow. As soon as she got done at the dentist's, she was going home and going to bed to sleep all day.

She was leaning across the desk to turn off the lamp when her phone began to ring.

"Not now," she muttered, and for a second she thought about letting it ring, then her conscience pricked and she picked it up. "Missing Persons—Detective Smith."

"Detective. It's Hershel Porter, Bordelaise P.D."

Sandy recognized the Southern drawl of the man she'd talked to before, and picked up a pen and paper as she sat back down in her chair.

"Yes, Chief. What can I do for you?" she asked.

"Nothing, ma'am," Hershel said. "It's what I can do for you. I have some information. We found your missing man's rental car today in a grove of trees on Morgan's Reach, the property he was going down to foreclose on."

Suddenly Sandy was all ears. "Austin Ball? You found him?"

"No, ma'am. Just the car. We checked the tag, and it was his rental, all right. And I have to tell you, the car looks like hell, and it was about twenty feet up in the air, caught in a stand of trees."

"Oh Lord," Sandy said, then rubbed at the new pain that shot up between her eyebrows. "This doesn't look good for my missing man, does it?"

"No, ma'am, it does not. Like I said, we don't

have a body, but the car was turned over to the state police's forensics lab."

"I would appreciate a copy of any reports," she said.

"Absolutely," Hershel said. "I'll be in touch. You take care, now."

"Yes. Thank you," Sandy said, and hung up.

Then she leaned back in her chair and groaned. Now she was going to have to make a detour before she could go home. She could call Marcey Ball and tell her what she'd learned, but this was pretty brutal news to break over the phone.

No. She was going to have to do this face-to-face.

With a weary sigh, she pushed herself out of the chair and headed for the parking lot.

Ten

Ten days ago, Marcey Ball would have said her world was perfect. Her husband was an amazing, loving man, just as excited as she was that they were about to become parents. They'd known for several months that the baby she was carrying was a girl, so every day since, and before he left for work, Austin first kissed Marcey, then her belly, goodbye, telling both his girls that he loved them.

Then he'd left home, just like every other workday, and disappeared. She still couldn't believe that such a perfect life could have taken such a horrible turn. She'd known almost from the start that Austin was in trouble. He'd decided to take the trip on Sunday, his normal day off, just so he'd be free to go with her to her doctor's appointment on Monday. It was supposed to have been a simple trip—down and back on the same day to deliver some papers for a client. No big deal. But when noon had come and gone, and he hadn't called, she'd felt uneasy. Austin always called.

She'd told herself any number of things could have come up while traveling. But when five o'clock came and he still hadn't called, and then he didn't come home, she couldn't come up with any more excuses. She'd started calling his cell—every thirty minutes—until midnight. At that point, she'd panicked and called his law partner, Paul Meacham, praying that he would know what was going on. He'd had no idea what was going on and had suggested he and his wife come over and wait with her, but she'd thanked him and turned down the offer. It wasn't until after that call was over that she'd cried. Then she'd sat in their house, in the dark, waiting for a miracle or daylight—whichever came first.

Morning had come but Austin had not, and she'd made the dreaded call to the police. She'd cried all the way through the call, as if the simple act of making it was the final proof that her husband was in trouble.

Her parents arrived the day after she reported him missing, but the longer they stayed, the more she wished they would go home. With each passing day without news, the sympathy on their faces was becoming intolerable to bear.

This morning she'd woken up to the smell of bacon frying. It only made her weep. Austin used to surprise her with breakfast in bed on the weekends. It had taken every ounce of energy she had to get up and go about the day as if it mattered, reminding herself that, if for no other reason, she had to hold on to her sanity for the baby—their baby.

And so this day, like all the others since Austin's disappearance, slowly passed. Her parents had offered to take her out for dinner, but she'd asked them to order in, instead. She was in the kitchen, making a cup of herbal tea, when the doorbell rang.

That will be dinner. God, help me to eat enough for the baby.

"I'll get it," her mother called.

Marcey went about pouring the hot water into her cup. She was about to stir in a dollop of honey when her mother appeared in the doorway.

"Um, Marcey…"

Marcey turned around. "Yes, Mom?" Then her heart sank. She could tell from her mother's expression that whoever was at the door was not the delivery boy from Wong's Canton Cuisine.

"What's wrong?"

Her mother sighed. "There's a Detective Smith from Missing Persons to talk to you."

All of a sudden the baby kicked. Hard. As if warning her that this wasn't going to be good news.

A wave of terror washed through Marcey. She wanted to run—to hide and never come out—because if she didn't hear the words, then the news couldn't be real. But her mother kept waiting for her to move, and finally Marcey lifted her chin, laid a protective hand over her belly and went to face her visitor.

As Marcey entered the living room, she saw Detective Smith standing at the fireplace, looking at one of the family photos on the mantel. From the back, she looked like any slim blonde in a gray pantsuit. But Marcey knew the badge the detective wore at her waist changed the picture drastically.

"That picture was taken on the beach in Oahu on our honeymoon," Marcey offered.

Sandy turned, then swallowed a sigh. The look on Marcey Ball's face was one she'd seen too many times, and no matter how often she delivered this news, it never got easier.

"Can we sit for a minute?" Sandy asked.

Aware of her parents standing stoically nearby, Marcey refused to move. Instinctively she squared her shoulders, readying herself for the blow.

"Just tell me. Have you found Austin?"

"No, ma'am. But the police in Bordelaise, Louisiana, found his rental car today."

Marcey moaned softly, unaware that she'd paled as she clutched at her belly. "Where?"

"On the property of the man he'd been going to see."

Marcey's heart thumped rapidly. "Then you have to talk to that man. He must have seen Austin. If he denies it, then he's hiding something."

Sandy hesitated, then said, wanting to get this

over with, "Not necessarily, Mrs. Ball. Remember I told you earlier that part of the state had a tornado the day of your husband's trip? From where the car was found, it seems obvious it was picked up by the tornado." Sandy took a deep breath. Damn, but she hated this part of the job. "It was in the tops of some trees, about twenty feet off the ground."

Marcey's face crumpled. "Oh my God. I knew it! I knew something awful had happened. What are they going to do? They have to keep looking. He could be hurt, too hurt to go get help."

"They'll keep looking," Sandy promised.

"Until they find his body," Marcey wailed, then covered her face and collapsed on the sofa, weeping loudly.

"I'm so sorry," Sandy said. "If I hear anything else, I'll let you know. Once again, I'm sorry my news wasn't better."

"I'll see you out," Marcey's mother said, and ushered Sandy out the door before rushing back to her daughter's side.

Sandy paused on the stoop long enough to dig out her car keys, then strode through the dark to her car.

"Son of a bitch," she muttered. Then, blinking tears from her eyes, she shoved the keys into the ignition and drove herself home.

Lance was glad to see the taillights of Joe's rental car as he headed back to Baton Rouge to catch his flight. He'd heard more preaching from Joe during this trip than he'd ever heard in church on Sunday.

But the relief of Joe's absence didn't last. Lance did evening chores without the usual amount of satisfaction. Knowing he no longer had a vested interest in Morgan's Reach had somehow changed the charm of feeding the few head of livestock and chickens into a thankless job. Harvesting the peanut and soybean crops later in the year would be nothing but hard, dusty work, since he knew there would be no financial gain for him at the end. He imagined himself no better than the slaves that had once lived and worked this land. Though he had no one but himself to blame, he was still bitter.

By the time he had finished and returned to the house, it was almost dark. As was his habit, he stood on the back porch, watching the stars appearing, and noted that it was going to be a full moon. Once he began hearing the distant grunts of bull gators and the call of the night birds, he went inside. But his bad mood continued to grow, and by the time he'd rummaged through the fridge for something to eat, he was beyond pissed. This just wasn't fair. Joe couldn't take this place away from him. He would find a way to get back in his brother's good graces, and when he did, he would talk him into returning his share of their birthright. Having decided life was somehow going to accommodate him again, his mood shifted. He reheated some shrimp etouffee that he and Joe had made earlier in the week and sat down to enjoy his meal.

As he ate, he had to admit that he missed having company at mealtime and was sorry Joe had left in such a huff. Outside, the wind began to rise, and he immediately thought of another storm. He reached for the TV remote on the sideboard and turned on the set, just to make sure that no threatening weather was coming his way. By the time he was through eating, the broadcast of the weather had come and gone, assuring Lance that the only thing approaching was a line of thunderstorms with a promise of rain. No tornado watches or warnings for the night.

He carried his dishes to the sink and put them to soak before looking for something sweet. The Morgan family had grown up with the notion that a meal wasn't over until dessert had been served, and Lance still held to the practice. And, he knew just what he was going to eat. The church ladies who'd served dinner today had packed up two pieces of pie and a cinnamon roll for him to bring home.

He dug the cinnamon roll out of the box, put it on a plate and popped it in the microwave to reheat as he made himself some coffee. Soon, the warm, homey scent of sweet spice began to drift throughout the kitchen, along with the aroma of fresh brewing coffee. Once the microwave dinged, he carried his sweet roll and coffee into the library. He had yet to go through the day's mail.

Three unpaid bills and two sympathy cards later, he reached for the sweet roll and took a big bite. The scent of cinnamon and the crunch of sugar glaze were as near to an aphrodisiac as any food Lance could think of.

"Um, good stuff," he said, as he licked a dollop of icing from his finger.

He was reaching for his coffee when something slid through the back of his mind so fast he almost missed it. His brows began to knit as he looked down at the sweet roll and the stripe of butter, sugar and cinnamon running through the dough. He kept seeing himself putting a roll just like this in front of Susan earlier today, and her abrupt refusal afterward.

I'm allergic to cinnamon.

His heart slammed hard against his rib cage, making his next breath short and shallow.

That wasn't right!

Susan wasn't allergic to cinnamon.

But Cari was.

He stood up, then turned in a circle, as if the answer to his quandary was somewhere close but still out of reach. The longer he thought about it, the more nervous he became. Maybe he was just forgetting. Maybe Susan was allergic, too, and he'd just forgotten. It stood to reason that if one family member was allergic, another could be, too. Especially since their mothers were identical twins and they'd looked so much alike. But he couldn't let go of the niggle of worry, and before long, he was going back over the entire day, from the time he'd seen her in the funeral home to the moment Mike Boudreaux had sent him packing.

He'd known both women all their lives. He knew the differences between Cari and Susan. Hell, he'd seen all there was to see of Carolina North. Cari and Susan both had long dark hair, but Cari's eyes were rounder than Susan's. The curve of Susan's chin wasn't as definitive as Cari's.

He snorted beneath his breath, reminding himself that he could tell them apart. He was just making a big deal out of nothing. Then he thought about the new hairstyle that had taken him aback, as well as the bandages all over her face. He'd been expecting to see Susan, so he had.

She'd been a bit standoffish in the viewing room, but it was obvious she'd been crying, and she'd worn dark glasses a good portion of the day. It wasn't supposed to be like old home week. She was in mourning. But when he'd started to hug her, she'd retaliated with a—

Don't touch me!

Again, he yo-yoed himself into a plausible explanation. Her reticence had been understandable. She had staples in her head and bandages everywhere. That remark could easily be explained away. As far as holding a grudge against him, Susan would do so in defense of Cari. She would certainly have known why his engagement to Cari had ended. And, he hadn't seen Susan alone in over two years, and even then, just from a distance. Getting caught with that stripper had put a damper on their family holiday visits.

He sat down, trying to remember if he'd ever heard anyone refer to Susan's allergy, and flashed on a moment from their childhood when he'd caused all kinds of havoc.

The four of them—he and Joe, Cari and Susan—had been playing on the grounds of Morgan's Reach. He'd just beaten Susan in a foot race, and she'd been so irked that she'd called him a cheater, then stuck her tongue out at him. It had been so red he'd thought her mouth was bleeding. He'd run screaming into the house to tell everyone Susan was dying.

His heart started beating erratically as he remembered Susan's dismay at the fuss, then her disgust as she'd pulled a box of Red Hots out of her pocket and called him a tattletale for ratting her out for eating candy.

Lance began to panic. Red Hots were truly red and truly hot. But hot with what?

"How…do I find out?" he muttered, as he paced the floor. Then all of a sudden he got it. The Internet! He would run a Google search for it. Everything was on the Internet.

He dashed into the library, past the place where he'd beaten Austin Ball to death and slid into the chair to boot up the computer, Susan's voice still ringing in his ears.

I'm allergic to cinnamon.

"This doesn't make sense," Lance muttered, as he waited for the computer to load. "I'm the one who found the bodies, and I damn well knew Cari better than most. I know what I saw at the scene. I saw her body. She was still wearing the same clothes she'd had on when—" all of a sudden, the hair stood up on the back of his neck "—when she saw me burying Ball's body in the woods." He swallowed past the knot in his throat, afraid to let himself consider what he was thinking, but the fear wouldn't go away.

What if Susan had been at the Norths' that weekend? What if it had been Susan who'd died and not Cari? He'd been the one to make the identification, based solely on those clothes and the expectation that Cari would have been there. God knows a facial identification would have been impossible. —

At that point he realized he was online. He hit the Google icon, then typed in Red Hot Candies. A couple of clicks later, he was reading the history of Red Hots, skimming past the fact that they had been created in the 1930s to the phrase "cinnamon hard candy," which threw him into shock.

Sweet Jesus. He shuddered. *I am so fucked.*

Susan couldn't have been allergic to cinnamon and have eaten that candy!

So if it was Cari who'd survived all along, then why this elaborate masquerade? Why didn't she just go to the police? Why didn't she tell what she'd seen?

Then it hit him. Oh shit! She did tell. Mike Boudreaux knew who she was. He had to. Who else had she told? How many others knew what he'd done?

His heart began to hammer out a warning.

Run, Lance, run!

She hadn't told the police, because when she'd run home for help, the tornado had hit.

Run, Lance, run!

She hadn't told, because when she found everyone dead, she was too injured herself to face him on her own.

Run, Lance, run!

And, even more crucially, she hadn't told, because she would have known he would move the body.

Run, Lance, run!

So what was she waiting for? A sign from God?

At that moment, a clap of thunder sounded so loud that it rattled the glass in the windows.

Run, Lance, run!

Lance jumped as if he'd been shot, then grabbed his car keys and raced out of the house. He was in the car and flying out of the driveway even as the first drops of rain began to fall. When he turned down the driveway that led to the North property, the back of his car fishtailed. The rich Louisiana land that grew thriving crops of peanuts and soybeans had turned into black gumbo.

"Crap," Lance grunted, as he straightened the wheels, just missing the fence.

Moments later he'd reached the place where the North house had stood. Despite the dark and the rain, he bolted out of the car and began running from one pile of refuse to another, stumbling about in the downpour with nothing but his headlights and the occasional flash of lightning to guide him.

Run, Lance, run!

Even though it made no sense, he continued to retrace the steps he'd taken the day he'd found the bodies, as if their ghosts might still be lingering with answers he'd missed the first time around.

The rain was beginning to abate, but the wind was rising, whipping the splintered trees and blowing loose bits of refuse across the yard. Lance was staring off into the darkness, oblivious to danger or discomfort. His thoughts were in chaos. He didn't know why he'd come here, but the troubles he'd thought were behind him were back—and in stereo.

Overwhelmed with rage and despair, he threw back his head, raised his fists to the night and screamed.

Suddenly there was a loud crash behind him. He spun just as a huge branch came crashing to the ground only feet from where he was standing.

Run, Lance, run!

Without waiting to see what was coming next, he made a beeline for his car.

Once inside, he slammed the door shut, then locked the car tight, even though no locks could protect him from what he was facing. Water was running from his hair into his eyes, dripping from his clothing onto the seats, puddling on the floor beneath his muddy shoes.

Twice he reached for the keys to start the engine, but each time he stopped, trembling too hard to drive.

So he sat, shaking from the wet and the shock until a good half hour had passed. Finally he pulled himself together enough to start the engine. The wheels spun in the thick, black mud before he gained traction, and then he was off. The storm was passing as quickly as it had arrived. Except for the muddy roads and the stiff wind blowing away the last of the clouds, it was as if it had never happened. It was just as well, because Lance didn't remember the drive home—only that the sight of Morgan's Reach was the beacon he needed to put his life back on track.

When he got inside the mudroom, he stripped out of his wet clothes and left them in a pile as he strode naked through the house. Rage warred with unadulterated panic as he stepped into the shower and turned on the faucets. He stood without moving until the hot water ran cold; then he dried off and crawled into bed without turning on the lights, as always, refusing to face what he couldn't handle.

But he couldn't escape that easily.

The moment he closed his eyes, one image after another, taken from the years and years of past indiscretions, flashed before his eyes, ending with the worst mistake of all. Murder. If he could, he would take it back. But it was too late. Austin Ball was rotting beneath the good delta land of Morgan's Reach, and Lance's troubles, which he'd thought were all over, were turning into nightmares.

He tossed and turned until he was unable to spend another moment in bed. With a muttered curse, he threw back the covers and stomped through the house to the library and his father's liquor cabinet. He grabbed a decanter of bourbon, a cut crystal shot glass and headed for the sofa.

In the morning, he would figure out how to get to Cari/Susan. He would strip off all the bandages and the sling and the hair gel, and look her square in the face. He would know then if what he suspected was true: that today the town of Bordelaise had buried a woman under the wrong name. If he was right, then it would be up to him to make sure the real Carolina North joined her family. He had no way of knowing how many other people knew the truth, but without Cari as a witness, and without a body, they couldn't touch him.

But that was tomorrow's agenda. Right now, he was about to get shit-faced drunk.

Cari slept all the way back to Baton Rouge. Looking at her, Mike knew that what he was feeling was crazy. They hadn't even known each other a week, and most of that time she'd either been in the hospital, struggling through grief or trying to figure out how to get herself out of the mess she was in. Still, there were the brief flashes of levity, and in the rare moments when he'd caught a true smile on her face, he'd known he wanted to be the one responsible for putting it there.

He didn't know if her amazing resemblance to Susan had cut through his usual reticence, or if it was just the woman herself. When he thought about all she'd gone through, and how tough and focused she'd been in her determination to save herself and bring a killer to justice, he was in awe. He had never known a woman with that kind of courage, and his admiration for her was tangled up with his growing attraction. All the way home, he kept thinking of her making the same trip all alone, with life-threatening injuries and the belief that a killer was on her trail.

And now that they'd finished the sad business of burying her family, there was another, uglier, task to be tackled. He didn't know how they were going to make it happen, but he was going to do everything in his power to help her find the murdered man's body. As soon as he got her home, he would fill Aaron in on what they were going to need to search, and then go from there.

As he neared the turnoff, Cari shifted in her seat, then moaned. Mike glanced at her once, then negotiated the turn and accelerated down the long, tree-lined driveway to his home. Normally the sight of the three-story plantation house and the live oaks dripping with Spanish moss gave him a good, cominghome feeling, but not today. He was too concerned about how his sleeping beauty was going to feel when he awakened her.

A few moments later he pulled around to the back of the property and parked only a few steps from the veranda. If she didn't wake up, it wouldn't be far to carry her inside. He killed the engine, pocketed the keys, then allowed himself a final moment to look his fill.

Her hair was tousled, her lips devoid of the gloss she'd used earlier. He could see dark smudges beneath her eyes and knew she'd exerted herself too much, but it couldn't be helped. However, it was the tiny beads of tears on her lashes that pushed him over the edge.

Without further hesitation, he reached for her hand.

"Carolina...sweetheart...wake up," he said softly.

Emerging from a dreamless sleep, Cari roused, then took a slow, deep breath.

"Hey, sleeping beauty, we're home," Mike said, and then got out and circled the car to help her out.

At the sound of his door slamming shut, reality surfaced. The tornado. The hospital. The funeral. She sat up with a jerk. But she'd moved too fast.

"Ow," she cried, then reached for the door, but Mike was already ahead of her.

"Let me," he said, as he slipped his hands under her arms and steadied her while she got out.

Cari grimaced. "It feels like someone glued my joints."

"You had a pretty long day," Mike said, then couldn't help himself and brushed a wisp of hair away from the corner of her eye.

His touch was as gentle as his voice. Cari wanted to hide in the shelter of his arms, but she couldn't let him fight all her battles, even though the idea was tempting.

"I know, but I had no choice. It was my family," Cari said, then glanced up and quietly added, "Thank you so much for being with me."

Mike's gut knotted. Empathy intertwined with longing, and she was close—so close. He cupped her face, intent on a simple kiss to her forehead, but she surprised him by tilting her head back and catching the kiss.

Mouth to mouth.

Breath to breath.

When Mike's hands slid down her neck and around her shoulders, Cari moaned.

He flinched and immediately let go. "I'm so sorry, honey…did I hurt you?"

"Yes," she said, and watched regret flash across his face.

"Damn it. I should have known better. Where do you hurt?"

"Here," Cari said, and laid his hand on her breasts, just above her heart.

His eyes widened in sudden understanding, then he sighed.

"Damn it, woman...you scared me," he said softly.

"No more than you're scaring me," she said.

"God, help me," he whispered, then centered his mouth on her lips and took his time removing the last of her good sense and all of her inhibitions.

When he finally pulled back, Cari's legs were shaking and her heart was hammering in her chest.

"Ah...Carolina...what have we done?"

She arched an eyebrow, then almost smiled. "Moved beyond proper social boundaries?"

Her sassiness was unexpected, and enchanting. He smiled as he shook his head and ran a finger along the curve of her lower lip.

"A definite understatement, I think. So, tough stuff...you've crossed more than boundaries today. I can see the exhaustion on your face, which means I could have chosen a better time to give in to my feelings."

"Help me off with this sling, will you?" Cari asked.

Mike eased it from around her neck, freeing her other arm. Cari immediately slipped her arms around his waist and hugged him. It was as unexpected as what she said next.

"I don't know what's happening here, and if it's nothing but a gesture of condolence, I'll take it as such. But…if you're leaning toward investigating what might turn into a relationship, don't let the staples and bruises stop you."

"I'm definitely leaning," he said.

"Me too," she said, then, before he could push the issue, picked up her purse from the front floorboard and slung it over her shoulder.

"What time is it?" she asked.

"Almost five."

She sighed. "Is that all? For obvious reasons, I want this day to be over."

Mike cupped the side of her face "I know, *cher,* and you have the rest of the evening to do as you wish. If you want to spend it in your room, I can have Songee bring you supper."

She slipped her hand into the crook of his arm, then changed the subject before she started to cry. "No need for anything that drastic, but I wonder if she might have some sweet tea already made? I'm suddenly thirsty."

"Songee always has sweet tea," Mike said, as he led the way up the back steps and into the house.

"I want to change clothes," Cari said.

"Me too," Mike said. "Would you like me to have Songee bring the tea to your room?"

"I think I would rather sit out on the veranda for a while and just listen to the quiet."

"Then that's what you should do," Mike said.

They made the trip up the stairs with Mike holding

on to Cari's elbow, steadying her weary steps. When they reached her room, he stopped her again.

"Do you need any help?" he asked.

Cari couldn't quite read the expression on his face, but she'd liked the kiss that they'd shared—a lot. And if she wasn't so damned tired and sick at heart, she would have liked to explore what else there was about him that she might like even better. But that was for later. Right now, she needed to put today far, far away. She could deal with the memories later.

"I think I can manage. Just give me a few minutes."

As she closed the door to her room, she didn't dare look back for fear he would see the truth of her feelings all over her face.

In a few minutes Cari had changed into a pair of Susan's jeans and a blue knit pullover, and was on her way downstairs. It felt good to be in sandals instead of heels, and she was looking forward to a little peace and quiet and some fresh air. As she passed Mike's office, she heard voices and realized he had company. After the events of the day, the last thing she wanted was more conversation, so she hurried past the door.

Songee was carrying a watering can toward the large potted palms in the foyer as Cari approached. She paused long enough to give Cari the once-over, then frowned.

"You don't look so good," she said. "I'm thinking you've had all of today you can handle. Mr. Mike said you were tired and thirsty, so I set some iced tea on the veranda for you. You go on outside now and just relax. It'll do you good."

Cari wanted to hug her neck for being so understanding. "Thank you, Songee," she said and slipped past.

"You're welcome," Songee said gently. "Take all the time you need. We eat lots of late suppers around here."

Cari exited through the French doors and out onto the veranda. As promised, there was a pitcher of iced tea and two glasses, along with a small plate of bar cookies, on the round wicker table.

Cari poured a glass of tea and then plumped the green cushions and eased herself down.

The glass was cold in her hand, the cushions soft at her back. Within moments, as she gazed out across the wide lawn to the boundary of trees beyond, she felt lighter, as if the sadness she'd been living with had just taken flight along with the snowy-white egrets she saw flying past.

She took a sip of the tea, savoring the cold, sweet taste and the clink of ice cubes against fine crystal, then set the glass aside as she leaned back and closed her eyes. The sun was beginning to set behind the trees, sending the dying warmth from the lengthening rays up the steps, then across the veranda to where she was sitting. A trio of butterflies flitted about the deep purple blooms of the wisteria hanging from the eaves of the porch, and in the live oaks, a blue jay was loudly objecting to the squirrel above its nest. These were sounds and scents that Cari knew, and they soothed her saddened soul.

Then, suddenly, there was a touch on the back of her hand.

She opened her eyes, then looked down and smiled. It was Daniel, Mike's little redheaded friend, which meant that must have been his father she'd heard in the office earlier. She couldn't help but notice that not only was Daniel barefoot, but he was wearing striped bib overalls without a shirt—perfect three-year-old attire for a warm Louisiana evening.

"Well, hello, Daniel. It's nice to see you again. Would you like some iced tea?"

He nodded solemnly, then crawled up into the other wicker chair and waited to be served.

Cari poured the glass only half-full, so it wouldn't be too heavy for him to hold, then handed it to him. He took a sip, then set the glass between his legs, eyeing the cookies.

"How about a cookie to go with that tea?" she asked.

"Yes, pwease," he said.

Cari handed him a cookie rich with chocolate chips and coconut, then licked the chocolate off her fingertips.

He ate the entire cookie without talking, savoring every bite as only a child could do. When he was finished, he wiped his hands on the napkin but forgot to wipe his mouth, leaving a tiny smudge of chocolate at the corner of his upper lip.

Although he was very quiet, he seemed at peace with their silence.

"What have you been doing today?" Cari asked.

"Oh. I's been pwaying with Woger."

Cari stifled a grin, remembering that Roger was the tomcat who couldn't make babies. Poor Roger.

"I'll bet Roger likes playing with you," she added.

He nodded. Then his brow knitted, and he fixed her with a curious look.

"My daddy says you is sad today."

Cari sighed. Out of the mouths of babes…

"Yes, I am," she said.

"He says yous mama and daddy went to heaven today."

Cari nodded. "Yes, they did."

"Can you go and visit?" he asked.

"No, I'm afraid not."

She could see the shock on his face, and imagined him trying to put himself in her place.

His voice suddenly shook. "You doesn't gets to see 'em no moah?"

Cari's heart hurt just thinking about it, but she was very conscious of the fact that if she answered wrong, she might not only confuse but frighten him.

"Oh…I'll see them again. I just have to get older first."

His mouth went slack, as if he couldn't quite grasp

the concept, but she could tell he was somewhat relieved that the parting wasn't permanent.

"Would you wike to see my fwend Mr. Toad?" Daniel asked.

Cari's vision blurred. "I would love to see Mr. Toad. Where does he live?" she asked.

"Him wives out yonder unner Uncle Mike's gahden shed."

Cari stood up and held out her hand. "Show me."

Daniel set his tea aside, then scrambled out of his chair and, with all the style of a true Southern gentleman in the making, took her by the hand and led her down the steps, as if she were too frail to walk by herself.

They were halfway across the lawn when Mike and Dan came out.

"There he is," Mike said, pointing toward the south end of the lawn. "Looks like he's taking Cari to see Mr. Toad."

Dan frowned. "I told him not to bother her today."

"I think he's just what the doctor ordered," Mike said, as he watched them walking hand in hand. "Give him a few more minutes, will you?"

Dan shrugged. "Sure. Nora's not going to be home for another hour anyway." Then he switched the subject. "How did today go, with the funerals and all?"

"It was rough on her," Mike said.

"She's pretty darn strong, isn't she?"

"Oh, yeah," Mike said, thinking of their plan to go back to Bordelaise to find a dead man.

"I can't imagine losing every member of my family at once and being the one to find them," Dan added.

Mike nodded, remembering how Cari's poise had finally shattered at the funeral home.

Then Dan chuckled and pointed. "Would you look at that? They're both down on their knees, looking under the shed."

Mike couldn't help but wish he was down there with them, nose level with the grass and eye to eye with Mr. Toad—and Carolina.

"He's all boy, isn't he, Dan? I envy you, you know. You've got the perfect life… Nora and Daniel and a tomcat who can't procreate."

Dan grinned. "Yeah, thanks to my college roommate for introducing me to Nora, and to the vet who recommended neutering." Then he glanced toward the shed again. "Hey, look! It appears Mr. Toad is feeling sociable today. If I'm not mistaken, Daniel just set him in Carolina's lap."

"Oh hell, I hope he doesn't pee on her," Mike said.

Suddenly they heard the sound of Cari's laughter and saw her holding the toad out in front of her while Daniel was pointing and backing up fast.

Mike chuckled. "Oops…too late. Mr. Toad has his own way of saying hello."

They were still smiling as Cari wisely put the toad back down. At that moment she happened to look toward the house. Mike waved. She waved back, then said something to Daniel before they started back.

It appeared that Daniel wasn't through trying to change Cari's mood, because he turned somersaults and cartwheels all the way. And as they reached the steps, he was still talking.

"I can whissel weally good…wissen to this." Then he puckered up his lips and blew.

As whistles went, it wasn't the best. There was a bit of sound and a lot of spit, but Cari seemed sufficiently impressed.

"That's amazing," she said, and then sat down on the steps and hugged him. "Thank you for showing me so many good things, Daniel."

He beamed, then looked up at the men. "Hi, guys," he said brightly.

Mike grinned. Dan beamed proudly.

"Hi yourself, little man," Dan said, and then held out his hand. "Tell everyone goodbye. We need to get home."

"Bye, evewyone," Daniel echoed.

"See you soon," Mike said. They shared a high five; then Dan and his son were gone.

Cari watched until they'd driven away. She was smiling as she turned to Mike.

"I met Mr. Toad, and now I need to wash my hands."

Mike grinned. "Yeah, I saw. So…how long do you think it's been since a toad peed on you?"

Cari smiled. "I'd be guessing, but I'd say…at least

twenty years." Then her smile slid sideways. "Who knew that a little redheaded boy and toad pee would be the pick-me-up I needed?"

Mike opened his arms.

She walked into them and buried her face against his chest. She could feel his heartbeat against her cheek and smell the musky scent of aftershave on his shirt. But it was the way he held her that let her know she was in the right place, as if she might break and as if he never wanted to let her go.

Eleven

Hershel Porter walked into his office and closed the door behind him. He was worn-out in so many ways he couldn't count and figured he'd aged a good ten years in the past week. Bordelaise was still in cleanup mode. Utility crews were close to having power restored in all the storm-stricken areas, but the only businesses booming right now were the ones that replaced roofs and windows. Two days ago they'd buried Mr. Warren from the nursing home, who'd died during the evacuation. Today they'd buried the Norths. He was heartsick about their deaths, but there was nothing he could have done to prevent them.

It was the stuff still undone that was weighing on his mind. This morning he'd gotten word from the state police that they were reclassifying the case of seven-year-old Bobby Earle as an abduction.

With regard to the four missing prisoners, he

didn't have one shred of evidence as to what had happened to them. There had been no sightings, no unidentified bodies found. He wanted to think the tornado had blown them to kingdom come, but until he had physical proof, he couldn't mark them off the list of concerns.

And, as if all that wasn't enough, there was that fellow from Chicago who'd gone missing. After finding his rental car in the trees today, it was a sure bet what had happened to him. It was just a matter of finding the body. Following procedure, Hershel had ordered the car to be sent to the state police lab for processing. Beyond that, all he could do was try to tamp down the level of chaos until order was completely returned to Bordelaise.

He glanced down at his desk and the paperwork that continued to pile up, hung his hat on a hook and reached for his coffee cup.

The telephone rang.

He frowned. Hadn't he just told Vera to hold his calls for a while? Irked, he answered more gruffly than normal.

"Chief Porter."

"Porter...Stewart Babcock. DEA. Out of Washington, D.C."

Hershel ignored the man's staccato manner of speaking and shifted mental gears. "What can I do for you?"

"I've been out of the country. Returned to the

office this morning. Found a report stating you'd arrested a Nick Aroya."

Hershel frowned. "Yes, along with three other men. What's your interest in him?"

"He's mine," Babcock said.

"What do you mean?"

"He's one of my best agents. Been undercover for months. What's it going to take to get him out? Drop the charges on all four men?"

Hershel sighed. It seemed this was his day for imparting bad news.

"Well, I hate to be the one to tell you this, but in a manner of speaking, they're already out."

"Good news."

"No, sir, it's not, because I didn't let them go. Last Sunday morning, our town was hit by a tornado. Among other things, it took the back off the jail. Those four prisoners are still among the missing."

Hershel waited for a comment. And waited.

"Uh…Babcock…you still there?"

Hershel heard a sigh, then a muffled curse.

"Yes, I'm here," Babcock said. "Are you saying they're dead?"

"No, sir. I'm saying we don't know what happened to them or where they are. So far, we've buried four people this week, and on top of those prisoners, I still have two missing—a seven-year-old boy, and an attorney from Chicago who had the misfortune of picking that day to come to Bordelaise on business.

The city and the surrounding area were hit hard. We've been limping along as best we can, but as you can imagine, our resources have been stretched pretty thin."

"I'll have a team there tomorrow," Babcock said.

"All right. Help from anywhere is appreciated."

"Do I need to tell you to keep what you've heard to yourself?"

Hershel bristled. "Hell no. I might be small-town stuff compared to you, but I'm not stupid, mister. Send down your big dogs. We'll do our best not to hurt their feelings."

Babcock sighed. "That came out wrong. But if by the grace of God we find them alive, I don't want Nick's cover blown."

"Yeah, well…you'd better be saying some big prayers up there, because if you do find them alive…it will damn sure *be* by the grace of God."

There was a click in his ear.

Hershel slammed the phone back on the cradle. "Damn Yankee," he muttered, then grabbed his hat and stomped out of the office, too pissed to tackle the paperwork piling up on his desk.

For Lance, sunrise came with a hangover. He woke up in the library on his father's leather sofa, confused as to why he was naked, and with the stopper to the bourbon decanter stuck in his mouth like a pacifier. If there'd been a naked woman next to him, it wouldn't have been quite so humiliating. But to know that he'd wasted a good drunk alone... That was something he hadn't done since high school.

Groaning beneath his breath, he spit out the stopper, then tried to sit up. But the room wouldn't stop spinning, and before he knew it, he was flat on his face on the floor and staring at what looked like a small piece of chicken meat stuck to the underside of the coffee table.

He wasted a couple of minutes trying to figure out how food could have gotten under the table when it hit him. This was where he'd beaten Austin Ball to a pulp with his high school baseball bat, and what he was looking at was most likely a piece of the man's flesh.

Panic hit, but vomit was faster. He threw up the entire contents of his stomach, including last night's supper and a quart and a half of bourbon. His belly was still in revolt as he tried to get up. He paused to retch, slipped in the mess, stood, then fell back in it again. By the time he got to his feet, he was bawling. He grabbed the nearest thing at hand, which happened to be the cut glass decanter, and threw it against the mantel of the fireplace, where it shattered into thousands of tiny shards. Then he began flinging everything within reach—books, pillow cushions, an antique writing pen from his father's desk—until the library looked like a tornado had hit it.

Gagging from the stench of his own vomit, he stumbled from the room and up the stairs to his bedroom, then into the shower. A short while later, he emerged—nearly sober, but with his rage still intact.

It was daunting to know that he was going to have to clean up the mess he'd made, but he had no money to pay someone else to do it—and no choice, either. He couldn't let anyone know he wasn't himself.

He began by brewing a pot of coffee. After he'd downed a couple of cups, he grabbed a broom, a mop and a bucket full of soapy water, and headed for the library. When he was finished inside, he went outside to do the morning chores. He'd already decided he was heading to Baton Rouge. Carolina North might think she'd pulled a fast one, but she had another think coming. Before he was through with her, she was going to wish she *had* died in that twister. Murdering for a second time wasn't a thing he looked forward to, but he didn't really have a choice. He had too much to lose to leave her alive.

Cari woke to the squawking of a pair of cockatoos in the trees outside her bedroom window. From the sounds, it appeared one of them was seriously ticked. She rolled out of bed and headed for the bathroom in a similar mood.

She'd been thinking about her next steps. After seeing a rep from her publishing company at the funerals, she'd made a risky decision. She was going to contact her agent and tell her what was going on. She trusted her completely and knew she would do whatever it took to make sure Cari's interests with her publisher would be protected.

She desperately wanted to get back to her home and see if there were any keepsakes to be salvaged. She also wanted to bury her dog. The thought of scavenging animals tearing at his faithful little body made her sad.

She needed a map of the parish, especially the area around Bordelaise, in the hopes it would trigger an idea as to where Lance could have moved the body. She could probably get one off the Internet. The tornado had hit within minutes of their encounter, so he couldn't have gone far from where she'd first seen him. He definitely would not have had time to get to the swampland to dump the body with the intent of turning it into gator food, because it wasn't possible to get there by car from where he'd been digging the grave.

And, it wasn't like he would have had time to dig a whole new grave with the storm that close, although he could have hidden the body and reburied it later. She sighed. He would have had all the time in the world to make *that* happen—assuming the tornado hadn't just picked up the body and carried it away to God knew where.

At any rate, she desperately wanted evidence before she went to the police, although there was no question that she *would* go to them eventually. The only positive notes in the whole mess were the missing person's report on the Chicago attorney and his car being found on Morgan's Reach. It would definitely lend credence to her claim, although, after her purposeful deception in letting the citizens of Bordelaise believe she was dead, she might have to fight public opinion falling on Lance's side. But she was ready to tilt at that windmill, whatever the cost.

After her shower, she'd opted for comfort, and dressed in jeans and a yellow knit shirt before going downstairs. As she neared the dining room, she could hear Songee's soft Southern drawl and Mike's sexy Cajun accent. When Mike suddenly burst into laughter, Cari stopped, letting the sound flow through her, remembering the feel of his mouth on her lips and—his hands on her shoulders, then cupping her backside as he pulled her to him.

There was every reason to believe they would make love. She knew she wanted to. She knew he returned the feeling. She didn't know what it might mean in the long run, or if that was even something she should consider. But she'd just been handed a very painful reminder of how short life could really be, and her heart was telling her to go for it. Now all she had to do was make time for sex between her continuing charade and finding a murder victim.

For a mystery writer? Piece of cake.

She ran a shaky hand through her hair, checking to see if the shaved part with the staples was concealed. There was a definite gap, which couldn't be helped, but her hair style was as good as it would get for quite a while. Then she tugged at the hem of her shirt, picked a piece of lint off her jeans and stepped into the dining room.

"Hey! Good morning," Mike said, as he jumped to his feet and quickly pulled out a chair for her. "Songee made waffles and some mean raspberry butter to go with them."

Cari's mouth actually watered. It was the first time she'd thought positively of putting food in her mouth in days, and she chalked it up to the relief of having the trauma of the funerals behind her.

"Sounds good," she said, smiling at Songee. "I would love to have one…with the raspberry butter."

"I will make a special one, just for you," Songee said, as she poured coffee in Cari's cup.

Mike watched the intent expression on Cari's face as she stirred sugar and cream into her cup, making a mental note that she liked two sugars and a buttload of cream, which he found oddly charming. He sighed. If he got turned on just watching Carolina fix a cup of coffee, he was a goner.

She looked at him over the rim of her cup and smiled.

The impact was like a fist to the gut. He hoped he was smiling back, but he couldn't be sure. His face felt funny, as if he'd suddenly lost tactile response. Damn. This was worse than he'd thought. He took a deep breath, then shifted mental gears.

"Did you rest well?"

A slight frown dipped between her brows. "Oddly enough, I did. I thought I would have nightmares about…about everything. I was sad, but that's to be expected, right?" Then she sighed. "I think I'm going to feel that way for a very long time."

"I think you're right," Mike said, then qualified his statement. "I was lost for a long time after my parents died. In fact, there are still times when the thought of never talking to them again makes me sad, but not for long. Time does help. But the bottom line was, I kept thinking of how upset they would have been to know I wasn't living my life to the fullest. After that, I began to realize that, by living the best I could, I was actually honoring them. I'm all that's left of them. It helped me cope."

Cari looked at him in quiet amazement. A gentleman and a philosopher? Yet another reason why he was so difficult to resist.

"That is probably the kindest, most sensible thing anyone has said to me since this whole nightmare began," she said.

Mike grinned ruefully. "That's me. Kind and sensible to the core."

"Shut up," she said. "You know what I mean."

Before he could answer, Songee was back with Cari's waffle.

"Eat it while it's hot," Songee said.

"Yes, ma'am." Cari eyed the sprinkling of

powdered sugar on the top, and the handful of fresh raspberries on the side, then scooped out a dollop of the raspberry butter from the bowl Mike pushed toward her.

Songee beamed, then arched an eyebrow at Mike. "Now why can't you be as agreeable?"

Mike grinned. "But I am. Ask Cari. I am kind and sensible…to the core. Right?"

Cari just shook her head as she spread butter across the waffle. "I know better than to take sides against the cook in the house."

Songee chuckled softly, then patted Cari's shoulder before exiting the room.

At that point, the phone began to ring.

"I'll get it. I'm expecting a call from Aaron," Mike said, as he jumped up from the table. "Excuse me. Back in a few."

Cari continued to eat and finished most of her waffle before pushing it aside. Then, since she was still on her own, she took her coffee outside and claimed what was becoming her favorite seat, one of the white wicker chairs with the green cushions.

Within minutes, Mike came out to join her, but instead of sitting in the other chair, he began to pace, and Cari realized this was probably how he did all his business: literally—thinking on his feet.

"I was right. The call was from Aaron. I don't know if you remember me mentioning him earlier. He's the head of security for Red Stick, Inc."

"Red Stick?"

He paused long enough to smile. "Hey…you should know that. Baton Rouge, translated means red stick, remember?"

Cari rolled her eyes. "Of course. At least I did, before the wind threw a two-by-four at my head. Sorry. Please continue."

He resumed pacing. "Anyway…Aaron is getting my motor home out of storage and heading to your place at Bordelaise to get it hooked up to utilities, etc. It will be stocked and ready to live in by the time we get there."

Cari's heart skipped a beat. This was really happening. "When can you get away?"

"I'm the boss, remember? I come and go when I want to. There's nothing pending right now, so this is a perfect time for me to be absent from the office, and I'm always available by phone and e-mail if something should arise."

Unconsciously Cari fisted her hands in her lap. "What if I can't find it?"

"The body?"

She nodded.

"Then you go to the police anyway and tell them what you saw, and why you played out the charade."

"I would so much rather have proof before it comes to that," she muttered.

Mike paused, then turned to face her. "Then we find proof. Aaron's already contacted the man I know with the cadaver dog. If we have to, we'll cover every square inch of land between the two properties and Bordelaise."

"But the property's such a mess! And I'm supposed to go back to the doctor in a few days to have my staples removed."

"One thing at a time, *cher,*" Mike said gently. "If you like, I can contact someone to begin cleaning up the property, but let's get there first and assess what needs to be done, okay?"

She nodded, then began to relax. It seemed that Mike was as good at mental organization as she was.

"Yes, that's a good idea," she said. "Besides, I'm hoping I'll be able to find a few keepsakes."

"Then we'll look for those, too," Mike said gently.

"As for your doctor visit, when that day comes, then we'll come back for it. In the meantime, we go hunting."

She shivered. "I'm a little nervous. The less I'm around Lance Morgan, the less chance I have of being recognized."

"Don't borrow trouble. We'll make it work, Carolina. Trust me."

She leaned back in the chair. "Oh, I trust you, implicitly. It's Lance who makes me uneasy. I've known him all my life, and while I will agree one hundred percent that as a man, he's worthless, I would never have thought him capable of such violence."

Mike stopped in front of her, then leaned down,

bracing his hands on the arms of her chair—so close he could see his reflection in her eyes.

"All men are capable of violence," he said softly. "But I would also add that the triggers that set them off are as varied as the men themselves."

Cari shivered. His mouth was only inches away from her face. If she wanted, all she had to do was lean forward and they would be kissing. The notion was tempting—tempting enough that her lips unconsciously parted. Finally she tore her gaze from his mouth to the green fire in his eyes.

"So what's *your* trigger?" she asked.

"Someone messing with my woman."

Cari shivered. "Do you have a woman?"

"I don't know," he said softly. "Do I?"

Before she could answer, he bent down.

The kiss started out as a gentle foray, but when he heard Cari moan, and then her lips parted beneath his, he pulled her up and out of the chair, and into his embrace.

Cari's arms went around his neck as his hands slid down to her hips.

Mike walked her two steps backward until she was pinned between the wall and his body, then finished what he'd started, kissing her over and over until she was out of breath and out of her mind.

It was Mike who finally stopped, and then only because he didn't want their first time making love to be outside on his veranda—in plain sight of God and the world. When it happened, he wanted her in his bed, in the dark, and the length of at least one night to get it right.

"Sweet Jesus," Mike whispered, but it wasn't enough. He cupped her face, then kissed each eyelid, then her cheeks, before moving down to claim her lips one last time. "You make me crazy," he said softly.

Thankful for the wall at her back, Cari put shaky fingers to her lips to see if they were really as hot as they felt.

"Careful," he said softly. "If you wipe away the kisses, I'll just have to put them all back again."

"What's happening here?" she whispered.

"Whatever you want to happen," Mike said. But he could tell she was rattled, and the last thing he wanted was to push her too far too fast. "So…how do you feel about taking a walk to visit Mr. Toad?"

The invitation was unexpected, but it was the perfect thing for him to say.

"Actually, I *would* like to see him—as long as he doesn't pee on me again."

Mike grinned. "It's your fault, you know."

Cari frowned. "Why?"

"Your charm and beauty are so vast that you rattle all males, even a fat, grumpy toad. Therefore, you must forgive him for his lack of manners."

Cari burst out laughing.

The hair crawled on the back of Mike's neck. Ah,

God…if he could bottle that sound, it would make magic.

He held out his hand, waiting for her to accept it. When she took it without hesitation, a wave of emotion swept through him so quickly it left him aching for more.

"Are you ready?" Cari asked.

"For you? Yes, ma'am," he said, and led the way off the steps and across the lawn.

The day was warm, with a slight breeze stirring the jacaranda and wisteria blossoms just enough to scent the air. A massive live oak was about fifty yards from the house. It had been growing there long before Mike Boudreaux's ancestors had ever set foot on American soil, weathering over two centuries' worth of hurricanes and wars. Silver-gray strands of Spanish moss hung from the branches like the shredded remnants of a widow's veil, and as they neared the old tree, a flock of cockatoos squawked, then took flight, as if angry at being disturbed.

"This place is so beautiful," she said. "Has it been in your family long?"

"About a hundred years. My ancestors weren't wealthy slave owners. My great-great-great-grandfather came to America as an indentured servant. It took him fifteen years to work off his contract. But instead of staying in Baton Rouge when he was free, the story goes that he took to the swamps, determined never to work under another man's hand again. The woman he married was almost twenty years younger than he was, and they had fourteen children, eleven of whom survived to adulthood.

"That's amazing," Cari said.

"What part?" Mike asked. "That he was indentured, or that he chose to live in the swamps among the mosquitoes and gators?"

Cari grinned. "No. That his poor wife gave birth to fourteen children. I think if that had been me, after baby number ten I would have met him at the door with a shotgun and threatened him with murder if he set foot in my bedroom again."

Mike chuckled. "I'll keep that in mind."

Cari's eyes widened, then she had the grace to blush. "Oh Lord…I didn't mean that…I, uh…only meant—"

"But I *did*…mean it," Mike responded.

Cari glanced up, caught the look in his eyes and shivered.

"Ok…and *I'll* keep *that* in mind," she said.

"I now consider myself forewarned," Mike said.

Cari smiled, then noticed they were almost at the shed. "Are we really going to see if the toad will come out?"

Mike's lips twitched as he met her gaze. "No. I just wanted to get you away from the house and all to myself."

"Lord save us all…a truly honest and honorable man."

Mike reached for her. When she didn't resist, he took her in his arms, then cupped her face.

"Honest, yes…but the longer I'm with you, the more difficult it becomes to stay honorable."

"Who asked you to?" Cari said softly, and watched Mike's nostrils flare as his eyes suddenly glittered.

"I'll remember that," he muttered, and then lowered his head and kissed her senseless.

Mike went into Baton Rouge after lunch, while Cari, with his permission, went into his office to use the computer, hoping to pull up some maps of the Bordelaise area. Even though she knew the woods like the back of her hand, she'd never looked at them from the standpoint of picking the best places to hide a body. She needed location reminders as to bayous, swampland, pasture and forests. And she needed to figure out timelines, as well.

Now that they'd found the rental car on Morgan's Reach, it stood to reason Lance hadn't used it to drive the body away, or he would have been caught in the tornado along with the car. So using the map and locating the place where he'd been digging the grave, then widening the area around it in a quarter-mile circle, seemed prudent. She didn't think he would have been able to get any farther carrying Austin Ball's dead weight.

Her other reason for using his office was that she wanted a private place to talk to her agent. She'd spent the better part of lunch with Mike discussing the wisdom of letting her agent know she wasn't dead. He offered his thoughts but reminded her that it was ultimately her career—her life—so it had to be her call.

Cari continued to be impressed. A man who believed she was capable of making her own decisions—and whose kisses made her crazy. So many reasons why he was impossible to resist. But every time she thought of what the future might bring with him, her thoughts rolled back to what she'd lost. Knowing her parents had become nothing but memories broke her heart all over again every time she thought about it. Then she reminded herself—*one thing at a time.*

Once she logged on, she quickly found several maps of her parish, then printed them out. Now that she'd accomplished one goal, she reached for the phone to call her agent.

She'd been with Meredith Bernstein for more than seven years—almost from the start of her career. She respected her, and knew how fortunate she was that, from the beginning, they'd clicked. She felt horribly guilty for having let her believe she had died, but knew once she explained, Meredith would surely forgive her. After all, how many clients ever came back from the grave?

She punched in the numbers, then scooted back in Mike's chair, relishing the soft leather and deep seat as she waited for her call to be answered.

"Meredith Bernstein."

"Meredith…it's me, Cari. Don't panic. I'm not dead, and I can explain everything."

The shriek hurt her ear. She winced as she held the receiver away, then waited for the noise to subside.

"Meredith...hello...are you there?"

"Is this someone's idea of a sick joke?" Meredith snapped.

Cari sighed. "It's not a joke. I'm in hiding." Then her voice broke. "My parents are dead, but it was my cousin, Susan, who died, who was buried in my place."

"Oh my God! Why? What happened? Where were you? I don't understand! Oh! Oh! I can't wait to tell Leslie. She'll be beside herself. We've both been in absolute mourning about you."

Cari rolled her eyes. Telling her editor, Leslie Wainger, was a complete no-no.

"No. Wait! You can't tell Leslie! You can't tell anyone. Not yet."

"But why? This is wonderful news!"

"Listen to me. This is serious."

She heard Meredith take a deep breath. "Okay, I'm calm now."

"I'm a witness to a murder."

A second shriek hurt her ear again.

Cari sighed. "Meredith."

"I'm calm. I'm calm. Now talk to me."

And so Cari began, relating what happened from the time she'd walked up on Lance burying the body to finding her whole family dead and realizing that her only way out was a dangerous masquerade.

"Wait! Wait! Are you telling me the killer is the

man you were engaged to a couple of years ago?" Meredith cried.

"Yes."

This time, the shriek was at least a half-dozen decibels down on the shriek-o-meter.

"What on earth? Do you know why? Did you know the man he killed?" Meredith asked.

Cari told her about what she knew up to this point, and what they planned to do next.

"I don't know," Meredith said. "It seems awfully dangerous, going back to try to find that body. It could be anywhere."

"I know. But I need that body to get myself out of the hole I'm in. I let everyone in my hometown believe I was dead. They buried me and my family, and mourned over all of us, and I sat there in the church and watched, pretending to be Susan."

There was a long silence, then Meredith launched yet another idea. "You do know you have to write about this, don't you? Talk about built-in promotion! You can call it something like…like… I know! Lazarus Rising."

"Lazarus was a man."

"I know that," Meredith said. "It's just an analogy. Never mind. It doesn't matter what you title it. You just make sure you live through this crazy mess to write it."

"I have every intention of doing that," Cari said. "And don't worry. Mike has already alerted his security chief. I won't be on my own."

Meredith's voice rose. "Who's Mike?"

"Oh, yeah. I forgot to mention…Susan's boss has become a sort of…knight in shining armor for me. He rescued me from the hospital, and I'm staying at his estate until we sort everything out. In fact, we're leaving tomorrow for Bordelaise, and we'll be staying on my property in his motor home until we find out what Lance did with the dead man."

"Oh my God…I am in heaven," Meredith said. "Not only are you alive, but you finally have a man in your life again."

Cari smiled to herself, although she had to admit, thinking about Mike as the "man in her life" wasn't a bad thing.

"One thing at a time. One thing at a time. Now… I've got to go. Just remember, I need you to keep this under wraps until I'm safe."

"I know. Mum's the word."

"Good. So…I'll be in touch," Cari said.

"Absolutely," Meredith said. "And, honey…I'm so sorry about your family, but so happy you called. You can trust me to keep your secret."

Cari's smile slipped. "I know," she said softly.

"Take care. Love you," Meredith said.

"Love you, too," Cari echoed, then hung up the phone.

Twelve

It wasn't until two days later that Mike and Cari were actually able to leave for Bordelaise, and even then, it took them until midmorning to get away. He'd had two overseas calls to make, and then Songee had stopped them on their way out the door with a picnic basket filled with food for the motor home.

Cari had seen the concern on the housekeeper's face and had been unable to look at her for fear of reading accusation in her eyes. There was no getting around the fact that it was Cari's fault Mike Boudreaux was involved in the mess that was her life.

Finally they had everything they thought they would need loaded into his Range Rover. Mike was still treating her as if she was fragile goods, although Cari knew she would find the strength to face what lay ahead.

Once they passed the city limits, her anxiety grew as to what she was getting into.

She wanted to be safe again, and to do that, she had to make her stand against Lance.

Miles passed. The sun rose higher in the sky, and she glanced over at Mike as he drove. He was unusually quiet, which made her anxious. She didn't know if he was regretting his promise to help her, or if he was thinking about the business duties he was leaving behind. Either way, she felt guilty. Her situation had put him in an untenable position. As Susan's friend and employer, he'd offered her shelter. Then one thing had led to another, and now he, too, was involved in a convoluted web of lies. She glanced at him once more, then looked away. What was done was done. There was no going back.

Cari didn't know that Mike was stewing in concerns of his own, concerns that had nothing to do with his own safety and everything to do with hers. He and Aaron had come up with a long list of ways to insure Cari's safety, but being a witness to a murder, albeit after the fact, was still a dangerous position in which to be.

Aaron's text this morning had given him a measure of relief. Mike's motor home was in place. Aaron had set it up, stocked it with food and connected to the utilities. He'd found what was left of Cari's dog after his arrival last night and buried it beneath some trees that were still standing. And, at Mike's request, he was going through the debris in the hopes of recovering some family memorabilia. It wasn't much, but it was all Mike could think of to do. The bulk of the search for the body was going to fall on Cari's shoulders. She was the one familiar with the area. And if Lance Morgan figured out what was going on, she was the one who would be in danger.

As for her charade, he wasn't one hundred percent convinced that she'd fooled Morgan, despite the fact that the man hadn't seemed suspicious. Mike knew that if she'd ever been his fiancée, no disguise would have fooled him. He already recognized her from her scent alone. He knew the shape of her face, the sound of her voice, the lilt of her laughter and the depth of her grief. She was sad, but she was strong. And she seemed as attracted to him as he was to her. As far as he was concerned, falling in love with her was a done deal. He'd never believed in love at first sight—but it wasn't the first time his beliefs had been challenged, and Carolina North had challenged him from the start.

They were about ten minutes away from the highway turnoff leading to her property when his cell phone rang. He saw Cari flinch as he picked it up, noticed it was Aaron and answered quickly.

"Hey. What's up?"

"Is Miss North with you?"

"Yes, why?"

"How far away are you?"

"Less than ten minutes."

"Then it can wait. I'll talk to her when you get here."

"About what?" Mike said.

"It's something I just found in the debris, and if you ask me, it's pretty damned amazing."

"Okay. See you in ten." Then Mike flipped the phone shut and laid it back down on the console between them.

"Is everything okay?" Cari asked.

"I think so. Aaron said he wanted to talk to you about something he found, but when he realized how close we were, he said he'd just wait and show you himself."

"Show me what?"

"I don't know, *cher.* But I asked him to go through the debris and see if he could find any family memorabilia that hadn't been ruined, so maybe it's something like that."

Cari's vision blurred. "Oh, Mike…"

He sighed. "I know today is going to be hell for you, and I can't bear to see you cry. I was just hoping to give you something tangible as a remembrance of you and your family."

"Well, right now these aren't sad tears, and it's not my fault you keep turning up on your damned white horse to save my day."

A lopsided grin tilted the corner of his mouth. "So…*cher*…are you saying I'm your white knight?"

"Yes, I am saying that," Cari said. "And just so you know, my editor, Leslie Wainger, would tell me that was such a cliché and to find another way to say it."

His smile widened. "Then you tell that Leslie I said no dice. As a kid, I dreamed of being a knight in shining armor and riding up on a white horse to save the princess in the tower, then living happy ever after."

Cari swallowed back tears. "Am I your princess?"

"Hell yes," Mike said softly, then reached across the seat and took her hand.

Cari shivered, then threaded her fingers through his and tightened her hold.

Mike felt her trembling, sensed her fear.

"Don't worry, *cher,*" he said. "I won't let you go."

Cari sighed, then pointed. "There's the turnoff."

Mike took it.

Cari shivered again. The last time she'd been on this road she'd been out of her mind with sorrow and fear. It was daunting to know she was coming back the same way.

Lance had mentally moved past the night he'd drunk himself into a stupor. Once he'd come to terms with his suspicion, that Carolina North was still alive, he'd started thinking of what had to happen next. But before he could make any firm plans, he heard a rumor in town that left him confused.

In the hardware store he'd run into Jim Bob Greeley, who'd told him about a stranger coming in to pick up some electrical equipment. According to Jim Bob, the man had just parked a motor home on the North property, so that Susan Blackwell would have a comfortable place to stay while overseeing the cleanup of the family land.

He'd been stunned by the news and had second thoughts about his conclusion. Maybe the Susan who'd come to the funerals was really Susan after all. If it *was* Cari, why would she come back around people who knew her well enough to see through her disguise? Then he remembered the cinnamon allergy and panicked all over again. Ultimately, the only way he could be sure was to stake out the property and get a really good look at her.

Jim Bob hadn't been sure about the timing of Susan's arrival, but Lance knew how to get around that. It was less than twenty minutes from Morgan land to the North property as the crow flew. All he had to do was get out his four-wheeler and take a little ride. And if someone saw him in the vicinity, the ride was perfectly innocent. It wasn't anything he hadn't done countless times before, looking for missing livestock.

Still, the news had shortened his trip into Bordelaise. Instead of stopping in at Mama Lou's Crab Shack for lunch, Lance had picked up a couple of burgers at the only fast-food place back in business and headed for home. He'd eaten the burgers as he drove, washing them down with a bottle of Pepsi, and ended the meal with a mint they'd tossed into the sack. It wasn't exactly his choice of dessert, but it was the only sweet available.

Once home, he'd changed into his usual work clothes: Wellington boots, a pair of jeans, a T-shirt, and one of his father's old Panama hats. The outfit would make his excuse all the more believable, should he be seen. All he needed was a pair of binoculars and he was good to go.

A short while later, he was on the four-wheeler and heading into the woods behind the barns.

Cari's first glimpse of where the family home had once stood was numbing. Instead of the rambling, single-story lowland house surrounded by massive trees and her mother's famous azaleas, it looked like a war zone. Some of the trees were missing their topmost branches, while others had been completely uprooted. The house and contents had been reduced to lumber and ruin, and strewn as far as the eye could see. Her car was still upside down out in the pasture, near most of the barn roof, along with the carcasses of some dead cattle.

Then she saw Mike's motor home. It wasn't exactly what she'd expected. It was huge and outwardly elaborate, a top-of-the-line showpiece of blue and silver. She could only imagine what it looked like inside. As he pulled up beside it and parked, she took a deep, shuddering breath, then clenched her fists, reminding herself of why she was there.

Mike hadn't taken his eyes off her since the moment they'd stopped. He'd known this would be difficult for her, but now that he saw it for himself, he felt sick to his stomach. That she'd lived through this was nothing short of a miracle.

But when he saw the muscles in her jaw clench, he could only imagine what was running through her mind. Desperate to shift her focus, he took her hand.

"*Cher*... Look at me."

Cari shuddered as she responded, only to find she was looking at him through a blur of tears. She swallowed around the knot in her throat as he tightened his grip.

"We will get through this together," he said softly. "I promise."

She nodded, then pulled loose from his grasp and swiped angrily at the tears.

"Let's go find your security chief. I need a piece of good news."

She got out of the Range Rover on her own and was already circling the motor home by the time Mike caught up with her.

"Careful," he said, as she sidestepped a precarious jumble of splintered lumber.

Cari shrugged it off. "That stuff is a lot scarier when it's coming at you faster than the speed of sound."

"Have mercy, woman," Mike muttered, as he took her by the hand. "Maybe you don't need coddling, but I do. I can't wrap my head around the fact that you lived through this."

Cari didn't answer, but she didn't pull away,

either. For Mike, it was enough. A few moments later he saw Aaron coming out from behind what was left of the barn, then wave.

"There's Aaron," Mike said.

From this distance, the only thing Cari could tell was that he wasn't quite as tall as Mike, and that he was bald. As he came closer, she guessed his age in the mid-forties, and knew if she was stereotyping him for one of her mystery stories, she would have guessed by the way he carried himself that he was ex-military. Good. She might be needing both muscle and firepower.

All of a sudden a gust of wind rattled through the area, loosening a strip of sheet iron that had been caught in the limbs of a tree only feet from where Cari was standing. Before she could react, Mike grabbed her arm and pulled her out of the way, just as the metal came crashing down behind her.

He spun her around and grabbed her by the shoulders. "Are you all right?"

"Yes, thanks to you," she said, then looked back at the ragged piece of sheet metal and shuddered.

At that moment Aaron came running up. "Wow! That was close!" he said, and slapped Mike on the shoulder in a familiar gesture of hello. "Quick moves, boss man." Then he eyed Cari curiously. He knew her story and was seriously impressed with how she'd taken the heat off herself until she was well enough to fight back.

He nodded at her. "Ma'am."

"Carolina, this is Aaron Lake. Aaron, for obvious reasons, Cari's answering to Susan."

Aaron grinned. "I'll just be calling you 'ma'am,' ma'am. That way I won't forget and get myself—or you—into trouble."

"Nice to meet you, Mr. Lake," Cari said.

"Aaron, please. Now…are you ready for some good news?"

Cari's chin quivered once, then lifted. "Yes… please."

"You guys follow me, then. You're not gonna believe this."

Cari fixed her gaze on the back of Aaron's shirt as he walked away, then, despite her earlier moment of independence, unconsciously reached for Mike's hand. She needed all her strength and his, too, to walk through this place without coming undone.

The pile of furniture and drywall under which her mother had been pinned had been moved—obviously during the recovery of her body. When they passed the remnant of wall where her father had been impaled, she stumbled but wouldn't look. There was no need. She saw the scene every night when she closed her eyes. As they approached the clearing where she'd found Susan's body, she noticed variegated shades of earth and realized that despite the rains that had followed the tornado, the ground was still saturated with her cousin's blood.

Jesus, help me, she prayed. She tightened her grip on Mike's hand as they walked. When she realized Aaron was talking, she made herself focus on what he was saying.

As they approached the ruins of the barn, he began to gesture with his arm. "Over there is where I was walking when I saw it...sitting out in the open without a scratch on it. I grew up in Oklahoma, and I've seen tornados do some crazy things just like this, though. Once, when I was a kid, an entire natural gas plant blew away just down the road from my house. Me and my dad were down there looking around afterward, and he showed me a piece of prairie grass that had been driven through a telephone pole without breaking the grass, like thread through the eye of a needle. Dangedest thing I ever saw. Threaded that grass through solid wood, leaving about six inches sticking out on either side. If I hadn't seen it, I would never have believed it possible."

Suddenly Cari realized that Aaron had stopped.

"Here it is," he said. "Look at that, will you?"

Cari stepped out from behind him, then froze.

Her mother's china cabinet was sitting out in the middle of the barnyard, with every plate, cup and dish that had been in it still on the shelves.

"Oh sweet Lord," she whispered, and then rushed forward and opened the glass doors, unable to believe what she was seeing. The outside of the cabinet was mud-splattered and dusty, but it was completely intact, as were the contents. "They're all here!" she cried, as she moved from the stack of dinner plates to the salad plates and bowls, then the coffee cups and her grandmother's crystal glasses. In the cabinets below, the bowls and platters nested one into the other, just like the last time Maggie North had put them up. When Cari pulled open the small shallow drawers and saw her grannie's silverware, she threw her hands in the air and then spun, her eyes shining with unshed tears.

"Mike! Look! Grannie's glasses and silver…and my mother's china! It's all here. I can't believe it."

Mike didn't know whether to laugh or cry. Her joy in the midst of such devastation was heart-wrenching.

"I'm so happy for you, *cher,*" he said. "I'm thinking we need to do a quick salvage job here…just in case of more bad weather."

"Yes!" she said, and began turning in a little circle, clutching her hands against her chest. Then she caught sight of Aaron again and threw herself in his arms. "Thank you."

Aaron grinned as he hugged her. "Well now, ma'am…I didn't have any hand in how this happened. I just found it."

"It doesn't matter," Cari insisted, then turned to Mike. "Can you drive the Range Rover over here? I want to get everything out now."

"Absolutely," he said. "Just let me grab a bunch of towels out of the motor home for packing.

And…I'll need to unload the suitcases so the back will be empty."

"I'll help," Aaron said, then added, "Uh…Mike said you guys had a dog. A black-and-white long-hair?"

Cari's eyes widened as she remembered Tippy. "Yes."

"I found him last night. Buried him under those trees over there. I laid that big rock on it to mark the place. Was that okay?"

A lump rose in Cari's throat. "It's more than okay," she said.

Aaron patted her awkwardly, then hurried after Mike, leaving her to visit Tippy's grave on her own.

Cari stopped at the mound of freshly turned earth, remembering the last time she'd seen Tippy alive. She'd been on the rise above the farm, and he'd been running for cover toward the barn.

"Poor Tippy," Cari said, her voice trembling. "I hope you're chasing lots of squirrels and butterflies. You earned the right to your own brand of heaven."

Impulsively she knelt at the grave and pressed her hand hard and deep into the loose dirt, then stood. Looking down at the imprint of her hand, it almost appeared as if she'd given the old dog one last pat on the back. After that, she turned and walked away.

Lance was on the rise above the North property, careful to stay hidden behind the trees. He'd parked the four-wheeler about fifty yards back, just to make sure the sound of the engine didn't alert anyone to his presence. He'd been there since just before 10:00 a.m., watching a bald, middle-aged man digging through the debris, and decided he must be the man Jim Bob Greeley had mentioned, then dismissed him.

He'd been on the rise almost two hours when he'd seen a black Range Rover suddenly appear around the bend in the driveway. At that point his heart had started to pound. That had to be them! Any minute now he would have his answer.

He lifted the binoculars to his eyes, focused them on the arriving vehicle and waited for them to park. When they parked off to the side, just out of his view, he cursed in frustration and shifted position to the other side of the trees and focused the binoculars again.

He saw Mike Boudreaux first and began to fidget. He hadn't expected the man to come with her. Boudreaux was a multimillionaire, for God's sake. Even if Susan was really Susan, why would he be here cleaning up storm debris?

Then, suddenly, he saw a woman coming out from behind the motor home. Her head was tilted down, as if she couldn't bear to look at her surroundings, but she walked like Cari, with a long, easy stride.

He saw Boudreaux take her hand. Then the woman lifted her head, and in that moment, Lance was seeing her—really seeing her—without bandages on her face or a sling around her neck, without the artifice of makeup or under the duress of a public funeral. The hair was different. But the oval-shaped face was the same. Round eyes. Curved lips with the lower just the tiniest bit fuller than the upper.

"Fucking A," Lance said, and let the binoculars fall until they dangled against his chest. It was just as he'd feared. Carolina North wasn't dead. Not only had she put one over on the entire town of Bordelaise, she'd put an even bigger one over on him. He knew why she'd come back, and he would bet money it had nothing to do with clearing property. She was going to try to find that body she'd seen him burying. And when she did, she would turn his ass over to the police.

Now that he knew for sure she was alive, he knew that he'd been right about what he had to do. Get rid of the only witness to Austin Ball's murder.

Frustrated and pissed, he stomped back toward his four-wheeler. He'd learned everything he needed to know. It was time to go home.

Hershel Porter was working a fender bender in front of the bank when his day dispatcher, Vera Samuels, called him on his radio.

"Porter here."

"Chief. Just got a call from Katie Earle. She said she came home from the grocery store and found a message from J.R. on the answering machine. I don't know the details, but it appears he's surfaced. Maybe now we'll find out what's happened to Bobby."

"Fan-freaking-tastic," Hershel muttered, then realized he was on the air. "Uh…10-4, Vera. I'll be heading over to Mrs. Earle's shortly."

"I'll let her know. Oh…and one other thing."

"What?"

"Um…a team of four men showed up here earlier asking for you. They said you were expecting them."

Hershel immediately remembered the DEA agents coming to try to find their man.

"Fine. Tell them I'll be in shortly."

Hershel finished writing up the ticket he was giving to Prentiss Johnson for pulling away from the curb without looking and banging into a car that had been passing by. That the driver of the second car happened to be a teenager was immaterial to Hershel. The kid was in the right, and Prentiss was just going to have to deal with it.

Hershel ripped the ticket off his pad and handed it to Prentiss. "If you need a copy of the accident report for your insurance, it'll be ready by tomorrow," he said.

Prentiss was still cursing as he drove off. The teenager, a boy named Junior Emerson, was still upset. Prentiss Johnson had put a huge dent in the front right fender of his father's car, shoving the metal hard against the tire and making the car unfit to drive.

"Daddy's gonna blame me for sure," Junior said, as he gazed morosely at the big dent in the white Chevy.

"Then you tell Daddy to give me a call," Hershel said. "I'll make sure he knows what happened."

"Yes, sir. I will, sir," Junior said, and then sat back on the curb to wait for the wrecker, as Hershel Porter sped off toward the Earle place.

Cari was stacking her mother's china on the extra bed in the motor home when Mike came in with the last load. She pointed to an empty spot beside a stack of plates. "I've made a place over there."

Mike put down the platters and bowls, then stepped back, examining the lot with a practiced eye. "Looks like you've got it pretty well secured."

Cari nodded. "I think so. I still can't believe it. It's like a sign from God, reminding me that I didn't really lose everything after all. And I didn't, you know? Besides this…I have memories. Precious memories."

Then Aaron came in behind them carrying a large cardboard box. "Here's the last of what I could salvage," he said, as he set the box down on the floor. "There are a few pictures, a couple of figurines… anything that wasn't completely ruined or too broken to reclaim is in there."

"Thank you. Thank you, both," Cari said, and dropped to her knees as she began to dig through the box.

Everything she touched, everything she saw, brought back a memory…a memory that brought tears to her eyes and a lump to her throat. All she had left of her world was these boxes.

Overwhelmed again by the scope of her loss, she covered her face and started to cry.

There was nothing Mike could do to make this better, but he wasn't going to let her grieve alone. He sat down on the floor beside her, then pulled her into his arms.

"Cry, *cher*...that's good, that's good. Cry it all out and know you're not alone."

Thirteen

Night was coming to Bordelaise, bringing with it a dark, moonless sky. The air was still, leaving it with a hot, muggy feel. Lightning bugs were beginning to appear. An owl hooted from the woods nearby, and in the distance, a whippoorwill's call lent a sad, lonely sound to the proceedings. Even though the sun had set and dusk was turning into night, Cari continued combing through the debris.

Mike had been beside her every step of the way, lifting the heavier pieces so she could search beneath and making sure she didn't come to any harm. As the day had passed, he'd watched her steps slow and her stride shorten. There was a smear of dust on her cheek and a thin coating on the legs of her jeans. He'd watched waves of fresh grief come and go on her face so often he was physically sick. Finally she stumbled across a jumble of broken rafters and came within an inch of running a nail through her tennis shoe and into her foot. That was when he called a halt.

"*Cher.* Enough."

As Cari straightened, a bead of sweat took a dive down the middle of her back. "What did you say?"

Mike stepped across what was left of a small rocking chair and took her by the shoulders.

"You've done enough for one day. You're so hot and tired you're beginning to stagger, and I, for one, do not want to see you injured again. Please, Carolina…it's time to go inside."

She might have argued, but the gentleness in his voice was her undoing.

"Yes, okay. I didn't know it was so late," she said, as she wiped the dust from her hands onto the legs of her jeans.

"Take my hand," Mike urged, as they moved toward the motor home. He knew she'd pushed herself beyond the limits of her endurance. He understood the anxiety that drove her, but it didn't stop him from feeling concerned.

Cari didn't know until they got inside how truly exhausted she was. Too weary to appreciate the luxurious furnishings or to cry another tear for the devastation of what had been her family home, she was still grateful for the air-conditioned comfort. The bits and pieces that she'd recovered from the wreckage were the only tangible memories she would ever have of her life before the storm and were well worth the effort it had taken to find them.

"You shower first," Mike said, and aimed her toward the bathroom.

Cari did as she was told, taking a clean nightgown from her suitcase before slipping inside the small, perfectly appointed bath. Conscious of the compact hot water heater and the need to share their resources, she didn't linger in the shower, even though the hot water felt wonderful on her aching body. She dried quickly, found some talcum powder and lotion on a shelf, for which she blessed whoever had stocked the camper, and was beginning to feel like a new woman by the time she pulled the nightgown over her head.

As she exited, she could hear Mike on the phone in the kitchen. From what she could tell, he was firming up tomorrow's plans with Aaron, although she hadn't seen the man since the middle of the afternoon. Just after three, another member of Mike's security team, Trent Joseph, had arrived in a red Jeep, picked Aaron up and driven away. From the snippets of conversation she was hearing, whatever they were planning had something to do with Lance.

She entered the bedroom, moving quietly on bare feet, then stopped in the doorway. Since she'd piled her mother's dishes on the extra bed earlier in the day, there was no getting around the fact that this was the only bed left. She also knew that Mike had made a big deal out of the blankets and pillows he'd carried into the living area earlier, obviously as an assurance that the bed would be hers alone.

She sighed.

There was no denying the attraction between them. If there was anything deeper than consideration and affection alongside that sexual attraction, only time would tell. What she did know was that the past week would have been hell without his care and attention. She knew he wanted her. The hard jut of his erection against her belly had been impossible to ignore, but to his credit, he'd never once pushed her to do something she wasn't ready to consider.

But that was then, and this was now. She did want him—in the most elemental of ways. She needed to be someone other than a woman on the run. She wanted to feel something besides gut-wrenching grief. Mike had given her so much already, but if he offered more tonight, she knew she was going to take it.

"Are you all right?" he asked.

Cari felt his hand on her shoulder and turned around. "Feeling much better, thank you."

"Give me five minutes to clean up and then we'll eat. In the meantime, I made some sweet tea. It's not as good as Songee's, but it's passable. Help yourself, *cher.* I won't be long."

Cari nodded, then tried not to stare as he pulled his T-shirt over his head and disappeared into the bathroom. It was the first time she'd seen his body, and while she wasn't surprised by the lean and muscled physique, the warm, olive cast of his skin was intriguing. She couldn't help imagining what the rest of him must be like, then shivered with sudden longing.

Startled by the emotion, she decided iced tea was in order and headed for the kitchenette. Ever the perfect host, Mike had set out a small plate of appetizers, along with the pitcher of tea. Cari chose a bite of ham roll and popped it in her mouth, then took her tea and sat down on the sofa. The small flat-screen television on the opposite wall was on. She found the remote and upped the volume, then curled her feet beneath her, letting the sound wash over her without actually focusing on what was being said.

She thought back over the events of the day. The trauma of coming back to the scene of so much death and devastation, followed by the joy of finding the china cabinet. The consideration that Aaron had shown by burying the family dog. The box of keepsakes that he'd found, as well as the bits and pieces of memorabilia she'd uncovered later. But even more, Mike's unfailing presence at her side, and his constant care for her comfort and safety.

A few moments later she heard the bathroom door open. She looked up just as Mike exited with a towel wrapped around his waist. She got a quick glimpse of long legs and a broad back before he slipped into the bedroom.

Startled by the surge of longing to follow him, she

jumped up from the sofa and went to the refrigerator to add some ice to her tea—anything to keep her mind off lying naked beneath Michael Boudreaux. She was putting a second ham roll in her mouth as Mike arrived.

"Those are good, aren't they, *cher?* I think it's the Dijon mustard Songee uses in the cream cheese that gives them such a kick."

He reached over her shoulder and took one for himself, then gave her a quick kiss on the back of her ear before he put the food in his mouth.

A sharp rush of longing shot through her so fast it made her weak, and at the same time, she was shocked at herself. She wasn't the kind of woman who fell into lust with a good-looking man. Then she shifted her inner guilt to the lifetime's worth of drama she'd lived through this past week. Maybe it was her instinct for self-preservation reminding her to tap into something life-affirming that was causing all these emotions. And maybe not. All she knew was, she needed to feel something besides sorrow.

Mike swallowed, then licked a smear of cream cheese from his thumb as he sorted through the covered dishes in the fridge. "We have some chicken salad sandwiches on croissants, Cajun potato salad, pickled okra and deviled eggs. And…my favorite dessert, bread pudding with raisins and Bourbon sauce."

Cari managed a smile. "Sounds like Songee knows the way to your heart."

Mike turned around, about to tease her, but the look in her eyes ended the thought.

"Food fills my stomach...not my heart," he said softly, then cupped her face with his hands, leaned down and slid a soft, searching kiss across her lips.

Cari moaned as she reached for him. Encircling his waist with her arms, she returned the kiss with intensity and the promise of more.

He took what she offered like a dying man in search of redemption, pulling her hard against him and then lifting her off her feet. He practically growled as he lowered her to the edge of the table. When he stepped between her legs, she shuddered.

"Ah...*cher,* do you know what you're doing to me? You are playing with fire."

Cari saw her reflection in the wild green of his eyes. She didn't have time to be shocked by the wanton woman she saw there.

"I know perfectly well what I'm doing, and I'm not asking you for promises. Just solace. I'm tired and broken, and, oh God...I'm empty...so empty. Fill me, Mike, please fill me."

She leaned forward until she was so close she could feel his breath on her face, then slid the tip of her tongue between his lips.

Mike grunted as if he'd been kicked, then picked her up from the table and carried her back to the bed. He paused long enough to slide the door shut, then dim the lights. Cari was already naked as he stepped out of his sweatpants and dropped his T-shirt on the floor. Within seconds, he was beside her on the bed.

While there was something to be said for taking one's sweet time, this wasn't the moment for delay. The tension of the past week and the buildup of their emotions faded in the face of unstoppable passion. In a tangle of arms and legs, they held on to each other in a frantic manner, as if losing contact would mean being lost themselves.

And then they kissed. Until their lips were swollen and their breath was gone.

And they touched. Until their skin was on fire and their bodies aching.

Then they stroked. Until they found the rhythm to the dance of love.

Nothing mattered but the desire to reach their impending climax, and to reach it together.

Cari was the first to beg, but she didn't have to ask twice. When Mike raised himself up and then over her, she was ready.

She felt him slide between her legs, then in.

She closed her eyes as he went deep.

When she wrapped her legs around his waist and her arms around his neck, a deep groan slid out from between his lips.

Cari sighed. "So good," she whispered. "Don't stop. Don't stop."

"Not until I die," he said softly, then began to rock and thrust, hammering into her body in a wild animal rhythm over and over, until she thought she might faint from the intensity.

Her climax came as suddenly as the tornado that had nearly ended her life. Consciousness burst behind her eyelids, disappearing in a white-hot flash of rushing blood and light.

Her cry shattered Mike's concentration instantly, blinding him to everything but the shattering feel of his own release. He groaned as he held her fast, while the echoes of his climax rocked his body just as he'd been rocking hers.

"Ah…sweet Lord…sweet Carolina. *La…petite morte,*" he muttered, then collapsed on top of her.

Cari was still riding her own aching echoes when she heard the words. She sighed, complete within herself as she held him fast against her. Only the French would have such a beautiful phrase for the moment of climax. *La petite morte*. The little death. When the heart stops and the body gives up to the culmination of true passion. So he'd done as he'd promised: he hadn't stopped until he'd died.

Finally he rose up on his elbows to look down at her.

Breath caught in the back of Cari's throat as she looked her fill in turn. Black hair, green eyes, and that smooth, olive complexion, coupled with those high cheekbones and sensuous mouth, were enough to make a woman weep. Then he spoke.

"Tell me, Carolina…does your heart still ache?"

She shivered. "No."

He kissed the right side of her mouth.

"And tell me, Carolina…are you still lost and empty?"

She cupped his face with her hands, memorizing the contours of his features, knowing this moment would be forever marked in her memory as the perfect act of healing and compassion.

"No, Michael. Not anymore. I'm full."

He kissed the other side of her mouth, then touched his forehead to hers. "While I, *mon cher,* have been emptied of all that I am," he said softly. Then he rolled onto his back and stared up at the ceiling above the bed. "And I can honestly say, I have never been so happy to oblige."

Cari smiled, then rolled over onto her side and slid her arm across his chest. She didn't want to think about tomorrow, or why she was so reluctant to let him go.

It was the way she turned to him instead of away that made Mike's heart leap with longing. He didn't know how he was going to make it happen, but for the first time in years, he knew what he wanted besides another successful business deal.

He wanted *her.* He wanted Carolina North—and not for just tonight. He wanted her in his world, in his bed—in his life. Every night and for the rest of his life. All he had to do was figure out how to get her in the same frame of mind.

He turned to face her, taking pride in the very satisfied expression on her face.

"I know you're full, *mon cher*...but are you still hungry? And before you answer, please say yes, because *I* am starving."

Cari laughed, then pushed herself up on one elbow. "Then I say, yes, Michael Boudreaux. I am very, very hungry...for food."

Mike smiled, then watched as she got out of bed without any hint of embarrassment, picked up her nightgown and slipped out of the room and into the bathroom. A short while later, he joined her in the kitchenette, where they ate Songee's cooking while going through the treasures Cari had found. With each one came a story. Mike let her talk, knowing that, with the telling, would come the first steps in healing, then eventually the time when remembering lost loved ones was a thing to savor.

Lance was a privileged son. He wasn't accustomed to doing without. He liked to think of himself as a gentleman farmer. The tractors he used had air-conditioned cabs, while he hired local help for the harder, heavier work. He'd studied crossbreeding cattle, as well as new techniques in farming. He liked fine wines, good food and hot sex, and not necessarily in that order. The fact that he was readying himself for a nighttime foray through the woods, on foot, at the mercy of mosquitoes and snakes, was indicative of how desperate his situation had become.

Being forced to literally hunt Cari down and kill

her was against his nature. He had acted impulsively and, yes, that had led him to killing Austin Ball, but he was not a cold-blooded killer. Or hadn't been. But once he followed through on his plan tonight, that was exactly what he would be. And he didn't only have to kill Cari. Through her deception, she'd pulled Michael Boudreaux into the situation, which meant he had to die, too.

He didn't have a firm plan as to how to accomplish that, because he wasn't sure what he would run into once he got there. All he knew was that they were in a motor home that, despite possessing all the bells and whistles, was basically still just a house on wheels. And all houses were alike in that they had doors and windows. This one had the added benefit of having a gasoline tank attached. Handy little thing, gasoline. Made engines run. Made fires burn hotter. An all-purpose liquid of life and death.

It occurred to him as he was dressing to leave that he should wear black. No need making a target of himself. He pulled a pair of black Nikes out of his closet. He thought about taking a handgun, but it would negate the whole impression of an accidental death if they were found with bullet wounds. Then he remembered the carcasses of dead animals still strewn about the countryside after the tornado and put a handgun in his pocket just in case he ran into some sharp-toothed scavenger having a late dinner.

On the way past his garden shed he picked up a rope, just in case, looped it over his shoulder and set off.

It took more than thirty minutes to get through the woods in the dark before he emerged from the trees to stand on the rise above the homestead. The lack of moonlight was to his benefit, although he couldn't see where the hell he was stepping unless he used his flashlight. But now that he was this close to success, he couldn't do anything to call attention to himself, so he put the flashlight in his pocket and hoped for the best.

He started down the hill with as much speed as he could safely manage, certain that whoever was in the motor home could neither hear nor see him from this distance. And since old Tippy had bought the farm during the storm, Lance didn't have to worry about a barking dog. He did worry about them waking up before they were overcome by smoke and trying to get out the door, so he needed to make sure he jammed that up in some way. But there was plenty of debris around, so he could figure something out after he got there. All he had to do was wedge some two-by-fours against the door. The boards would burn up in the fire, so no one would know they'd been there. The deaths wouldn't look like anything but a horrible accident.

As he started down the slope, his focus was on the two yellow squares of light coming from the motor home. It meant they were still awake. But they wouldn't be awake forever. He would just get in place and wait them out. A faint scent of dead flesh drifted past his nose, but he brushed it aside. It wasn't the first time he'd caught wind of the smell, but since it was dead, whatever it was, it represented no threat to him.

He wouldn't think about the possibility that Mike had told Cari's story to others, or that he wasn't the only one she had told. Did it even matter? If she'd already told the authorities, he would already have been hauled in for questioning, at the very least. Whatever she might have told anyone else would only be hearsay evidence and, without a body, unlikely to stick. Ball's car had been found in the treetops. Common sense dictated a similar fate happening to Ball. He knew he could make this work—if he could just silence Carolina.

He was halfway down the back slope when he heard rustling in the grass off to his right. He stopped, listening intently, but the sounds had stopped when he did. He chalked it up to night critters and his own nerves, and started forward.

Again he heard something moving through the grass and swung his flashlight toward the sounds. All he saw was the rotting carcass of one of Frank North's cows and a lot of tall, dead grass. He wrinkled his nose at the sight, although it did affirm the source of what he'd been smelling. It also alerted him to the fact that he could have walked up on feeding scavengers, which wasn't good. His hand automatically went to the pocket with the handgun, and he patted it once, taking comfort in the outline of heavy steel.

It was the sudden and shrill scream off to his right that stopped his heart. He'd grown up hearing that sound in the night, but never this close or this threatening. He grabbed the handgun from his pocket as he swung the flashlight in the direction of the sound.

It was the reflection of his flashlight off the big cat's eyes that sent his heart into overdrive. When he realized he was between the cat and the carcass, he knew what was coming next. When the cat moved toward him, he swung the handgun up and fired. Once directly at the cat, then a second and third time at the blur of its retreating form.

Just as he was thanking his lucky stars for his foresight in bringing the gun, he realized what he'd done. Wildly he turned just as a door opened down at the motor home. There was a moment when Mike Boudreaux was silhouetted against the light, and then he disappeared. That was when Lance knew for sure that the surprise he'd planned had gone south.

"Well, shit," he muttered, squeezing off a fourth shot and turning to bolt for home just as he heard someone shout.

"Don't move!"

At the same moment, he was caught in the glare of a handheld spotlight. Before he could think beyond that, another voice yelled at him from behind.

"Drop the gun!"

That was when he lost it. He started to run, when a shot rang out. Suddenly *he'd* become the sitting duck.

"Don't shoot! Don't shoot!" he screamed, and he dropped the gun as two men came out of the darkness.

Mike and Cari had been sitting at the small table in the kitchenette, looking at her reclaimed treasures. She was still wearing her nightgown, and Mike had on a pair of sweatpants. He was laughing at one of her stories about the summer she and Susan turned eleven and came down with chicken pox at the same church picnic. Between them, they had managed to infect thirteen other kids from her Sunday school class. He was still smiling when he heard the first shot. Within a heartbeat, he was on his feet and shoving Cari to the floor as the second shot rang out, followed by a third.

"Get down!" he yelled. "And stay down!"

He made a run for the bedroom, and came back seconds later wearing shoes and carrying a gun.

"Mike! No!" she screamed, but before she could stop him, he was gone.

When she heard the fourth shot a moment later, her heart nearly stopped. Was someone shooting at Mike? What in God's name was going on?

Desperate to know what was happening, she jumped up and turned out the lights. If someone was shooting at them, she wasn't going to be an easy target. Then she went into a crouch and felt her way to the bedroom, where she found her tennis shoes and quickly put them on before heading back to the door. It might not be the smartest thing she'd ever done, but she wasn't going to sit inside this tin box and wait to see if a good guy or a bad guy came through the door. She slipped outside, feeling along the ground until she found a good-size piece of lumber to use as a weapon, and disappeared into the darkness.

She realized there were lights on the hillside above the barn and knew that whatever was going on, was happening up there. She heard shouting, followed by Mike's voice, yelling something up the hill. She couldn't make out what he was saying, but the fact that he was alive and talking was enough. She froze, waiting beside the pile of rubble with the makeshift club still in her hands, and watched the bobbing lights as they started down the slope.

Lance had always been a man who thought fast on his feet. It was a necessary skill for his wayward lifestyle, but it wasn't doing him much good tonight. The two men who'd come out of the darkness were strangers to him. Both big and burly, the kind of build he associated with bodyguards. The older of the two was clearly the one in charge. From what Lance could see, he was in his mid-forties, with a bald head and a pissed-off look on his face. The other was younger but bigger, which didn't bode well for Lance. He was a lover, not a fighter, despite having graduated to killer.

When they retrieved his gun, then tied him up with his own rope before marching him down the hill, he knew he'd reached the height of humiliation and was as close to being ruined as he'd ever been. With every step he took, his mind was whirling from one scenario to another, trying to find a story that would fit with where he'd been caught and what he'd been carrying.

"I don't understand!" he kept saying, as they pulled him along. "I didn't do anything but protect myself from a panther. You must have seen it. It was coming at me. I had to shoot. Who are you people? What right do you have to treat me like this?"

All of a sudden he became aware of another figure coming toward them up the hill. He cursed beneath his breath. It had to be Boudreaux.

He was so fucked.

Then he heard Mike shout.

"Aaron?"

"We're here," the big bald man said, and pulled on the rope, causing Lance to stumble to his knees in the dark.

"Look out, damn it!" Lance cried, and then rocked back on his heels and looked up to find Mike Boudreaux towering over him.

The first thought that ran through his mind was that the man was built more like a dockworker than a high-powered money man. It was impossible to miss the guy's rock-hard abs, and muscular arms and shoulders, or the fact that he was only wearing a pair of sweatpants and tennis shoes. He wanted to be pissed off that the man had been with Cari, then remembered that he'd been planning to kill her.

"I demand to know what's going on!" Lance said.

Mike reached out, grabbed the rope tied around Lance Morgan's wrists and yanked him upright.

"You're trespassing, so you've forfeited your right to demand anything, Morgan. And while we're on the subject, what the hell are you doing on North property with a gun?"

"I was looking for some lost livestock," he said, settling on the best of his lousy options.

Mike snorted. "In the dark?"

"There's a flashlight in my pocket," Lance muttered. "And I had a rope so that when I found them, I could lead them home, but your goons have tied me up with it."

"What if I don't believe you?" Mike said softly.

Lance shivered. He knew why Boudreaux would distrust him. Cari and her big fat mouth.

"Then I guess you'll just have to call the parish police," Lance said, and tried to pretend the notion of Boudreaux doing just that didn't scare the hell out of him. "Is Susan down there with you? If she is, ask her. She'll confirm that the cows were always knocking down fences. I've come here plenty of times looking for cattle, just like her uncle came onto Morgan's Reach doing the same thing."

Lance glared. He knew the bastard was lying, but he also knew he had them over a barrel.

"What were you shooting at?" he asked.

"A panther," Lance said. "I accidentally walked between it and the carcass of a cow, which it must have come back to feed on. It came at me, so I fired to scare it off. These men must have seen it."

Aaron nodded. "Yes, there was a panther there, and it did run off after he fired. But I've been following this guy ever since he walked onto the property, and he didn't once look for a break in the fence anywhere."

Lance jerked as if he'd been punched. "You were following me? What the fuck for?"

"Looking for looters," Mike lied. "They've already been on the property once."

"Oh," Lance said. "Well…I am not a looter. I'm a well-respected member of this community, and as such, you had no—"

"Sorry, boss," Aaron said. "I guess it was too dark for us to see the 'well-respected' sign on his butt."

Lance glared at the man, but considering the fact that the others were the ones with the guns, he restrained himself from making more enemies.

"So…am I free to go?" he asked.

Mike shrugged. "It's not up to me to say. This is Susan's property, not mine. I think she's the one to ask."

Lance felt sick. He didn't want to face Cari. He'd never been able to lie to her and get away with it. Still, what other choice did he have?

"Whatever," he muttered, then let himself be led the rest of the way down to the motor home.

Cari was so scared she was shaking. Everything had come to a halt a few minutes ago, and she didn't know why. The lights had stopped moving, and she could no longer hear anyone talking. All she knew was that Mike was up there with God knew who, and she was down here in her nightgown and tennis shoes with nothing but a piece of lumber for a weapon.

Just as she was thinking about going inside and finding her cell phone to call the police, the lights began to move again. When she realized they were coming this way, she didn't know whether to be relieved or worry even more. Uncertain as to who was approaching, she stepped behind the trunk of a nearby tree with her makeshift club raised, ready to fight.

A few minutes passed before she began to hear the murmur of voices again. When she recognized Mike's voice, then Aaron Lake's, she began to relax. If Mike was with his security team, he was surely safe.

Mike hadn't noticed until they were closer that the lights were all off inside. He could only imagine Cari's fear, and while he was anxious to make her feel better, he didn't think Lance Morgan being on the hill above her place with a gun was going to do it.

Lance couldn't be any happier about having to face Cari, but he wasn't letting on. He was walking between the security guards with his head up and his shoulders back, full of defiance and indignation.

Just as they were passing a shattered tree and a large pile of debris between where the barn and the house had once stood, Mike called out.

"We're coming in!"

In that moment Cari stepped out from behind the tree trunk, holding a two-by-four as if she was about to swing at a pitch. Wearing the gauzy, ankle-length cotton nightgown, she looked like a misdirected fairy godmother with an oversize wand.

Startled, Mike took a step sideways.

Between her sudden appearance and Boudreaux's quick sidestep, Lance's brain computed imminent danger. Tied up and unable to fight for himself, he screamed, then threw his arms across his face.

In the poorly lit scene, all Cari was aware of was Mike's sudden movement, followed by an unexpected scream. By the time Lance threw his arms up in self-defense, she was already swinging.

The blow hit Lance at waist level, knocking the breath out of him. He went down without a sound, then sat sprawled on the ground, gasping like a fish out of water.

By that time Aaron and Trent had carefully moved themselves out of harm's way, leaving nothing but their spotlights trained on the downed man.

Cari took a step forward, peering down, then crying out in disbelief.

"Oh! For the love of God. Is that Lance?"

Mike was laughing so hard he could hardly answer. "It was," he said, and then took the board out of Cari's hands and tossed it aside before she could do any more damage.

Aaron was grinning widely. "Good one, ma'am. If you ever decide you want to do something besides work for the boss, I'll make an opening for you on my team."

Still reeling from the fear of believing they'd been shot at earlier, Cari kicked the bottom of Lance's shoe.

"Lance! Was that you who fired those shots?"

He leaned forward, desperately wanting to curse every bone in her body, but he couldn't find the breath. Someone thumped him on the back a couple of times, then yanked him to his feet. The suddenness of the motion made him gasp, which drew fresh oxygen back into his lungs.

"Jesus Christ, Susan," he muttered, as he coughed and hacked. "You are a freakin' menace."

Cari started to panic. She hadn't been prepared to face anyone without some sort of disguise, but then she realized the cover of darkness would do all that was needed. Slowing her speech down to mimic Susan's, she lit into him with both barrels.

"You're calling me a menace when you were the one shooting at us? Are you out of your mind? What in hell were you thinking?"

Lance rounded on her as if they were children

again and she'd just burst his balloon. "I was thinking, as I was looking for the cattle that had gotten out, that I might need protection in the dark. That's what I was thinking. And I was fucking right! I shot at a panther who was eating on the carcass of one of your uncle Frank's cows so it wouldn't eat me. That's what I was doing."

Then he grabbed his belly and doubled over again. "Damn it to hell, that hurt," he moaned. "Besides, it's not like you haven't heard gunshots out here your entire life."

She glared. "Well, smartass. It's not every day there are four escaped prisoners yet to be accounted for. When I heard that first shot, that's the first thing I thought of."

Lance cursed himself for forgetting about that. "Oh. Right. I didn't think."

Cari rolled her eyes. "And what else is new?"

Lance glared.

Ignoring him, she turned to the other men. "Was there really a panther?"

"Yes, ma'am," Aaron said.

"It came for me, so I shot at it. I didn't know anyone was even on the property," Lance said.

"Um...that's not exactly true," Trent Joseph said. "You saw the lights in the motor home. I know because I saw you stop to look at them."

Lance turned on him, blustering his way through yet another flimsy explanation. "Well...yes...of course I saw them then. What I meant to say was that I didn't know anyone was here until I got here."

Cari snorted. "Fine. Your explanation has been made. Now that you've scared an entire year off my life, you can take your sorry ass home."

Lance yanked at the rope tied around him, waited for Trent to untie it, and then wadded it up into a messy coil and extended his hand to Aaron. "My weapon…if you please."

Aaron emptied the bullets out into the dirt and then handed back the gun.

"What the hell?" Lance cried. "I might need those. That panther is still out there…somewhere."

Mike pointed toward his Range Rover. "Trent will take you home. And I would suggest that the next time your cattle get out, you choose a better way to look for them than after dark, on foot, on someone else's property."

Lance stomped off toward the car, Trent on his heels.

They heard the door slam, then Mike pointed toward the motor home. "Aaron, the car keys are on the little shelf over the sink. Maybe you'd better ride along. Give the sorry bastard something to think about with one armed man behind him and another in the seat beside him."

"You got it, boss," Aaron said, and jogged off after the others.

A few moments later the lights came on, then Aaron came back out on the run. Mike and Cari watched until the taillights of the vehicle were disappearing up the driveway. At that point, he turned to face her.

"You are something fierce, Carolina. Remind me not to startle you ever again."

"Well, what was I supposed to think? We hear gunshots, then you disappear up on the hill while I'm back here imagining God knows what. All I could think was, I'm going down fighting."

Mike grinned, then swung her off her feet and into his arms.

"I read you loud and clear, *cher.* All I ask is that I get to be on your side in the next war, okay? Now…come inside before the skeeters eat you up."

"Mosquitoes are the least of my problems," Cari said. "And just for the record, I didn't fully believe Lance, did you?"

"No, ma'am, I did not," he said.

"Then what do you think this means? Do you think he suspects something?"

"I wouldn't want to bet your life on it," Mike said.

"Crap," Cari muttered. "All the more reason to make this a quick and successful search."

It was daybreak when Cari woke abruptly. She sat straight up in bed, her heart pounding and her fingers knotted in the covers. In a panic, she grabbed Mike's arm and shook him awake.

"Mike! Wake up!"

He woke instantly and was reaching for his pants when Cari grabbed his arm.

"I think Lance knows who I am."

His heart dropped, although he wasn't surprised. "What makes you say that?"

"It was something he said last night. At the time, it didn't click."

"What was it?" Mike asked.

"Last night, when he was yelling at me for hitting him in the stomach, he said, 'It's not like you haven't heard gunshots out here your entire life.'"

"I don't follow."

Cari's shoulders slumped. "That statement wouldn't apply to Susan. Her whole life was spent in cities. Not once did she ever live out in the country. She only visited. The family was here often, but not often enough to make Lance say something like that."

"Well, hell," Mike said. "This changes everything. I need to notify Aaron, and you need to think about talking to the parish police *before* you start searching for that body, not afterward."

Fourteen

Lance hadn't slept a wink. He'd done morning chores before daylight while thinking about what lay ahead. His belly still hurt from the blow Cari had delivered last night, and his feelings were still raw from being trussed up like a prize pig and dragged down the hill to face her. The only saving grace of the entire debacle was knowing he'd put one over on her. She didn't know he was on to her, and that would be his edge. He knew why she'd come back here, and it had nothing to do with reclaiming her property. She was going to look for the body. That meant he had no time to waste. Somehow—someway—this had to be her last day on earth, or he would have to resort to plan B, which, for Lance, was six feet under. Problem was, he wasn't sure he had the guts to kill himself.

Falling in love with Carolina was the first impulsive thing Mike Boudreaux had ever done in his life.

As a kid on the streets, not even the sharpest-tongued bully with the biggest fists had been able to goad him into a fight unless he had a stake in the outcome. He'd always known what he wanted out of life and gone after it in a cool, methodical way. Normally he was the man with the plan—the business shark who knew how to turn failing companies around without losing his shirt in the process. He did nothing without an in-depth study and hours of preparation.

But he had never been faced with a woman like Carolina North—a woman strong enough to bury her own identity to right a wrong. He just hadn't known it when he'd been standing at the bedside of a stranger, waiting for her to wake up and explain her impersonation, hadn't realized that he would be head over heels in love with her before the end of the week.

Now his problem was figuring out how to keep her safe until Lance Morgan was behind bars, although she'd done a fair job of taking care of herself last night when she'd downed Morgan with a piece of broken lumber. That had been priceless. Hearing those shots last night had rattled him, and it had been a tense few minutes as he'd run up the hill toward Aaron and Trent, not knowing for sure what he would find. Her revelation this morning that she was sure Lance Morgan knew who she was, was even more unsettling.

Today was going to be a long one. He had to get her into Bordelaise, convince the parish police she wasn't crazy, then begin the search for the body, even though the man with the cadaver dog couldn't get here until later in the evening. Cari had maps and a starting point, which was the original grave.

He pulled a knit shirt over his head, dropped his cell phone into the back pocket of his Levi's and headed for the kitchen area. Cari was microwaving some of Songee's ham biscuits for breakfast, and he'd started the coffee while she was dressing. As soon as they ate, they were heading into Bordelaise.

"Hey, good-lookin'," he said, as Cari handed him a ham biscuit. "I don't know which looks better, you or this biscuit."

"It better be me," she said, then wiped her hands on the seat of her jeans and flicked a biscuit crumb off her T-shirt.

Mike grinned, eyeing her short spiky hair, and then swooped in for a kiss that left her reeling. Before she could comment, he took a big bite of the biscuit, then rolled his eyes as he chewed. After he swallowed, he pretended to study the difference between her kiss and the bite he'd just taken.

"Oh…stop it," she said. "I don't want you to lie, and I don't want to know you'd rather have biscuits."

Mike laughed out loud, picked up another biscuit and his coffee cup.

"So, *cher*…you ready to go face the music and confess your masquerade?"

Cari sighed. "No, but it has to be done."

"That's my girl," he said.

As they were moving toward the door, a knock sounded, then Aaron yelled from outside, "Hey, boss, it's me!"

"Come in," Mike called back.

Aaron walked in and immediately eyed the ham biscuits.

"There's more," Cari said. "Help yourself."

"Yes, ma'am. Don't mind if I do," Aaron said.

"Are you and Trent ready to go?" Mike asked.

Aaron nodded as he picked up a biscuit.

"What did Lance do after you dropped him off last night?"

"I can't say what he did inside, but I *can* say he didn't come back out until early this morning to feed the animals. You know…he makes a big deal out of what he does, but it sure doesn't amount to much. He's got ten head of cattle, a few chickens and some barn cats."

Cari sighed. "It used to be more. So much more. His father raised horses and bred Hereford cattle. His mother was a professional artist and pretty well-known for her paintings of the Louisiana swamps. The family was a good family. His brother, Joe, is a super guy. It was Lance that they spoiled. When Joe finds out what Lance has done, it'll destroy him."

Mike cupped the back of Cari's neck.

"It's not your fault, and it's not your problem. All that's happening to Lance Morgan is nothing more than what he's brought on himself, so don't start claiming all the guilt. You hear?"

Cari nodded. "I hear."

"Okay, then. We'll keep an eye on Morgan," Aaron said, as he grabbed one last ham biscuit. "For Trent," he said, and bolted out the door.

Mike grinned. "What do you want to bet that Trent never sees that biscuit?"

"I'll bet you're right, and that's all I'll bet," she said.

Mike laughed.

Cari loved the way Mike's eyes crinkled at the corners when he smiled, and when he laughed, the sound was like balm to her badly wounded heart. She'd never gotten this close to a man this fast in her life. It was scary and exciting, and like standing on the edge of a cliff, waiting for it to go out from under her. But she wanted it—and him—bad enough not to step back. If she fell, so be it. Knowing him, making love with him—it would all be worth it.

Mike's focus shifted when he saw her expression flatten. He knew she was struggling, both with the revelation of her resurrection and with what would happen when she told what she'd seen. And yet, when he thought about what was at stake, and how a tornado and a twist of fate had brought them together, he knew what was happening was meant to be. And even if this wasn't the perfect setting, it was the right time to say what he'd known for days. He slid his hands down the sides of her hips, then pulled her close.

"What would you think if I told you that when this was over, I don't want us to be over, too?"

Breath caught in the back of Cari's throat as her eyes filled with tears. "I would think that we were feeling the same things."

Mike sighed with both relief and understanding. "I know today isn't going to be champagne and roses, but it's going to be all right. I just wanted you to know that, whatever happens, we're in it together, okay?"

"You aren't just saying this out of loyalty to Susan?"

"*Cher*...I adored Susan, but I would never think about happily-ever-after with any woman just to please someone else. I'm as serious as I've ever been, and as sure as I've ever been that this is right."

Cari's vision blurred. "Oh, Mike..."

His expression crumpled. "No...no, *cher*...no... this wasn't meant to make you sad," he said, and began kissing her eyes, then her cheeks, then her lips, trying to coax a smile back on her face.

"It's just that...my parents will never know you," she whispered.

"I know, *cher*...and mine will never know you, either, but think about this. We both loved Susan, and if it wasn't for her, we might never have met."

A wry smile tilted the corners of her mouth. "This is true...and she would be gloating about it, too. So, about this long-term stuff...we can discuss it after this mess is over, okay?"

"Okay," he agreed.

She kissed the hollow at the base of his throat, then leaned back and looked up. "And…when I'm me again, we'll talk about happily-ever-afters, too."

An ache was building, fired by his desire for her and a fear that no matter what they did to keep her safe, it wouldn't be enough. Still, it would do no good to let it show, and he managed to return her teasing.

"Why do I get the feeling I'm no longer the one in charge?"

Cari grinned. "My daddy used to say, 'If Mama ain't happy, ain't nobody happy.'"

Mike touched his forehead to hers, then brushed a soft kiss across her lips. "Sounds like your daddy was a pretty smart man."

"He was." Then she changed the subject before it made her cry. "So…you've totally rattled my head and my heart today, and I thank you for it. I have a feeling this will be as good as it gets until this mess is over. Are you ready to be my witness and to bail me out of jail if the need arises?"

Mike was still grinning as he grabbed his coffee and biscuits. "Right behind you, *cher.*"

Vera Samuels was dumping the old coffee grounds into the wastebasket in preparation for making a fresh pot of coffee when the door to the police department opened behind her.

"Be right with you," she said, then quickly added

a new filter, coffee, and slid the pot beneath the reservoir and turned on the machine. She picked up her coffee cup as she turned around.

"Oh. Miss Blackwell, it's you. How can I—"

When the words died on her lips, Cari realized her masquerade was over. Minus bandages, bruises and sunglasses, the new hairdo wasn't enough to disguise her true identity, especially from someone who'd known her as long as Vera had.

"Now, Vera…take a deep breath. Before you freak out, let me assure you that you're not imagining things."

Vera screamed. The thick pottery-style cup hit the floor with a loud pop, shattering into a dozen pieces as she covered her face with her hands and started reciting the Lord's Prayer as loud and as fast as she could.

Cari gave Mike a wild look, then rolled her eyes, grabbed Vera by the shoulders, and started talking.

"Vera. Stop. Stop. You're not losing your mind. You're not imagining things. It's me, Carolina. I'm not dead, okay?"

Vera choked, then shuddered as she peered through the fingers splayed over her face.

"How did this happen?" she asked, then didn't wait for an answer. Instead she threw her arms around Cari's neck and hugged her fiercely. "Oh my God, my God…you're not dead. You're—" All of a sudden she drew back and fixed Cari with a shocked expression. "Why did you come to the funerals and pretend you were Susan?"

"It's a really long story, and I need to talk to Hershel. Is he in?" Cari asked.

Vera nodded, then started crying again.

"Oh, honey…don't cry," Cari said, and looked to Mike for help, but he just held up his hands with a "no way, Jose" expression on his face.

The last thing he wanted was to have a crying woman he didn't know dumped in his lap.

"How come you're not dead?" Vera wailed. "Who died? Who did we bury?"

Cari sighed. "Susan. You buried my cousin, Susan."

As the reality of it all began to sink in, Vera began to chant, "It's a miracle. A miracle!"

"Not for Susan, it's not," Cari said, but not even that harsh reminder could dim Vera's joy.

Hershel Porter figured the coffee must be ready by now and left his office in search of a cup.

The first thing he saw when he reached the outer office was Vera laughing and hugging some woman. He didn't like emotional scenes and wondered what the hell he'd walked in on. Then he recognized the man who'd accompanied Susan Blackwell to the North funerals and caught his eye.

"What's going on?" he asked.

Vera tore herself loose from Cari's arms and swung her around. "Chief, look! It's Cari North. She's not dead. She's not dead after all."

Hershel's eyes bugged, and his mouth dropped. For a moment it felt as if he'd been sucker punched.

"Cari? Is it really you?" he asked, eyeing the short hair and fading bruises.

She sighed. "Yes, it's me. And…we need to talk."

"You think?" Hershel waved her toward his office. "Vera. Hold my calls."

"Yes, sir," Vera said.

Then Cari said, "Vera…you have to promise not to tell anyone about this. Not yet."

"But—"

"You can't," Cari said. "It's a matter of life and death."

Vera's eyes widened, then her jaw set. She hadn't worked in the police department for the past ten years without learning a thing or two about staying mum.

"Not a word," she vowed, then pulled herself together and began sweeping up broken crockery as Cari and Mike followed the police chief back into his office.

"Sit," Hershel said, pointing to a pair of chairs on the opposite side of his desk.

"Happy to," Mike said. "But you're going to be the one who needs to sit to hear this story."

Hershel frowned, then sat down and leaned forward, resting his elbows on the desk as he fixed Cari with a cautious stare.

"How the hell did this mixup happen, and why did

you masquerade as your cousin the day of the funerals? It *was* you…right? You knowingly came to Bordelaise and watched us bury you. So tell me why."

Cari sighed. "It's a long story, but the ugly end of it is, I accidentally walked up on Lance Morgan out in the woods between our properties just minutes before the tornado hit. He was in the act of digging a grave, and there was a dead man wrapped up in what looked like a rug lying there."

Hershel stood up with a jerk. "What the hell are you saying? That Morgan murdered someone?"

"I didn't see the man die. I only saw Lance in the act of burying him."

"Holy shit," Hershel muttered, then shoved his hands through his hair in disbelief. "Who was it? Could you identify the dead man?"

"I don't think so," Cari said.

Hershel sat back down, then grabbed a legal pad and a pen. He had a bad feeling that he'd just found out what happened to the missing lawyer. "Start talking."

And so Cari did, starting from the moment she'd walked up on the scene, describing the black car, the fact that Lance had given chase but never caught her, and on to the time the tornado hit and what had happened afterward. By the time she got to the end of the story, tears were running down her face.

"I came to, in pain and bloody, found my father impaled on a wall by a piece of lumber, my mother dead beneath a pile of furniture and Susan dead with her face...gone. I kept going in and out of consciousness, remembering that I'd seen Lance trying to hide one murder victim and didn't want to end up being the second. Susan's car hadn't been damaged. I managed to drive into Baton Rouge. I barely remember the trip, only that I passed out at a stoplight. By the time I came to in a hospital, everyone had assumed I was Susan because I had her purse, her identification, and was driving her car. And we looked so much alike."

"Like freakin' twins," Hershel muttered, then eyed Mike curiously. "Where do you fit into this mess?"

"Someone notified me that my personal assistant, Susan Blackwell, was in the hospital, unconscious. I rushed there, only to find an impostor. I was all ready to call the police on her myself, then she woke up. I realized she was Susan's cousin, who I'd heard about for years but never met, then I heard her story and...well..."

"He took me home with him," Cari said. "He's fed me and clothed me, and helped me bury my family. I haven't legally committed any kind of fraud because I haven't spent any of Susan's money—or any of mine. I've made no legal claims on Susan's property in Baton Rouge. I've just been waiting to be well enough to start the search."

"The search for what?" Hershel asked.

"The body. I'd just lived through a tornado. I'd seen my parents dead. My cousin dead. I had a hole in my head that took eleven staples to close. I figured no one would believe me. You know what he is… Bordelaise's golden boy. The heir to Morgan's Reach. I figured I would need the body or no one would believe a thing I was saying."

Hershel was beginning to understand the dilemma she'd faced.

"So did you find it?"

"Not yet. We just got back yesterday. I spent the day going through the debris, trying to find some keepsakes. As for finding the body, even without looking, I know it's not where I saw him digging. Lance isn't stupid. I saw him climbing out of the hole to give chase, and I took off running and didn't look back. I don't know what happened, but I'm guessing he went back and covered up the hole, then hid the body somewhere else. Thinking that if I did go to the authorities, it would be my word against his. And you know our history…he could have claimed I was just trying to pay him back for the stunt he pulled that broke our engagement."

Hershel's frown deepened as he began to understand her reasoning. "Okay. I get that. But why didn't you say something to me at the funeral? I'd just told you about a man going missing, remember?"

"And once again, I had no body to show you. But what I did have, and still do, is a head full of staples. Wrap your mind around what a good defense attorney could do with that. Besides, Lance showed up last night with a gun. Said he was looking for lost cattle, but I didn't believe him."

"Damn, woman. Your mess is bigger than anything you write about in your books."

Cari smiled. "You read my books?"

He shrugged, then looked a little embarrassed. "Now, Carolina, you know everyone in Bordelaise reads your books. It's kinda like blowing out the candles on a birthday cake and shooting off firecrackers on the Fourth of July. You're one of us. That makes it tradition…you know?"

Cari looked away as a fresh set of tears began to flow.

Mike sighed. "Oh hell. Now you've done it."

Hershel looked rattled, then cleared his throat and changed the subject.

"So what made you come tell me now? Before you have a body?"

"Lance knows I'm not Susan."

"How do you know that?" Hershel asked.

"It's a long story, but trust me…he knows."

"Which means her life is in danger again," Mike pointed out.

Hershel shook his head. "I just don't get it. Why would Lance kill this man? If the man you saw him burying was, in fact, the missing attorney from Chicago, why did he kill him? We know he owed money on the property, but it's been paid. And he didn't owe it to the lawyer, anyway."

"I don't know why. And it doesn't matter. He still

did it," Cari said, then turned to Mike. "Tell him about what your security team discovered?"

Mike stood. Without thinking, he began to pace.

"This is what we know, and how we figured it out. Right after hearing Cari's story, I ran a background check on Lance Morgan. Found out he owed a Chicago loan shark named Dominic Martinelli almost a quarter of a million dollars, and that he'd defaulted on the loan. Then we found out a lawyer named Austin Ball, who represented Martinelli, had come to Bordelaise to serve foreclosure papers and disappeared. With his connection to Morgan and what Cari had seen, we guessed he was most likely the dead man Cari had seen, but we couldn't prove it."

Hershel sighed. "But the loan's been paid. What reason would Morgan have to kill the man if the loan got paid?"

Cari picked up the story. "The loan wasn't paid off until after the lawyer disappeared, since he was coming down here to serve foreclosure papers. I doubt Joe Morgan found out about the foreclosure until after the fact. The family has always bought Lance out of every mess he's been in, and everyone knows it. Joe is the only one left now. The job fell to him."

"Do you think he knew about the murder?" Hershel asked.

"Lord no!" Cari cried. "And I know when he finds out, it's going to devastate him."

Hershel nodded, then remembered something

Mike had said earlier. "Cari, you saw a car at the site where Morgan was burying the body, right?"

"Yes."

"Can you tell me what kind of car it was?"

Cari frowned. "I'm not good with makes and models, and I was looking at the body in the rug and Lance standing in the grave, but I know it was a black, newer model car, and I'm pretty sure the tag indicated a rental."

"Son of a bitch," Hershel said, thinking of the car they'd found in the treetops on Morgan's Reach and traced to Ball. "I wish you had come to me with this from the start."

Cari sighed. "You were in the middle of a disaster area. You have missing prisoners, a missing child and you didn't even know about Austin Ball being missing until days later. If I'd walked into this office with a hole in my head and blood all over me and told you this story, what would you have thought?"

Hershel's shoulders slumped. "That you were hallucinating and sent you to the hospital."

"And I can promise you, Lance would have found a way to silence me permanently before I ever got out."

"It's hard to wrap my mind around this," Hershel said. "Morgan is from a good family. He just isn't the killer type. Besides that, he was the one who found the bodies at your family farm, and he seemed absolutely devastated."

"Just what's the 'killer type'? And what do you

suppose Lance was doing at the farm so soon after the tornado hit? I'd bet cash money he was looking for me," Cari said. "He must have thought he'd just won the lottery when he found everybody dead. Lance is a man who believes he's entitled to whatever he desires, and he feels no remorse for anything. All he gets is pissed when he's caught. And trust me, I can attest to that personally."

Hershel flushed, remembering the big stink when Cari had caught Lance in bed with a stripper from Baton Rouge, and the uproar that had followed when she'd thrown her engagement ring in his face.

"Okay. I'm in," Hershel said. "I'll have him brought in for questioning, so he doesn't have a chance to run. In the meantime, I'll find a judge and get a warrant to search his house. We've already got cause to search the property, given where the car was found."

At that moment there was a knock on the door, then Vera poked her head in. "Sorry to disturb you, Chief, but after what's going on, I knew you needed to see this."

Hershel frowned. "What? Were you listening at the door?"

Vera glared. "Read the report," she said, then winked at Cari as she left the office.

"Excuse me a minute," Hershel said, as he scanned the text. Cari saw his eyes widen, then he looked up. "Talk about timing. Yours is pretty good."

"Why?" Mike asked.

"This is a report from the state crime lab where we sent the car for testing. They found traces of blood in the trunk that matches Austin Ball's DNA. Not in the front seat. Not in the backseat. Just in the trunk."

Cari got it immediately. All her years of weaving clues through her stories had given her quick insight into a lot of the way the police worked.

"They would have been expecting Austin Ball's blood to be anywhere inside the car—*except* the trunk. I mean…if he was supposedly driving the car when the storm caught up with him and he got hurt. But not in the trunk."

"Exactly," said Hershel. "With this report and what you've just told me, I have all evidence I need for a warrant. What I do need from you is a written statement attesting to everything you've just said."

Cari pulled several folded sheets of paper from her purse and laid them on Hershel's desk. "Signed and dated," she said, then smiled. "Police procedure… right?"

Hershel shook his head.

"If you ever decide to go into a business other than writing mystery stories, you might want to give me a call."

Cari grinned. "That's the second offer I've had in two days. I might have to rethink my career."

"Oh…hell…no," Mike said, then thought to add, "Please."

Cari looked at him, then burst into laughter.

All Mike could think was that this was the first time he'd made Carolina laugh. Really laugh. It was a good way to end a stressful morning.

Fifteen

Lance was pulling out of the bank parking lot when he happened to look across the street toward the police department. What he saw sent him into a tailspin of disbelief. This couldn't be happening!

Cari North and Mike Boudreaux were on their way inside, and she wasn't wearing bandages or sunglasses or anything else that would disguise who she really was. He hit the steering wheel with the flat of his hand. She was going to tell what she'd seen! He just knew it. But why now? What should he do? Walk in and face her down? Blame it all on her head wound? No. That wouldn't be smart. It would appear too defensive. He would just go home. There was no reason for Hershel Porter to believe her. Why would he? A murderer needed a motive, and thanks to Joe, he no longer had one.

A new wave of panic hit as he remembered the missing person's report and the car they'd found on his property. What if they got suspicious and found out Ball had been on his way with foreclosure papers—*before* Joe had paid off the loan? Then sanity surfaced. Why would they bother? The man had died in the tornado. End of story.

But he wasn't happy. He felt as if he were standing on swampy ground and waiting to sink, even as he gunned the engine and sped out of Bordelaise. He kept an eye on the rearview mirror all the way home, for fear he would see police cars on his tail. He didn't know what had prompted Cari to come forth now, but he suspected that what he'd done last night had been the push she'd needed. Damn his bad luck and that stupid panther for messing everything up.

As he turned off the highway and sped down the driveway to Morgan's Reach, he couldn't help but wonder if this would be the last time he would ever be here. His reign as heir to Morgan's Reach was already over, thanks to Joe. And Morgan blood was too blue to endure a life behind bars. He would rather die than go through that kind of humiliation. Should he take his chances and wait and see what happened? Should he run? He had a friend who could get him to Mexico. It would be a simple thing to get from there to South America. He had a passport and—

Then he remembered. If he used the passport, they would just stop him at the border. All of a sudden he realized how ill-prepared he was to be a man on the run. In that moment he was overwhelmed by a visceral longing for his parents. If only they hadn't died, none of this would be happening.

As he turned the corner, his vision blurred. The magnificence of the fine old house was like a diamond against the verdant green of the trees and grass. And if that wasn't enough of a reminder of what he had to lose, a pair of white cockatoos lifted off from a tree and flew across his line of vision. This had been his own Garden of Eden. He'd killed to keep from losing it, and now, in a horrible twist of fate, in order to stay alive, he might have to leave it.

"Ah, God," Lance cried and burst into tears.

Hershel Porter was at the Quick Stop gassing up his cruiser while waiting for his deputies. He'd sent Mike and Cari back to her home place with a promise that he would call just as soon as they had Lance Morgan in custody. After that, they were free to do what they could to find Austin Ball's body. And with that thought, he remembered he hadn't notified that Chicago detective about the latest break in the case.

He reached for his cell phone, and within moments, they were connected.

"Chief Porter! What can I do for you?"

"It's what I can do for you that matters," he said. "We have news."

"You've found Austin Ball's body?"

He heard the lilt of hope in her voice and hated that he was going to ruin it.

"No."

"Damn," Sandy Smith muttered.

"But we had a big shift in the investigation. We have a witness attesting to the fact that your missing man was murdered. We're about to go out and pick up our suspect. Oh…and you should be getting a report from the forensics lab at the Louisiana State Crime Bureau with another interesting development."

"What?" she asked.

"They found blood in the trunk of that rental car that matched Austin Ball's DNA."

"In the trunk? But—"

"Yeah. Hard to figure out how a guy's blood would be in the trunk if he was supposed to be driving when the tornado hit, right?"

"I'll be damned," she said. "How did all this break?"

"Eyewitness came forward claiming she'd seen Lance Morgan trying to bury a body out in the woods between his place and hers."

"Where the hell has she been all this time?" Sandy snapped.

"It's a long story, but she's the only survivor in her family and still has a headful of staples to show for what the tornado did to her."

"Oh. Sorry."

"Me too, ma'am."

"Keep me posted."

"Will do."

He dropped his cell phone back in his pocket just

as the pump kicked off, hung up the hose and was about to get in the car when a police cruiser pulled up beside him with two of his deputies inside. Lee Tullius was behind the wheel.

"We're ready," Lee said. "The warrant is forthcoming, and someone from the parish crime lab is meeting us at the residence."

Hershel sighed. "Then let's go. The sooner we get this over with, the better I'll feel."

"We'll follow you," Lee said.

A few moments later, the two police cruisers headed out of town.

Cari was sitting on the step of the motor home, staring out across the debris to the pasture beyond. Mike was inside on the phone, dealing with a glitch that had occurred during the proposed buyout of a telecom company. She'd urged him to do what he needed, even if it meant going back to Baton Rouge and flying out to San Francisco himself. He'd given her a look of disbelief, then kissed her senseless before getting on the phone. She had to admit, it was reassuring to know she wasn't doing all this on her own.

It hurt to look at the devastation around her, and know that everything and everyone in her entire family was gone. Even though she would have the debris cleaned up, she didn't want to rebuild here. There were too many ghosts, and too many ugly memories of how they'd died.

As she sat, a mockingbird flew up and landed on the ground beneath what had once been a willow tree, then proceeded to squawk at her from a distance, as if to complain about his lot in life.

"Yeah, well…my day hasn't been so hot, either," she said back, then grinned when the bird turned its tail to her and began pecking at the ground. "Just like a male. No interest in you if he can't get what he wants."

Mike had just hung up and was about to rejoin Cari when his cell phone rang. He answered without looking at caller ID, only to hear Aaron's voice. It was the thread of panic in it that made the hair rise on the back of his neck. Aaron wasn't the kind of man to panic without cause.

"Boss! I just found Trent. He's unconscious, with a lump on his head the size of an egg, and Morgan is nowhere in sight."

"Call an ambulance," Mike said, as he glanced out the window to make sure Cari was all right. She was still sitting on the steps. "I'll notify Porter. It's probably going to be a wasted trip to Morgan's Reach, now. Lance must have gotten wind of what's up and gone on the run."

Aaron disconnected. Mike scanned through his call list, found the sheriff's number and hit redial. Porter picked up on the second ring.

"Hershel Porter."

"Chief. This is Mike Boudreaux. One of the men

I sent to keep watch on Morgan's property has been found unconscious with a big knot on his head. I'd lay odds Morgan is on the run. Cari is determined to begin the search for the body, although now that I know this, I'm going to suggest we go back to Baton Rouge until you have that S.O.B. in custody. Problem is, I'm not sure she's going to go for that."

"If she's determined to start her search, tell her to wait until we get there," Porter said. "It won't take long to determine if Lance is gone, and then we'll be on our way."

"Will do," Mike said, and clicked off, then hurried outside to fill Cari in. She looked over her shoulder as he opened the door behind her. "Hey, *cher*...got room for me on that step?"

Cari smiled as she scooted to the side.

Mike sat down beside her, then slid an arm around her shoulders and gave her a quick hug. "Feelin' okay?"

She shrugged. "It's hard to put how I feel into words."

Mike pulled back, then lifted a stray lock of hair from near her eye before he leaned over and kissed her.

The pull of his lips mirrored the ache in her belly. If they weren't in such a mess, she would have made him take her to bed.

"That was nice...very nice," she said softly.

"I have news," he said.

Her eyes narrowed. "So was that a 'you feel

sorry for me' kiss or a 'balm for what you're about to tell me' kiss?"

"You forgot the 'just because I love you' kiss."

Cari's eyes narrowed as she studied the expression on his face. "No. In this instance, I don't think it applies."

"You're probably right," Mike admitted.

"Talk to me."

"I just got off the phone with Aaron. He found Trent unconscious, with a goose egg on his head. I told him to call an ambulance, then I called Porter. Cari…I hate to say this, but Morgan is probably already on the run."

"Oh my God," she breathed, and stood abruptly. "What are we going to do? What *can* we do?"

"We aren't going to do anything about Morgan," Mike said. "That's up to Chief Porter. What I want to do is take you back to Baton Rouge until the danger has passed."

The disbelief that spread across her face was not unexpected.

"No. Hell no. I came to find a dead man, remember? As sad as I am, and as terrible as all this is…there's a woman back in Chicago who needs to bury her husband just like I buried my family. And since I was probably the last person, except for Lance, to see him, I can't turn my back on that. I have to look for his body."

Mike didn't bother to argue or to point out that the

police would also be looking for Austin Ball's body. But his appreciation of Carolina kept growing. "You sure you're up for that?"

Cari looked at Mike, then reached for his hand. "I am up for whatever it takes."

A surge of pride swept through him. With her determination to see this through, he felt anything was possible, even finding a dead man in the middle of the Louisiana swamps.

"That's what I figured you'd say. I told Porter you would probably want to start the search, but he asked you to wait for him and his men. They're on the way."

"Then we wait," Cari said, despair for what was happening almost overwhelming her as Mike went back inside for supplies.

Within fifteen minutes, four police cars were pulling up near the motor home. Cari watched as Hershel and his deputies got out.

"I hear you've got some ideas about where we should look, Cari," Hershel said, as he approached.

Mike exited the motor home with a backpack slung over one shoulder.

"We're ready when you are, Chief, but as far as I'm concerned, this is Carolina's search. I have a man coming down from Savannah with a cadaver dog, but he won't be able to get here until late this evening."

Hershel's eyes widened as he looked at Cari. "You're still serious about doing this?"

She nodded, ignoring the slight tremor in her muscles.

"I don't see how I have any other choice. Just give me a minute to change my shoes and I'll be ready to go."

She went inside, leaving the men to talk among themselves.

Sixteen

By the time Cari came out of the motor home, another half dozen police cars were in the yard, along with almost a dozen policemen, some from neighboring parishes.

Mike was waiting for her at the bottom of the steps.

"I need to go to the site of the first grave and start from there," she said.

"Okay, *cher.* We'll make it happen."

Apparently the news was already spreading that Carolina North wasn't dead, because from where Cari was standing, she could see cars lining the road up beyond the driveway, and people standing at the edge of the fence line, trying to get a glimpse of her and figure out what was happening. None of them yet knew that Bordelaise's golden boy was on the run, but they would. The bigger shock would come when they realized why.

Hershel Porter eyed Cari carefully. He hadn't forgotten about her recent injuries. The last thing he wanted was to find out she had lived through the tornado only to do too much, too soon, and end up back in the hospital.

"You doin' all right, girl?" he asked.

She shrugged as she eyed the onlookers. "Doesn't take long for word to get out around here, does it?"

"Too many people have police scanners. I reckon most of them know we're gathered here for a reason, because they heard us put out a call over the radio for extra help. But they don't know why. I also know, because Lee Tullius told me, that the word is out you're alive. Vera said someone saw you leaving the department earlier this morning, and before she knew it, the news was all over town."

Cari shrugged. "I guess it doesn't matter now, right, Mike?"

"No. You don't need to keep it a secret anymore, *cher.* And I know that has to be a relief in itself."

"Yes. I've been so torn about letting everyone think I was dead. Even going so far as to watch them cry at my funeral. I felt awful about everything…but I had no choice, did I?"

Hershel patted her gently on the shoulder. "No, you didn't. And it's all right, girl. When everyone finds out the truth of this mess, they're going to think you're some kind of heroine right out of a book."

"I don't feel very heroic," Cari said. "And I'd give anything not to have to try to find that poor man's body, but I just don't think I could live with myself if I didn't follow through."

"Time to get started, then," Hershel said, and waved at a half dozen men waiting beside one of the cruisers. As they approached, he introduced them to Cari.

"Men, this here is Carolina North. The man with her is Mike Boudreaux. Miss North is a witness to the crime we believe Lance Morgan has committed. And I say 'believe' because at this point, he has not been officially charged, although it's pretty damn obvious to me that he's on the run for a reason. Anyway…she's going to lead us to where she first saw Morgan digging a grave."

The men eyed Cari curiously. She could tell they were hesitant to believe she knew what she was talking about, so she gave them the same once-over, then asked, "You guys planning to dig with your hands or what?"

They looked taken aback and headed for their cruisers.

"Follow me," Cari said when the men returned with their shovels, and led the way past the piles of debris and up the slope to the woods beyond where the barn once stood.

Mike held her hand as they walked, steadying her as they moved over uneven ground, helping her as they climbed over a fence, giving her a pull as they started up a steep slope. The silence within the group was telling—proof of the gravity of their purpose. Every so often Cari could hear the squawk of a radio as information passed back and forth from Hershel to the men he'd left behind at Lance's house.

The scent of putrefying flesh got stronger as they approached the crest of the hill. When they passed by what was left of a cow's rotting carcass, a black cloud of flies lifted, circled, then settled back again.

Cari quickly looked away, and finally they reached the verge of the woods. Even though the air was hot and humid beneath the trees, there were plenty of branches that had escaped the worst of the tornado and provided welcome shelter from the sun.

Mike kept a close eye on Cari, making sure she wasn't pushing herself past her physical limits, although it soon became apparent that she was at home here in this place. He'd heard her talk about how she and Susan and the Morgan brothers had played in the woods between their properties. How they'd waded creeks and climbed trees, all without caution for life and limb, fearless from the simple fact that they were children—and mortality was a concept they didn't know or understand. He couldn't help but wonder, after what she'd seen, if it had ruined the magic and memories of their childhood. But it was obvious from the way Cari was focused that she was not, at the moment, worrying about that herself.

It took about ten minutes for them to reach the

place where she'd caught Lance digging. As soon as she approached the clearing, she began to slow down.

"It was just up ahead by that pair of big pines," she told Hershel. "Lance had driven the car in from that way…see the path? It's nothing more than a narrow lane, but it's been in use for years, although mostly for four-wheelers."

When they reached the area, she stopped, then pointed to a very obvious indentation in the earth.

"This is where he was digging when I walked up on him. He was more than knee deep in the hole, with his back to me. At first I didn't know who he was, and he didn't know I was there. The body was between us, in what I first thought was a big pile of rags, but then I figured out it was a multicolored rug."

"What did you do?" Hershel said, eyeing the depression in the earth. It was obvious someone had been digging there recently, although the hole had been filled back in.

Cari grimaced. "At first, nothing. I couldn't figure out what he was doing. Then the wind blew the corner of the rug aside and I saw the dead man. I couldn't see his features…just the blood…so much blood. That's when I screamed. And that's when Lance turned around. It's hard to say who was more shocked. Him or me."

She shuddered, then wiped a shaky hand across her face as Mike tucked her close against his side.

Just the feel of his arm around her was all the reminder she needed that she wasn't in this alone.

One of the deputies coughed, then turned away. Hershel looked up.

"This is not the time for me to find out you faint at the sight of blood, boy."

The deputy looked taken aback but didn't comment.

"What happened next?" Mike asked.

"When Lance saw me, he looked like he'd seen a ghost. Then, when he began climbing out of the grave to come after me, I turned and ran for home. The storm was on top of us. The wind was rising. It was starting to rain. I know he started after me, but I don't know why he stopped."

"Lots of people make strange decisions in moments of crisis," Mike offered.

Hershel nodded. "Yeah, he was probably so focused on hiding what he'd done, that that became more important. And obviously, he could no longer leave the body here." Then he asked, "Did you have your cell phone with you?"

"Yes, but I couldn't get a signal. It was because of the storm, I guess. God. I was so scared. Then I lost the phone somewhere along the path to the house. Either when I fell…or maybe when that branch fell on me."

Mike paled. These were details he was hearing for the first time, and the thought of what she must have endured made him sick.

"For God's sake, Carolina, you're stopping my heart here."

Cari shrugged. "There's no pretty way to explain what happened. Even after I realized I'd lost the phone, I didn't really worry. Lance had disappeared, and I knew when I got home I would tell Mom and Dad, and they'd call Chief Porter, and everything would be okay." Her chin quivered, as she added, "Only…it wasn't."

"You know these woods," Hershel said. "You know Lance, probably better than anyone else. Put yourself in his place and think. With a storm on top of you and no time to think what to do next, where would you hide a body?"

"I've asked myself that same question a thousand times," she said. "I can think of places, but I have no idea if they're the right places. I do know he didn't have time to get to the swamps before the storm hit, so unless he took it there later, he had to have hidden it somewhere close."

"So what do you want to do?" Hershel asked.

Cari shrugged. "Start with the obvious places first," she said. "There's a kind of clearing up ahead where we used to play. The ground is soft, and there aren't many trees."

"Lead the way," Hershel said.

For the next three hours they combed the area in every direction, wading creeks as they looked along the banks, moving in an ever-widening circle until they were all hot, tired, bug-bitten and out of sorts. It took everything Cari had to put one foot in front of the other.

About two hours into the search, Aaron Lake had joined them.

When Mike saw him coming, he hoped for good news.

"I can tell you for certain, I will not bitch the next time you send me someplace cold," Aaron said, then took out his handkerchief and swiped at the sweat running down his face.

"How's Trent?" Mike asked.

"Got a headache and a concussion, but he's going to be okay."

"Did he know what happened?" Mike asked.

"Just that he heard something behind him in the woods but got coldcocked before he could turn around."

"Lance," Cari said, then felt sick all over again.

Mike saw the desolation in her eyes. "Hey, Chief. I think we need to rest a bit. Cari isn't going to say so, but she's about on her last legs."

"Absolutely," Hershel said. "I could use a rest myself."

Cari was so hot she was shaking, so she didn't argue. When Mike handed her a bottle of water, she took it gratefully and sank to the ground while he and Aaron moved away, obviously going into explanations they didn't want her to hear. That was fine with her. She'd seen and heard just about all she could take.

Hershel glanced at his watch, then frowned. "When did Mike say that man with the cadaver dog was due to arrive?"

"Late...probably too late to run him today."

Hershel nodded, then took off his hat and sat down on a nearby rock as his deputies hunted their own places to rest.

"I'm sorry," Cari said. Her voice was trembling.

"You have nothing to be sorry for, girl," Hershel said softly.

"I know, but I'm still the one who's dragged everyone all over the place for the past...how long?"

"Three-plus hours," Hershel said, glancing at his watch again.

"Oh Lord," Cari said, then pulled her knees up under her chin and rested her head on them. Moments later, she looked up. "I think you need to call Joe."

Hershel frowned. "Why? What could he possibly do to help us find a body?"

"He might remember a place to look that I haven't thought of."

"Oh. Right," Hershel said. "Give me a minute to get him on the phone," he said and walked away.

She was watching the sheriff's back when Mike reappeared. "Eat this," he said.

She looked at the energy bar he was holding and tried not to gag.

He frowned. “I know you’re not hungry. But you have to keep up your strength.”

She took the bar without comment and ate, while Mike sat beside her, watching her every move. Finally she washed the last of it down with a long drink of the water he’d given her earlier; then, at his urging, she stretched out beside him and laid her head in his lap.

Her eyes closed. And in the quiet of the clearing her body relaxed, and her thoughts turned to a new plan of action.

A couple of minutes passed, and then Hershel came back. “Joe Morgan is on the phone. He wants to talk to you.”

“Thanks,” Cari said, as she took the phone. Then she got up and walked away. Other than the day she’d called the funeral home to make arrangements for her family, this had to be the worst phone conversation she would ever have.

“Joe. This is Cari.” She heard a gasp, then a choking sound, and realized he was crying. “Joe…I’m so sorry.”

“Jesus, Carolina. Tell me this isn’t happening.”

“But it is,” Cari said softly. “It’s true. All of it.”

“He killed a man?”

“I didn’t see him kill him. But I saw him trying to bury a body. It was rolled up in a big bright-colored rug.”

Joe gasped. “The missing rug from the library. Oh Lord.”

Cari started to cry. She knew exactly how he was feeling.

"Dear God," Joe murmured. "I left him in anger. I told him that no matter what he screwed up next, he was on his own, and I never got a chance to say I'm sorry. I can only imagine how panicked he must be."

"Don't think like that. You have nothing to apologize for. Lance is the one who needed to be sorry, and the sad thing is…the only real thing he was sorry about was getting caught."

"We all spoiled him," Joe said. "All of us. And yet I would have bet my life he wasn't the kind of man who could commit murder. Nothing is important enough to kill a man over. Not even Morgan's Reach."

"And yet you bought him out of trouble to make sure it stayed in the family," Cari reminded him.

"I know. I know. Like I said, we all spoiled him. But I didn't know about anyone being killed. You have to believe me."

"I do. But I have something to ask you now. And it's important that you help me as best you can. It's the only thing we can do for the widow of the man Lance murdered."

"Anything," Joe said. "Just name it."

Cari quickly told him where they were and what they'd been doing, including where Lance had begun digging the first grave.

"I need to know…where do you think he would have gone next? He didn't drive any farther. He

couldn't have, because the woods were too thick
and we know he didn't take the body back t
Morgan's Reach, because he *would* have driven bac
there. And since Morgan's Reach wasn't hit bad b
the tornado, but the car was, he must have left the ca
here, and that's how it wound up in the trees. S
Lance couldn't have gone far from the first grave site
because the tornado came right through the wood
here within ten minutes of me seeing him. What d
you think? Where would he go?"

"Oh Lord, Cari, don't ask me that. It could b
anywhere," Joe said. "We played all over those woods.

"I know."

"Maybe...maybe the creek bank. It's soft there.
wouldn't have taken long to dig down."

"We've been there, and just about everywhere els
I could think of during the past three hours."

"Oh. Well then...I don't know," Joe said an
changed the subject. "I know I haven't said it yet, bu
I'm really glad you're alive."

"Thank you," Cari said. "So am I."

His voice broke again. "I'm just sorry you wer
so scared of what my brother might do to you tha
you had to hide. Chief Porter said he hurt a man wh
works for Boudreaux today."

"Yes."

"God. I just can't wrap my mind around all this
It's as if I never really knew him. I don't know wh
he's running. This was obviously not premeditated

He's young enough he could serve his time and still get—"

"Joe, stop and think," Cari said. "Can you imagine Lance in prison?"

There was a long moment of silence. So long that Cari thought he'd hung up. "Joe? Are you still there?"

"I'm here," he said. "And you're right. He wouldn't be able to endure that."

"We can talk about all this later. Right now, I need you to help me think. We have to figure out where Lance would have gone."

Mike had been standing back a bit, giving Cari the space she needed to deal with her old friend's anguish. But he could still hear her side of the conversation, and something she'd said triggered an idea, and he moved closer.

"Cari…excuse me for interrupting…but maybe if you two could remember where you all used to hide. You said you used to play everywhere here…even places you weren't supposed to, so where did you go when you were hiding from each other?"

Instantly an image popped into Cari's mind. "Oh my God… Joe. Did you hear what Mike said? I think I might know where he went."

"Yes. But what does hiding when we were kids have anything to do with—" Then he stopped. "Oh shit."

"The old pirates' cave," they said in unison.

"I'll call you," Cari said, disconnected and handed the phone to Mike as she yelled at the chief.

"Hershel! Bring the men. I think I might know where the body is."

They gathered around her quickly, waiting to hear.

"What did he say?" Hershel asked.

"There's a cave. It's a place where we used to hide when we were kids." She slid her hand in Mike's. "Mike is the one who triggered the thought. I haven't been there in years, but it's not far."

She kept hold of Mike's hand, talking excitedly now as she led them away.

"About three hundred years ago, most of this land was either swamp or under water. Time, and some of the levees around Baton Rouge and Bordelaise, changed the water table. Even though we're on solid land now, in the old days, you would have had to come in here in flat bottom boats. Old-timers used to say that the pirate Jean Lafitte had a stronghold in here somewhere, and that he used it to stash his loot and, when necessary, hide from the law."

"You found Lafitte's stronghold?" Mike asked.

"No. At least, I don't think so. But there *is* a cave, and we pretended it was the pirates' cave. You know kids."

"You think he might have hidden the body in there?" Hershel asked.

"I don't know," Cari said. "But it's certainly possible."

They waded through thick underbrush and downed tree limbs, swatting at the occasional mosquito and sidestepping anything that looked as if it might harbor snakes. Without warning, they emerged from the trees into a small, oval-shaped clearing.

The grass was about ankle-high, and the underbrush was almost as thick as the trees. The remnants of a couple of old cypress stumps were prominent landmarks—proof of what the water level had once been.

Cari stopped. It didn't look exactly like it used to. There was so much more growth. But she knew what was back there.

"It'll be over there," she said, as they approached a wall of bushes and swamp grass.

"I don't see a damned thing but solid brush," Hershel said.

Cari started to push through a thicket when Mike caught her arm, stopping her.

"Let us, *cher.* Aaron…come with me."

She didn't argue. She watched as he got a flashlight out of the backpack, then dropped the pack at her feet and started forward.

"You two, go with them," Hershel said, pointing to a couple of his deputies.

The rest of them stayed back with the chief and Cari, watching as the four men stepped into the thicket, then disappeared almost instantly.

The silence among those waiting was palpable. No one spoke. No one moved. It was as if the world had stopped and was waiting for a signal to take another breath.

Suddenly someone yelled from inside the cave.

"In here!"

Hershel pointed at Cari. "You. Don't move."

She didn't have to be told twice.

She sat down on one of the old cypress stumps, exhausted and heartsick in every pore of her body. She tried to remember the happy times and laughter that had echoed in this place. The picnics they'd had. Susan always insisting on carrying the food, and Joe insisting on being the one to dole it out, while she and Lance had waited to be fed, like hungry puppies waiting for dinner. And always, everyone arguing over who got the biggest piece of watermelon, and who got the last of Maggie North's famous lemon bars.

Then, all of a sudden, everything hit her. The ache for what she'd lost was so fierce, the enormity of what had happened so great, that she buried her face in her hands and began to sob.

Mike, Aaron and the two deputies walked into the cave, almost without knowing where the bushes ended and the cave began. One moment they'd been in chest-high brush and the next they were in darkness. They reached for their flashlights and quickly swept the area. The first thing they noticed was that the ceiling sloped inward. The men were too tall and had to bend down slightly to move around.

The air was cooler inside, and Mike could understand what a draw this place would have been for children raised in the heat and humidity of a Louisiana summer. The floor of the cave was littered with leaves and small twigs, and as he moved farther in, they began to find bits and pieces of animal bones.

"Oh hell," one of the deputies muttered, as he swept his path with his flashlight. "Some panther's most likely been using this as a den. I hope to hell we don't walk up on him."

"We've been making so much noise, it would be long gone by now," Mike said.

"Yeah. I guess you're right," the deputy answered.

Mike swung the beam of his flashlight around the area, eyeing the thicket of roots from the greenery above that had grown down through the ceiling of the cave like tattered curtains, then aiming the beam farther back.

"There!" he said suddenly, as the light revealed a large mound of dirt toward the back of the cave.

The men hurried forward and quickly found a shovel that had been left behind, lying between the wall and the pile of dirt.

"This hasn't been here long," Aaron said. "Look. The wood on the handle is still smooth and clean."

"Except for the blood spots," Mike said, aiming his flashlight at the dark stains near the metal spade.

"Yep, I see them," Aaron said, and leaned the shovel against the wall as one of the deputies ran back to the mouth of the cave and shouted, "In here!"

Mike stepped aside as the small cave suddenly

filled with men. But Cari was nowhere in sight. When the chief appeared, his first thought was for her.

"Where's Cari?"

"I made her stay outside."

Mike nodded, then aimed his flashlight toward the mound as the men began to dig.

Cari was wiping away tears and staring blindly out across the clearing when a raccoon suddenly waddled out from beneath some bushes nearby, then stopped. It took her a few seconds to realize the animal wasn't looking at her but rather at something behind her.

The hair crawled on the back of her neck. Her heart began to pound. She knew before she heard the quiet sarcasm in the voice that she was no longer alone.

"Carolina. Carolina. What in hell am I going to do with you?"

Cari gasped, then jumped to her feet. Lance was so close she could see a vein pulsing in his neck. Then her gaze moved to the handgun in the waistband of his jeans.

"Lance! I'm not Carolina. I'm—"

"Can the act, Cari, I know who you are."

She felt sick. She wanted to call out, but the men were too far away to help her, and Lance had the gun. If she said or did the wrong thing and set him off, she would be dead before they could get out of the cave.

"What are you doing here?" she asked.

"What do you think?" he countered.

A chill ran through her. This couldn't be happening. God wouldn't allow her to live through a tornado just to let her be murdered now.

"How did you know I wasn't Susan? No one else suspected."

A sad look came and went in Lance's eyes so fast that Cari almost missed it.

Then he shrugged.

"Susan isn't allergic to cinnamon."

"I know that, but what—" she began, then sighed. That day at the funeral when he'd offered her a cinnamon roll, she'd told him without thinking that she was allergic. "Well, hell."

Lance's lips twisted into a wry grimace. "Yeah, I've had a lot of those moments myself lately."

"What are you going to do?" she asked.

He shrugged again. "I haven't quite decided. You know it's going to be my word against yours. And you're the one with the most recent hole in your head. A good lawyer can put a spin on anything. Then there are the missing prisoners. They could have done this."

"They wouldn't have bothered to bury the body. And they wouldn't ever have found this place. It's so overgrown, if I hadn't known the cave was there, we would have walked right past it. And…if the prisoners had come across a car, what are the odds that they would have left it for a tornado to take? I'd be driving it away if I was on the run, wouldn't you?"

Lance frowned, but he wouldn't give up. "Like I said. A good lawyer can—"

"There's more than just my word now," she said and watched him visibly flinch.

"Like what?"

"You know the car they pulled out of the trees on your property?" she said, playing for time, hoping he would see the pointlessness of shooting her.

"Yeah? What about it?"

"Chief Porter sent it off to the state crime lab. The report came back today that there was blood in it. The DNA was a match to Austin Ball."

The blood drained from Lance's face so fast Cari thought he would faint.

Then he began to bluster.

"Well, of course there was blood. He got caught in a tornado, remember?"

"I thought you just said he got caught by the missing prisoners, who buried him in the cave. So why would there be blood in the car?"

"Well…because…because they killed him in it," Lance muttered.

Cari shook her head. "Right, and then buried his body in a cave. Not. Unfortunately for you, Lance, the blood was in the trunk. *Only* the trunk. And even if they threw his body in the trunk after he was dead, how did his body wind up here and the car in the treetops? Because you and I both know this place is only accessible on foot."

"Well, hell," he said, echoing her earlier words.

And as they stood there staring at each other, Cari could see acceptance sweeping over Lance's face.

He knew it was over.

Cari was afraid to say more for fear of saying the wrong thing. But she could tell her news had taken all the defiance out of him. It was now apparent that his word against hers was no longer a viable defense. She could see him coming undone.

His body began to shake, and his skin was ashen. He kept swallowing and blinking, as if choking back tears, but as unexpectedly sorry as she found herself feeling for what was happening to him, she was even sorrier for the man he'd killed.

Suddenly the bushes at the front of the cave began rustling, and before Cari could shout a warning, Mike emerged.

In seconds Lance had the gun in his hand and a finger to his lips, motioning with the pistol for Mike to come stand beside Cari.

Mike's heart skipped a frantic beat. All the help they needed was less than ten feet away, and he couldn't call out for fear of getting Cari killed.

"Damn it, Morgan. You don't want to do this," he said, and then pushed Cari slightly behind him so that he was shielding her with his body.

The gesture wasn't lost on Lance. He grimaced through tears. "Ever the gentleman, right, Boudreaux?"

Mike stepped forward.

Lance swung the gun up toward Mike's face. His expression had gone from defeated to wild, and Cari knew he was on the verge of losing control.

"Lance! No!" she begged, and dashed out from behind Mike with her hands in the air, as if to shield him instead.

"Oh my God!" Lance cried, as snot began running from his nose. "Both of you are freakin' pathetic. Who wants to die for love first? How about I just shoot the both of you and get this misery over with?"

"No, Lance. Don't!" Cari cried.

Mike reached for Cari while talking to Lance. "Easy, Lance, easy. Just let me stand beside Carolina…please."

A tiny fleck of spit appeared at the corner of Lance's mouth, but he didn't speak. It was as if he'd lost the capacity to form words.

"Lance?" Mike asked, still waiting for permission to move.

"Back! Get back…both of you!" Lance yelled.

Cari's thoughts were in free fall. She had to do something. Say something. Anything that might calm Lance down. Then she remembered.

"Chief Porter said you were the one who found Mom and Dad."

Lance blinked. It was the even tone of her voice that got through his panic. He shuddered, as if a cold wind had just blown down the back of his neck, then nodded.

"Yes. After I—" He glanced toward the cave, then

shifted mental gears. “After the storm had passed, I headed home. When I realized Morgan’s Reach was safe, I thought of your family.”

Cari knew there was another reason why he’d gone to her home that day, and it had nothing to do with rescuing anyone. Still, this wasn’t the time to say anything about that.

“Thank you for making sure they were found so soon.”

He nodded. “It was…it was—” A sob came up his throat. “Awful. I’m so sorry about them.”

“It wasn’t your fault,” Cari said swiftly. “The tornado killed them.”

Mike had managed to move slightly until he was standing beside Cari with his hand on the small of her back. It was the only solace he could offer. One wrong move could set Morgan off.

“Yes, the tornado…” Lance said, and then his voice trailed off as his gaze slid to Cari’s face. “Do you ever wonder why things happen the way they do?”

She nodded.

“Me too,” Lance said. “You know, I miss my parents…a lot. I love Morgan’s Reach, probably more than anything else on earth, but I didn’t know how to take good care of her.”

“I know,” Cari said. “I’m so sorry.”

Lance shuddered. “Oh God, Cari. I fucked up big-time.”

“I know,” Cari said, then took a deep breath. She

had to ask. She had to know. "Why, Lance? Why did you kill that man? His death wouldn't have changed anything that was happening."

Lance shrugged, then wiped his nose with the back of his hand. "I don't know. It just happened. He pulled foreclosure papers out of his briefcase, and I just…" He sighed. "I just went blank. By the time I came to my senses, he was dead." Then his gaze narrowed. "If only you hadn't been there…in that place and in that moment." His eyes filled with anguish. "Why, Cari? Why were you there?"

"I was following the blood drops. I thought someone was hurt."

Lance rolled his eyes, then waved the gun in the air. "And you…ever the do-gooder, had to follow them, didn't you? Did it ever occur to you it could have been an injured animal? That you might have been putting your life in danger?"

"Yes."

Lance swayed on his feet, then managed a wry smile. "You haven't changed a bit from the kid you used to be."

"You have," Cari said.

Mike gasped, then held his breath. Cari wasn't pulling any punches, and he could tell Lance didn't like that.

"Shut your mouth," Lance said, and pointed the gun straight at her face.

Cari's gut knotted, but as long as she could keep him talking, he wasn't shooting.

"I know you were the first on the scene at my house after the storm."

Lance frowned. "We just covered that. So what?"

"Why did you really come?" she asked.

Lance's lips thinned as a muscle jerked at the side of his jaw.

"Just leave it alone, Carolina," he snapped.

"If you'd found me that day…injured but alive. What would you have done?"

He jerked as if she'd just slapped him. It shouldn't have been a shock. It wasn't anything he hadn't asked himself all the way there that day. But the need for a definitive answer had been taken away when he'd found everyone dead, letting him keep a measure of his self-image intact. Now she'd breeched that tenuous barrier between himself and insanity.

"Never mind," Cari said. "You don't have to say it. I can see it in your eyes."

"I told you to shut up!" Lance yelled, and waved the gun at her again.

Mike grabbed Cari's elbow and gave it a squeeze in warning.

She felt his concern, but she knew something about Lance that Mike didn't. Lance didn't have it in him to be a cold-blooded killer. He'd killed, but it had been without premeditation. What was happening to him now had to be his worst nightmare. She wanted to weep for what she was witnessing. She'd never seen a human being self-destruct so visibly. That she'd known him intimately made it all the more painful. But if she was going to die, she deserved to know.

"If Mom and Dad had been alive, and you knew for a fact that I'd already told them what I'd seen, would you have killed them, too?"

Lance choked on a sob, then fired the gun into the air.

"Shut up!" he screamed. "Just shut the fuck up!"

Mike grabbed Cari and spun her around, then threw her to the ground and covered her with his body just as the sheriff and his deputies came rushing out of the cave.

Lance took one look at the police rushing out, then back at Cari, sheltered beneath Mike Boudreaux's body. She had been his first love. Always. And he'd thrown her away as casually as he might toss a paper cup in the trash. It had taken years for him to realize that just like there was only one Morgan's Reach, there was also only one Carolina North.

Mike held his breath, waiting for the shot.

Hershel Porter was drawing his gun as Lance shifted his aim.

"No, Lance, no!" Hershel shouted.

A shot rang out.

Mike flinched as Cari screamed.

"Son of a bitch," he heard someone say, then lifted himself off Cari far enough to look up. His stomach heaved. He cursed softly beneath his breath, then quickly turned away.

"What?" Cari asked, as she struggled to get free.

"No, *cher*, no. Don't look," Mike said, as he helped her to her feet.

"What happened?" Cari cried.

"He's gone," Mike said.

Cari pushed him aside in disbelief.

Lance was on his back, the gun still in his right hand, a gaping hole on the same side of his face. But she was so deeply in shock that the emotional impact of what she was seeing wasn't sinking in. How had the sheriff shot him at that angle when he had been on the other side of the clearing? Then the truth registered, and the ground seemed to shift beneath her feet.

Hershel hadn't shot Lance Morgan. Lance had pulled the trigger on himself.

She didn't even notice when she started to scream. She was coming apart from the inside out, and there was nothing she could do to stop it. One minute the sky was above her, the next, everything went black.

Mike's arms were already around her. He caught her before she fell.

Hershel came forward, his gun still in his hand.

"There was nothing I could do to stop him," he mumbled, still rattled that he'd watched a man he'd known so well put a gun to his head and pull the trigger. He swiped a shaky hand across his face, then glanced at Cari. "Is she hurt?"

"Not by a bullet," Mike said, as he held her close.

Hershel nodded, then turned to the deputies. "Lee, radio the office. Tell Vera to call the coroner, then tell her how to get here."

Lee looked rattled. "Chief, we've wound around so many times, I don't reckon I know exactly where here is."

"I do," Aaron offered. "I'll help."

The two men walked away as Hershel glanced toward Lance's body, then back at Mike. "This is gonna be real rough for Joe Morgan to hear. I'd rather do anything than have to call him with this news."

Mike didn't have any answers for the harried officer. He was too focused on getting Cari away from the scene. Quickly he carried her to the other side of the clearing, then eased himself down onto a stump, still holding her cradled against his chest.

Hershel followed. "Want me to call an ambulance for her? Not sure how close they can get, but…"

Mike looked down. Her cheek was streaked with dirt and tears, and there were still fading bruises beneath her skin. She'd been through so damn much. But he kept thinking of how determined she'd been, how strong in standing up to Lance, and shook his head. "Medicine can't fix what's wrong with her. Just let me know when it's okay for us to go. I want to get her back to Baton Rouge as soon as possible."

At that moment, Cari moaned.

Mike's eyes narrowed anxiously. She was coming to, but in what condition?

Cari opened her eyes. The first thing she saw was Mike. Her Mike. The big man with the tender touch. All she wanted was to go home. Then it hit her.

There was no home.

But there was Mike.

And, with the grace of God, they had a lifetime ahead of them to make a home together.

Mike's face was a blur. Her voice was shaking. "Away…take me away from here. Please."

"Yes, *cher*…I will. You did a good job today, but the job is over. We're going home."

Hershel patted her arm. "This paperwork is on me, girl. Like the man said…you did a good thing today, but now it's time for me to do my job. You two go on. If I need something, I know how to get in touch. Okay?"

"Very okay," Cari said, then took Mike by the hand as they walked away. Moments later, they disappeared into the trees and never looked back.

There wasn't much for Hershel to do now except wait for the coroner. He would call Joe Morgan later. Right now, there was another call that had to take precedence. He reached for his cell phone and put in a call to the Chicago P.D., then asked for Detective Sandy Smith. As soon as he heard her voice, he started talking.

"I got some news for you. It's not good, but it's what you needed to hear. We found Austin Ball's body. Decomp is already pretty bad due to the heat and humidity here, but his identification was still in his pocket, and the foreclosure papers he'd come to serve were underneath him, along with a baseball bat, which we're assuming was the murder weapon."

"Oh Lord," Sandy said. "What about the perp?"

"He's dead. Suicide."

Sandy sighed. "You tell your witness for me that her help was appreciated."

"Yes, ma'am," Hershel said. "And you tell your widow for me how sorry we are for her loss."

"Yes. I will," Sandy said. "Send me copies of all your reports and…as bad as the news was, thanks for calling."

"Yes, ma'am," Hershel said, and hung up.

He glanced at his watch. Still time enough to get back into Bordelaise and see what that DEA crew was up to. See if they'd come up with any fresh leads on the missing prisoners. After that, he needed to stop by Katie Earle's. Word was her husband, J.R., was due to arrive at any time. Surely to God the man would have news about their missing son, and he would be able to slot in a few more pieces to the puzzles remaining in Bordelaise before he put his head on a pillow tonight.

It was growing dark in Chicago. Like Hershel, Sandy Smith had one last call to make before her day was over. She punched in the number of Marcey Ball's home, and waited for someone to pick up. The news she had to give wouldn't be good, but it would be closure, which, in Missing Persons, was more than she usually had to offer.

Suddenly she heard the soft, trembling voice of Marcey Ball answer the call.

"Mrs. Ball. This is Detective Smith. We have news."

Seventeen

Six months later

Cari leaned back in her chair with a sigh of relief. The complete manuscript of her latest work—a book she was going to call *Blown Away*—was in the computer. She'd just typed *The End*, which were usually her favorite words. This time, though, the story was different. This was the first time she'd written something that wasn't fiction. The story of the murder, of living through a tornado, then being a witness to her own funeral and to the suicide of a lifelong friend, had been the most difficult thing she'd ever had to write. But it was a story that had to be told.

The news of her resurrection and the reason behind it had swept the publishing world, even the national news. Once the wire services had picked up on it, there had been no stopping the onslaught of coverage. In the midst of correcting court records, moving Susan's body to the Blackwell family mausoleum, and the final cleanup of her family's land, Cari's life had become public property.

For the first two months after the truth was revealed, everything Carolina North did was considered newsworthy, right down to the enormous engagement ring that appeared on her finger about a month after the story hit the headlines. The fact that Fortune 500 business magnate Michael Boudreaux was finally taking a wife—a wife who happened to be famous mystery writer Carolina North—just added to the story's romance and mystique.

Their engagement had been public, but their wedding had not been. One weekend they'd hosted a dinner party for their closest friends, but instead of serving dessert after the meal, a priest had appeared and performed an impromptu wedding for Cari and Mike.

It was not lost upon the guests that neither bride nor groom had one living family member to stand up with them. But it was also noted, that neither one had let that ruin the moment. When the news was announced at the table, and the priest moved into place, the room became a hive of excitement. Chairs were pushed back. Last sips of wine were abandoned as Cari rose from her chair and took Mike's hand.

It had been little Daniel who'd put everything in perspective when he'd appeared in the doorway holding a small pillow with the wedding rings attached.

"I gots da wings!" he'd crowed.

"And I gots the girl," Mike echoed.

It had been Cari's laughter they remembered afterward, along with the expression on Mike's face when Cari had said the words "I do."

Their honeymoon had been brief—a four-day trip to Honolulu, with the promise of a longer honeymoon in Paris when Cari finished the book she was writing.

And, in an odd way, the retelling of her story had been healing in a way she had not expected. It had given her the chance to recall the precious memories of her youth and the wonderful life she'd lived in Bordelaise. It had made the way it all ended a little easier to bear. And, as Mike often reminded her, good memories were best when in constant use.

But now the manuscript was done. It was time to send it off.

Cari opened a new e-mail, sent a quick note to her editor, copied the message to her agent and attached the finished manuscript to the message.

It was out of her hands.

Oh, there would be the line edits and copy edits, and the final draft to go through later, but that was down the road. All she wanted to do now was sleep.

Mike was due home from Los Angeles tonight. She had a bottle of champagne cooling, and Songee had made his favorite dessert, bread pudding with raisins and Bourbon sauce.

They would share the bubbly and the dessert, and make sweet, sweet love in the night.

And then would come Paris and the rest of their lives.

It was a good beginning.

* * * * *

PAMELA CALLOW

Haunted by the death of her sister and wounded by her ex-fiancé's accusations, Kate Lange throws herself into her new career at a high-powered law firm.

When the grandmother of a lonely private school student seeks her counsel, Kate thinks it's just another custody case. But then the teen is brutally murdered. And it isn't only Kate who wonders if her legal advice led to the girl's death.

Put on notice by Randall Barrett, the firm's charismatic managing partner, Kate must fight for her career, for her reputation—and for redemption. But this fight leads Kate into the surgically skilled hands of the Body Butcher.

DAMAGED

Available wherever books are sold.

www.MIRABooks.com

MPC2750